Candy is the pawn of immensely depraved and sophisticated immortals and caught up in their maneuverings as their empire prepares for war with our Earth. As the helpless captive of one warlord who is intent on betraying her master, Candy is subjected to every level of servitude the Kami Empire requires from its slaves.

From a living tomb of bondage and pain she is delivered to the beasthood and its clever torments. She is even delivered into the hideously cruel and dreaded Underworld from which no slave has ever returned.

But Candy's destiny is stranger than any slave's has ever been and as war is prepared around her, she sinks ever lower into a slavery from which only her beloved master can save her from.

This book is a work of fiction. Names, characters, places, and incidents either are products of the author's imagination or are used fictitiously. Any resemblance to actual events or locales or persons, living or dead, is entirely coincidental.

Dragon Candy: Bondage Plaything
Copyright © 2023 Talia Skye
ISBN: 978-1-4874-3587-5
Cover art by Martine Jardin

Published by eXtasy Books Inc

Look for us online at:
www.eXtasybooks.com

Dragon Candy: Bondage Plaything
Dragon Candy 3

By

Talia Skye

CHAPTER ONE

Xiao once again listened helplessly as Lady Uzume strolled down from the upper reaches of the prison, set down some heavy items, and then stepped out before her captive. Xiao gave a shocked gasp when she saw the plexus of leather straps clutching to the woman's hips and from her crotch jutted a large black manhood. For a moment, Xiao assumed that the woman had magically conjured herself a real penis but then she saw that it was a separate toy, worn to imitate, but still just as effective on someone as restrained as she.

"Like it, slave?" she purred and grabbed the phallus at its base. Stepping forward, she started to rub the head of the toy around Xiao's face and laughed as she cringed and whimpered.

With a heartless cackle, she quickly installed a ball gag and then sashayed around the pillory. She leaned down and Xiao heard the rattle of chains before she felt cool steel closing about her wrists. The cuffs clicked and tightened and then a much larger one was installed around the base of her neck. The feel of naked steel was an unusual one. The material was too valuable to waste save on the most important and functional purposes. Squandering it on something as strange as restraint was puzzling to say the least and to Xiao it almost felt like jewellery of the most extravagant kind.

The straps on her left leg were unfastened and her ankle pulled forward until her knee was up by her breast before another cuff snatched hold of it. When her leg went limp, she found that it was connected to another chain, one that reached up and linked her wrists and collar. The other leg was similarly captured and Uzume opened the pillory and hauled her languid form from the padded surfaces.

The tyrant dropped her to the floor and closed the cuffs another few teeth to ensure they were fixed tightly to the areas that had previously been enclosed in leather. She then moved a small switch on the surface that locked them to prevent anymore closure, but only the correct key could coerce them into opening.

A glint of metal caught the light and Uzume revealed that small key in her fingers. After deliberately getting her captive's attention she stood up and slid the item into the front of her thong. With a slight wriggle she inserted the item and gave a shudder as its chill surfaces entered her body.

Xiao lurked on the floor, remaining on all fours as the five cuffs kept her in a curtailed squat. She stretched out against the impositions and when the chains snapped taut and revealed the maximum degrees of her movement, she instead looked around.

At the base of the stairs was a wooden bucket and a large scrubbing brush. Uzume marched to it and grabbed a leather stem from which a bushel of long thick straps emerged.

"Well, what are you waiting for? Get to it!" snarled Uzume.

The woman gathered the ends of the straps in one fist and yanked to make them snap together with a sharp cry.

Xiao started to scuttle over to the items and gave barks of pain when she accidentally knelt on the trailing chains. Keeping her legs wide and her hands close together, she dragged the weighty lengths beneath her and grabbed the brush as soon as she arrived.

The flogger flew in an overhead arc and descended across her back. The brutal signal made her jolt as heat spread through the assailed region. Uzume let the tentacles loiter on her for a moment and then trailed them aside. The leather slithered against her skin and fell away before being carried in another full circle. This time they swept down into the crease of her rear and the tips spanked to her pussy. Xiao gave a shriek and jumped up, only to be stalled by the collar. She dragged her hands up with her and then collapsed back to the ground, pressing her cheek to the wood and holding to the brush for strength as the scathing fires in her loins made her sob and chew on her gag.

"Get to work, slave!" ordered Uzume, and the flogger dropped across a wide expanse of her back to push her down towards the ground. The straps remained on her as a warning and Xiao humbly reached up, dropped the brush in the water, and started to scrub diligently at the timbers.

"Come on, slut. Faster! I want this done before sundown!" growled Uzume but left the flogger in place. Xiao scrubbed as quickly as she could, throwing her upper body into each shove as she felt the leather shifting on her back.

An arbitrary jerk carried the flogger aside and Xiao cringed in anticipation of another stroke.

"No delays!"

Uzume stepped behind her and after using the side of her boot to offer a light kick into Xiao's bottom, she laid the weapon to the base of her back. Xiao's hindquarters sank towards the ground, and she recommenced her work with new gusto.

"Yes, much better. But get that arse up! Show me your pussy!"

Xiao shuddered at the coarse attitude and the derision with which she was being regarded. Nevertheless, the flogger and the woman's brutal tones were not to be denied and so even though it savaged her with derogation to do so, she brought her legs inward and elevated her rear.

She felt a boot step onto her buttock and then jab the heel into her.

"Legs apart! Nice and wide!"

Scrubbing and weeping, Xiao drew her knees apart and arched her front down towards the ground to comply. It made scrubbing even harder, but she persevered as best she could.

"Yes, much better. Maybe I should fuck this tight little hole," murmured Uzume.

The rounded toe of her boot reached up and nuzzled between Xiao's rear. She wriggled the end against her sphincter, digging into it and churning it around.

"Would you like that? Hmmm?"

Xiao's eyes widened with humiliation as she was abused. She could not believe that another being could be so disgustingly depraved. The Kami were like nothing she could have expected. They gained intense satisfaction from the most bizarre and unseemly behaviour and acts, as though all composure and conscious had been stripped from them. Truly they were devils incarnate and if she did not accept their obloquy, they would brutalise her instead.

"Would it be fun for you, slave? To feel me rape your arse? Maybe I should have you beg for it first."

Xiao tried to ignore the animus coming from the woman and focus instead on her task. It became harder when her captor shifted her foot up and started to prod at her rear with her heel. When she acquired no response, she put the sole back into place and gave a vituperative shove that threw Xiao forward and dropped her onto her front. She landed into the puddle of water and onto her chains. The uneven links afflicted her front and she rolled and struggled to get back up off them. Pressing hands and knees into the coils was a further trial and then Uzume started to apply the flogger again. The leather dropped down onto her back and rear, spanking her with venom until she was again scrubbing the floor.

Uzume paced around the demeaned form of Xiao and continued to offer insult and crass comments that she interspersed with a bilious application of the flogger.

Xiao was made to scrub every inch of the floor, often being called upon to repeat an area that was deemed unsuitable. These areas were the hardest to finish because Uzume beat her with alacrity while she rectified her mistake.

Eventually though, the room was finished, and Xiao sagged from fatigue. Uzume hung her flogger on a hook on the wall and took down a bamboo cane with a curved handle and a wickedly lithe length.

"You're not done yet, slave. There's more!"

Xiao gave a resigned sigh as she anticipated being ushered to another storey and made to repeat her entire ordeal over again. Instead the elegant leather-clad leg of her oppressor stamped down between her chained wrists.

Xiao let go of the brush with one hand and drew backwards. Uzume swung her foot back and kicked the utensil from her grasp. Xiao gave a brief squeak and clutched the battered fingers to her breast as she looked up Uzume. The tyrant leaned down and grabbed the back of her plait before yanking up. The harsh pull made Xiao drop her face back down whereupon the rear of the gag was set free. The buckle was drawn up, twisting her head around and dragging the bloated orb from her lips.

Uzume placed the handle of the cane under her armpit and then held it there so the same hand could grab the tip and then hoist the weapon high into the air. She hooked the handle into a ringlet in the ceiling above them and with the freed hand she grabbed Xiao. She sank fingers and thumb into her cheeks to purse her lips together. She snarled and applied more pressure, digging in and making her jiggle in her kneeling pose.

"Mmmm. This makes your mouth look like your bottom. Maybe I should fuck this hole first."

Uzume tossed the ball gag aside and started to trace her forefinger around the puckered orifice.

"Maybe that would be preferable for you though. You seem virginal, but maybe the men of your village have already made use of this opening," she mused cruelly.

The finger started to push into her mouth and then ride back and forth. The woman pushed in and squeezed her other hand to ensure Xiao's lips were kept pressed to the intruder. The thought of having a male use her in such a way had never occurred to Xiao. Her life had been kept away from such things and to be taken in such a manner was outlandish and absurd, yet through Uzume's actions she could now see how it could be done and it horrified her.

The woman giggled as she saw the confusion written in Xiao's eyes. The finger slipped out and tapped her nose.

"Tongue. Out. Now."

Xiao pushed and managed to strain the organ through the tight hole.

"Now use your tongue, slave."

Uzume used the hold to her slave's face and threw her back down at her feet before straightening up and folding her arms across her chest. Xiao started to rise but Uzume merely lifted her other leg and placed her boot between her shoulder blades. The heel gathered fresh weight and demanded that she lower while guiding her towards the other boot.

"Lick it," ordered Uzume and took the cane back down from its lofty anchor.

Fearful of the consequences of disobedience, Xiao swallowed her pride and started to lap at the red leather. She spread saliva on the hide and traced around the toe and instep before hoisting the tip up and down the dagger heel. When she reached the woman's ankles, Uzume took the subjugating boot from her back and stood with legs apart to let Xiao curl round and round, rising higher with every lap.

"Veeeery good, slave. It's so pleasing to watch that impudent rear swinging in the air as you work and worship my legs."

There was a hum of displaced air, and the tip of the cane sank into Xiao's left buttock. She jerked into a ball and quaked. The assailed area seemed to bloat with a thumping havoc that refused to fade.

"No slacking!" snapped Uzume and applied another swipe to Xiao's other cheek. The second detonation of lucid pain made her throw her head down and embrace the toe of the boot in her mouth. She sucked on it for comfort and security as she flashed her tongue to the hide and quaked from the awful effects of the cane. As the scorching pulse started to ebb, she let her jaws widen so she could start to lick easier.

When she reached Uzume's heel, another stinging swipe landed on the side of her thigh. The stroke made her rear tumble aside and slap to the floor. She clutched her arms to her chest and her shins tangled upon themselves as she jolted and fought to endure the withering amerce. Sprawled on her side, it was easier to swing her head left and right and lick the heel, but another stroke to her hip again corrupted her efforts.

Uzume turned around and stamped her heels down to gain Xiao's attention.

"From ankle to hem in single laps, slave. Do it! Do it, now!"

Xiao rolled onto her front and gasped for breath before she set free her tongue and laid it the warm leather. Shivering, she trailed the organ all the way up the long, elegant legs and stopped just before she trespassed onto skin. The leather rippled with sultry motions as the woman clearly savoured both Xiao's plight and the feel of a subservient tongue upon her footwear.

When she had attended the rear of the boot, Uzume turned around and had her attend the front. After she had made her eighth voyage from floor to upper thigh, Uzume grabbed her by the plait.

"Suck."

The dildo prodded her lips and caused Xiao to give a repelled spasm.

"I said suck it, slave!"

"I ca-" she began, and the woman exploited the protestation to throw her hips forward and sink the toy into Xiao's mouth. Her eyes bulged as it breached the back of her throat and made her retch. Uzume let go at the same moment and this caused Xiao to catapult herself away and collapse onto her flank where she continued to cough and gurgle.

A moment later, her reactions became far more drastic as the cane started to rain down upon her. The bilious rod hissed through the air and laid itself to her thighs and rear, and when she flipped over to defend the regions, it filled the fronts of them with equal servings of harrowing.

The intensity of the caning was more than Xiao could stand and she became a mindless creature of response. There was no ability to fight or try and escape, all she could do was throw herself around on the floor. She was even ignorant of the times when she travelled across her chains and pained her body.

Screaming for mercy and wailing in despair, Xiao convulsed and wrenched at her restraints while trying in vain to defend her abused body.

The withering blizzard of swipes stopped, and Xiao was left in a tight bundle, sobbing and quaking as every searing line continued to pound with a steady and remorseless pulse of its own. Slick with sweat and with tears streaking her face, she wept freely and became dizzy from the strange intoxicating surge that ran through her mind. The pain had been more than she dared believe possible and the stark contrast to an unpunished state was enough of a decline to bring a creepy form of rapture.

Uzume used the toe of her boot to kick Xiao's thighs apart and then she leant her toe to her prisoner's groin. The sole of the boot started to stroke with small and precise movements. Still phased by the caning, Xiao only registered a sultry pleasure and not the manner in which it was being delivered. She gave a groan and trembled as the toe continued to tease her loins and the sound of moisture cackling against the leather suddenly snapped her from her torpor.

"Oh God! No! Stop! No!" she cried and threw her thighs together against the boot while trying to scuttle away.

"Goddess!" corrected Uzume and made Xiao shriek as she laid her most brutal stroke yet. Employing all of her considerable strength, the weapon dropped with meteoric intent and caused her breast to ripple from the impact. The single stroke dropped her back to the floor and her chest arched into the air as her jaws stretched wide and a long and soul-torn howl raged in her throat.

Xiao clamped her hands to the site of woe and dropped back to the floor. She entered a sobbing fit of despair and her oppressor's foot exploited her quiescent state and again started to tease her. Appraised of the penalty for resisting, Xiao laid where she was and just accepted this dissolute attack. As demeaning as it was, the pleasure of being played with was at least mitigating the throbbing angst lurking in the countless rosy stripes that were crossing her body. Some were already darkening into crimson streaks, and these were the ones that were throbbing the most distinctly.

"Yeeesss, you like that, don't you. You can offer this virginal façade, but I know there's a wanton little whore in there somewhere, and I intend to find her!" said Uzume with a sibilant and libidinous purr.

Xiao bit her tongue and declined to retort. The foot started to find its work easier as it conjured fresh moisture from its subject and Xiao started to lose herself to the play. She hated everything this woman did to her, but the skill with which she was being manipulated could not be resisted. All she knew here was pain, so what could be the harm in embracing this vague moment of pleasure?

The toe started to work harder, and Xiao's breathing deepened as her belly rolled and her knees swayed in the air. Her hips began to roll her loins and she pushed up to grind herself against the toe with every increasing enthusiasm.

"Yes, there we are. Look at you on the floor. Fucking my toe like a horny little slut. That's it, slave. I want to see you come against the boot of your Goddess!"

The words were an insult that snapped her from her trance and Xiao thrust her hindquarters back to the ground to try and escape. If she allowed herself to give in and climax, she would have given in to the desires of this vile devil. Was Uzume trying to seduce her, defile her, make her willingly subject herself to these twisted pleasures and heinous pains? Sorcery was clearly afoot, and Xiao had to fight it lest she lose her soul.

"If that's what you want, then so be it."

The cane shot forth on an underarm swing that caused its hissing tip to land in the very area that had been so full of rhapsody just seconds ago. The effect was catastrophic. Xiao's world vanished amidst a sheet of effulgent misery, and she shot out from under the cane. Rolling across the floor like a leaf in the wind, she eventually crashed into the wall. Xiao dropped down and shrivelled into a ball, her breath jumping in and out as she screamed and howled for deliverance from the unbelievable level of pain.

Finally she heard the sound of Uzume walking over to her and through blurred and tear-filled eyes she saw the tip of the cane. Xiao whimpered and quavered under its shadow. She was utterly defeated by its impossible potency.

"You want another caning, slave?" asked the woman.

Xiao's tardy response resulted in the bamboo tip prodding at a particularly vivid intersection of welts. The assaulted flesh responded poorly to the bullying and the fresh influx of pain forced words from Xiao's listless mouth.

"No, Goddess. Please, I'll do whatever you want. Just no more of the cane. I . . . I can't survive it."

"Nonsense. You can take much more, and you will. But for now, I want to see this cringing bitch suck this cock and masturbate as she does it."

The defamation of such a deed struck her like a slap, but it was nothing compared to the kisses of the cane. With a resigned push, Xiao managed to pull herself back up onto her knees whereupon her eyes greeted the jutting erect replica.

"Weeeeell," hummed Uzume.

Xiao opened her mouth and slotted it onto the toy. Closing her lips, she mimicked the motions that Uzume had shown with her finger.

Uzume stood to attention and watched her efforts with stark amusement.

"That's it. Take it nice and deep," she murmured.

Xiao pushed further and recoiled as it made her gag. Uzume just laughed.

"And don't forget to play with yourself, slut," she hissed and grabbed the back of Xiao's head before offering a small pelvic thrust to repeat the trauma. Xiao gurgled and retched before dropping her manacled hands into position. Masturbation was a rare indulgence for Xiao. Due to the dangers of slavers, raiders, rapists, and kidnappers she was always being watched, even at night. The opportunity rarely came and when it did, it was usually in the halcyon splendour of her secret lake. Now she was being forced to do something she dearly loved, but could hardly ever embrace because of publicity. This made performing for another person a potent taboo and Xiao found trouble in complying. Even the fake fellatio was easier on her.

Xiao tightened her oral hold and started to stroke her

humid loins.

"No teeth!" snarled Uzume and offered some light slaps to Xiao's cheeks by way of correction.

Xiao hastened her autoerotic activity to compensate for the minor fury that was now saturating her cheeks. She hollowed her cheeks with suction and tried to keep her jaws apart to a degree where the toy would not scrape against her teeth as she hauled on it with her mouth.

Attending the toy started to become easier as she continued to dance her digits to her sex, stroking her lips and pawing at her clit with faster and more drastic movements. Soon, the pleasure was weaving its magic on her, and her hips began to sway as she started to suck with greater devotion and murmur with delight.

Suddenly, Uzume revealed that she was now aroused beyond tolerance. After placing a hand to Xiao's cheek she simply shoved her to one side. The dildo stretched her mouth as she slithered from it and then dropped to the floor, collapsing down onto her moistened hands before her body struck the ground.

Before she could react, Uzume jumped behind her, grabbed her plait, and hauled up. She slapped the other hand under her chin to apply another grapple and then thrust. The dildo rushed into Xiao and opened her for the first time.

Uzume's holds were tested to their limit as Xiao jerked with a monstrous pulse of reaction. The pain of penetration immediately swirled around the rapture of having the saliva sodden length glide into her already wet channel. Xiao screamed even more potently than when she was being caned and this wail rose in octaves when Uzume drew back and then thrust into her again.

Xiao tried to leap away and escape the penetration, but Uzume held tight and continued to jolt back and plough the toy into her captive. Xiao's hands jumped back to try and fend the woman off, but the chain brought her efforts to an abrupt halt.

Screeching for mercy against this excruciating bliss, Xiao was ravished with cold-blooded fury until she swore that she would be torn apart by another thrust. The pleasure of being ravished was unlike anything she had experienced, it had a deep, potent quality that she found terrifying and exhilarating.

Uzume again flung her aside and off the toy before she got up, leaving her captive to quake on the ground and recover from the pleasure in the same way she permitted her moments to recuperate from the pain of chastisement.

"I'm going to give you a choice, slave. I can jump on you and fuck you until you come. Or you can go free. I can give you sexual release, or physical release. Your choice."

Xiao spun her head around and regarded the woman.

"Y . . . you're serious. I can leave?" she burbled, not able to believe that an offer of freedom was being made. Was it true or just some cruel trick designed to further batter her psyche?

"If you want to. Do you?"

The savagery of the molestation was still haunting her pussy and Xiao knew that if she felt that succulent device in her a moment longer, she would not be able to defy and would beg for the chance to orgasm. Penetration had shown her a form of pleasure that she had never felt before, and she was intrigued to see how much further it would take her. She had to get out. Now.

"I want to leave. I want my freedom."

"As you wish. First, you'll need the key to those cuffs," she said and began to unbuckle the harness. The toy came away and she flung it aside before standing with legs astride and hands on hips.

"Well, come and get it then."

"B . . . but it's . . . I . . . I mean . . ."

"Your feeble gibberish won't get it out, slave. Only your tongue will."

"Oh please, don't make me do that. Just let me take it out with my hands. Isn't that bad enough."

"If I'm to let you go free, I believe I can lay down the parameters. So, if you want the key to uncuff yourself, you'll have to take it by force, from my pussy. Understand?"

"Y . . . yes, Goddess."

Xiao crawled forward on hands and knees with chains dragging and rattling beneath her. She stopped at the woman's feet and rose up. With a final resigned glance upward she looked at the red leather thong and swallowed.

"Take down my underwear first."

Xiao took the sides and drew down to pull them out from under the corset and then she dragged them down to Uzume's ankles. The smooth-shaven sex of the woman appeared, and Xiao filled her mind with the recall of what she had endured here, and the possibility of escaping it if she could just perform this one final act of derogation.

With a sudden mental bluster of commitment she leaned in, closed her eyes, and stretched her tongue into the wet sex of her tormentor. Uzume stiffened and groaned aloud as she felt the entry and instantly clenched her channel.

Xiao squeezed her hands into fists and pushed her tongue against the internal muscles of the woman. The organ burned from strain as she tried to get deep enough to find the key, but Uzume was not making it easy. Xiao started to push with steady motions, trying to wear down the internal defences but this just seemed to excite the woman and bolster her resistance. Xiao pushed her lips to those of the woman and swirled her tongue around to try and locate the elusive key. Uzume shuddered against her.

"Oh yes, slave. Almost there. All . . . most . . . I . . ." panted Uzume, and in an uncharacteristic act she placed her hands about the back of Xiao's head and neck and pulled her in. Even so, she still held her pussy tight so Xiao had to fight harder to slither around and find her means of redemption. Uzume's words gave Xiao heart, for they meant that she was close to getting the key. When she increased her efforts, Uzume jerked and cried out. With a long howl she convulsed and held forcefully to Xiao.

A metal taste spread on Xiao's tongue as the key slithered free and dropped onto her tongue. Uzume staggered back, seemingly exhausted by her fight and now drained in defeat.

Xiao seized the chance and started to uncuff herself. The wet key slipped against the metal as her hands trembled and the taste of the woman continued to hang on her tongue. The cuffs sprang open and fell from her extremities before she fumbled for the one on her neck. When she found the hole and opened the collar, she scampered onto her feet.

"I can go now?"

"Pardon?" said Uzume with a sultry purr while she leaned against the wall.

"You said I could go free!"

"So I did. Come this way."

Uzume pulled up her thong, strolled past her, and walked onto the stairs. Xiao could not believe her luck. By resisting Uzume had she proved herself immune to seduction? Could the Kami only keep an innocent for a certain duration and if they failed to corrupt them, then they had to set them free?

Xiao followed the woman down to another chamber that was clearly some sort of lounge or reception hall. The floor had several deep fur rugs and on the other side of the room was a dense double door. Uzume walked over to it and turned round. A wicked glower was now on her lips.

"All you have to do is get by me," she growled.

"Bu . . . but you . . . you said I . . ."

"I said that if you got the key you could go free. You have

freed yourself. You are free. You wanted to leave. We left the chamber in which I was holding you. I mentioned nothing of total freedom, but am willing to let you try and grab it."

"Monster!" screamed Xiao, her tolerance finally gone.

She ran at the woman with hands outstretched and fingers twisted into claws to gouge at her. If she could quickly disable the woman, she could open the door and run away.

Uzume side stepped, and a knee jumped up and sank into Xiao's stomach, doubling her over with a startled croak. With her breath stolen and a ghastly throb in her belly, Xiao was momentarily crippled.

Uzume chuckled and grabbed her sides to spin her about and then place her foot to Xiao's bottom. A disdainful shove sent her careening across the room to drop at the bottom of the steps.

"If that's the best you've got, you may as well put the cuffs back on and march yourself back upstairs, slut. Then I'll fuck you so hard, you'll faint."

Xiao coughed and straightened up. With another ferocious charge she ran at her enemy and desperately tried to grab her. Uzume moved almost faster than Xiao could keep track of and suddenly a pair of slim hands clamped about her outstretched wrists. The strength in them and in Uzume's stance stopped Xiao dead in her tracks and as her arms folded on the last of her momentum, a swift knee between her legs lifted her feet from the floor. When she landed and her legs folded under her, Uzume threw aside and sent Xiao into a clumsy sprawl.

Mewling and holding her aching pussy, she gave a shriek and struggled as hands grabbed her left ankle and turned it. The rending sorrow in the joint caused her to roll over onto her front. The instep of a thighboot nudged into the back of her neck and pushed her face into the floor. A moment later she wailed as her ankle was turned further, twisting her leg and making her squirm and flounder. She tried to reach back and move the pinning foot, but she had no leverage and nowhere near the strength.

"Say you want to be my slave!" ordered Uzume.

"Never! I hate you!" she shrieked.

"Hate me all you want, but you'll still be my slave, and I want you to ask for it!" hissed Uzume. She hoisted the ankle higher and turned it to make Xiao shriek even louder.

"Noooooo!" she roared definitely.

Uzume let go and backed up towards the door. She stood poised on her heels as Xiao awkwardly got back to her feet and limped to the wall to catch her breath.

"The only way out of here is either back upstairs to be my slave, or through me to freedom. Come on, you weak little tramp. Let's see if you have any backbone, or have you been pampered all your life and don't have any fight in you."

Xiao gave a cry of indignation and rushed back at the woman with all the venom she could muster. Uzume ducked and let the attacking arms sail overhead. She sprang up, grabbed shoulders, deviated Xiao's impetus, and delivered her into the door she so desperately sought.

A flash of white signalled the connection and Xiao bounced from the timbers with a jarring thud. Just as her senses cleared, she saw red stretch before her eyes and the back of Uzume's leg suddenly hooked around the front of her throat and jerked back and down. Xiao was folded backward until the woman's other thigh met the small of her back. Xiao screamed from the pose as she was contorted over Uzume's thigh, the back of her head now on the ground. Arched into an incredible bow over the woman's leg, her arms rushed out to claw at her, only to be grabbed at the wrist and then turned to lock them into position and make every joint thunder with distress.

"Say you want to be my slave!" she ordered. The tyrant

turned her holds before pushing and arching Xiao even further.

"No! No! No!" she bellowed and threw her legs up to try and cast her knees into Uzume's head. The woman stretched back, and the incoming limbs flashed past and sailed over Xiao's body, causing her to perform a backwards roll that devolved into a disorganised tumble when her wrists were released.

Uzume returned to the door and stood with arms folded across her breasts.

"Is that it. Are we done?" she asked coolly and then examined her nails to check for any damage caused by Xiao's trivial offensives.

"Let me go!" howled Xiao and again charged, employing all her lingering strength.

Uzume performed a sudden pirouette and Xiao caught a brief glimpse of red and black before a scathing slap dodged her arms and crossed her cheek. The ferocity threw her head aside and the pirouette continued and dropped so that a shin could swing out and take her feet from under her.

Xiao landed on her back and the wind was thrown from her lungs. Uzume skipped forward, dropped a foot on either side of the prostrate girl, nudged her arms in against her sides and then dropped down onto her. The woman's legs clenched in and squeezed Xiao's arms to her sides, leaving her hands pawing impotently at the boots and heels.

She squirmed and Uzume let her discover just how helpless she was.

"Ready to be mine, slave?"

"No!" barked Xiao and a slap stung her cheek before striking the other.

"How about now?"

"Get off me, you demon!"

Uzume clapped a hand across Xiao's mouth and the other

pinched her nose shut to stop her breath. Xiao jerked and fought to get away but there was nothing she could do.

"Admit you want to be my slave."

The hand on her mouth lifted a little. Xiao tried to think of something to say, but was lost for words. The woman slapped her cheeks a few more times and each swipe stole away more of Xiao's ability to defy.

"Well? Do you? Answer me!"

Uzume curled an arm back across her body and held the back of the hand towards Xiao. Readying to slam it down onto her face, the vile creature grinned malignantly.

"Okay, okay . . . I . . . I . . ."

"Yes?" purred Uzume, and the muscles of the limb visibly flexed as she readied to deliver a hearty smack.

"Please, Goddess, let me be your slave," she uttered miserably. There was no point fighting any more. She was vanquished and she knew it.

"Good. Now pick up your cuffs, go back upstairs, and lock yourself back in them," she said lightly while climbing off of the defeated form.

Xiao rolled over and started to crawl towards her restraints. She picked them up and trudged drearily upstairs, readying to once again surrender to their control and become the property of this sadistic monster.

Lady Uzume heard the drawbridge being operated and with a huff of irritation wandered upstairs after her slave. She padlocked the middle of her chains to a ring in the wall and told her to kiss each of her nipples in gratitude. The slave complied with sombre reverence, and each peck made Uzume quiver with glee at having so effectively subjugated her property. After complimenting her slaves act of obeisance, she hurried back downstairs.

Uzume's heart was still racing from the fight, and she tried to calm herself while waiting for the portcullis to rise.

When the knock came, she opened the doors and stepped out onto the drawbridge as two officers of the Mitama laid the body of Masuda down on the ground and then remained on their knees. The warriors' armour was cracked in places and every inch of surface was riddled with dozens of impact craters from arrow and bullet. Finally, the integrity of his protective shell had failed under this withering abuse and then eaten through the woven discs of dense material beneath. Dried lines of red emerged from six holes across his chest.

"Tell me what happened," she uttered sombrely.

"Masuda was planning to circumvent the mountains and commence an attack on the Provincial towns along Calolloom Lake. He was sure that the army would retreat to tackle the threat, but they emerged from the mountains and began a march towards our position here. The Wani battalions intercepted them and held firm. Masuda led the cavalry against the flank of the enemy as they emerged, but even so, their numbers were too vast and although we managed to break their lines, they have fled into the peaks and are regrouping. The Wani have dug in to defend our retreat so we might inform you, Lady Uzume, but they are unlikely to hold for long."

"Masuda was a great man and a loyal servant of the Kami. This will not be the last chapter in his career. Ready all forces. I will not leave our Wani to stand alone while we crawl back to the Empire in disgrace. Ready my mount. We go to finish what my second in command started."

"Bu . . . I . . . Lady Uzume, we are outnumbered at least fifty to one. A Kami of your status cannot be-"

"Do not presume to tell a Kami what they can or cannot do," she said sternly.

"My absolute apologies, Lady Uzume. It is just . . . well . . .

they are so many . . . we are so few. We must not let you be put in jeopardy, th-"

"I am Kami in the Great Houses of Fire. I ride with those who worship me, and I will lead us to victory. Then we will return to the Empire and give Masuda a fitting burial, one that is proudly cloaked in victory, not stained with defeat."

"I conquer!" roared the officers.

"*We* conquer," corrected Uzume and both men jerked as though struck. Their deity was riding with them into war. All trace of doubt was now gone.

Uzume turned to go and gather her armour. The supply force would be despatched to begin the return voyage and take Xiao out of harm's way. Lady Uzume would ride with her forces and engage the enemy. Defeat was certain, and she would have to retreat, but by reinforcing the Wani she was sending a powerful message. To the Empire, the Wani were expendable and would accept catastrophic losses on the whim of the Kami, by siding with them, and fighting to save them, she would astound Toyotama-hiko and make him believe that she cared a great deal about these loyal foot soldiers. His seduction would come even more swiftly because of it. If she perished in the fight, her replacement would be propositioned instead, just as she had anticipated and, in some ways, hoped for.

Destiny would now decide the fate of Uzume, her slave, and that of the Empire.

CHAPTER TWO

Candy's hopes were confirmed, and the aftermath of orgasm allowed her to acquire a few periods of fitful snoozing even in the eerie pose that the frame demanded. The *V* shaped metal frame held her ankles out and her wrists midway along each strut before the apex formed a collar that captured her throat. A ring at the back kept her suspended in the air and utterly vulnerable. All she had wanted to do was rest and recover but the bondage made this difficult, fortunately, a concubine had thrust a thigh between her splayed legs and brought her to climax. When she wailed from the bliss, the sound sensitive shock collar that embraced her neck then punished her viciously, and brought her once more into the terribly addictive realm where pain and pleasure merged into a sinister and intoxicating force. As trying as it was, the exhaustion from this encounter had at least let her gain some much needed sleep.

The sound of the pressure door being opened roused her, but not to a degree where she truly awoke.

A slap skimmed her breast and then returned to swat the other. The startling sound and the lucid flash of pain caused her to cry out. Candy immediately gave a brief squawk of frightened horror that dropped into a bemused gurgle when the collar failed to react to her noises.

"Wake up, slave!" came a stern male voice and the hand returned to start spanking her breasts. The light swats oscillated from side to side, each impact making the flesh flop from side to side.

"I'm awake! I'm awake!" she cried as the attack continued.

The alluring visage of the Supreme Warlord of Water was standing before her, and he was dressed only in a flowing silken robe. His muscular arms were casually abusing her as she thrashed and tried to get away or at least shield the targets. Upon seeing Warlord Toyo-tama-hiko she quickly tried to mitigate any damage her rash words might cause.

"Master! Please! I'm awake!" she whimpered.

The slaps stopped and he merely grabbed her nipples in callous pinches and squeezed. Candy shuddered and her limbs remained tensed. Her feet curled in and her hands furled into fists as he added more power to the hold. Having acquired a great deal of recent experience in staying quiet, Candy stifled her responses and merely looked at him while her face reddened with strain.

Toyo-tama-hiko continued to tighten his pinch and then rolled the nipples. The rings were pulsating within the flesh as they were forced outward. A gurgle appeared in her throat, but she still managed to stay quiet.

"Good," he remarked.

The pinches came away and Candy's body relaxed. The peaks of her breasts were now reverberating with a stern pulse as circulation rushed back in, but the fight to stay silent had been the real trial.

The Warlord folded his arms before his strong chest and merely stared at her. Candy kept her eyes lowered and remained patient.

"You were the water concubine at the edge of the western abyss, were you not?" he said with toneless gravity.

Candy could not formulate an answer and so chose to remain quiet, feigning awe or fear while she ran through the possibilities. Was he certain of this? Had she committed a transgression? Would honesty serve her, or would it condemn her? The penalties would be grave, and she was afraid of inspiring his wrath.

"Speak," he barked, and spanked her breasts with four harsh swats that made her jump against her bonds and squeak with shock.

"I . . . I was swimming and saw some sort of military outpost. That's all," she stammered.

"What sort of military?" he asked firmly and then grabbed her nipple rings.

The Warlord grinned malignantly and started to gradually pull towards him. Candy gave a hiss of despair as her rings started to draw at her flesh and stretch the tender tips. The more he pulled, the more the pain gathered and from fearing serious trauma, her words tumbled out.

"I saw the Water Wani. I saw the secret army you're breeding in the depths!"

The Warlord released his captives and as though to apologise for his evil, he leaned in and kissed them. His tongue curled through the ring he had abused and flicked it about while the tip of his organ slithered back and forth, tickling the very summit of each breast. Candy's eyes rolled and a deep resonant moan rumbled from her throat.

"Hmmm, this poses a problem for me. One I will have to consider at length."

The Warlord stepped back and continued to stare at her. At some unspoken command, a pair of naked females marched through the doors.

The two women swiftly unfastened her ankles and let them drop to the floor. Candy arched onto tiptoe and grimaced as her joints and muscles thundered with deep aches from her long and awkward containment.

Her hands dropped to her sides, and she clutched them to her body as they too suffered the bilious effects of freedom from the frame. Finally, her collar was opened and as her legs wilted beneath her, the two Imbe caught her under the shoulders and hoisted her back up.

With her head sagging forward, Candy saw that the stern bruises created by the canes had almost vanished. Her time in the frame had either been considerably longer than she had thought, or the gel the maid had applied in the wake of climax was some sort of regenerative agent to help her body speed its recovery.

The smooth stone passages of the undersea world wandered by, and her feet slipped and skipped against the floor. Stumbling against the holds of the women, Candy was summarily taken to a new and luxurious chamber.

A domed ceiling offered the standard view of the ocean depths, with its flocks of mermaids and clouds of dazzlingly coloured tropical fish. A series of ornate lamps emerged from the walls and cast up dancing spires of flame that amply illuminated the room.

The middle of the chamber was dominated by a sunken Jacuzzi. The waters were tinted with pale pink hue and steam curled up to fill the room with a delicate scent. Around the edge were a few exquisite vases and pots, some of them holding a plant, others holding a variety of brushes, bottles, and other items.

Candy was brought to the waters and the women merely stepped in and brought her with them. She was turned around and laid back before her arms were hoisted up and entered into a pair of dense rubber shackles that lurked just beneath the surface of the water. The pair of buckles were pulled tight, leaving some slim chains to reach out and snag a dense ring on the perimeter of the bath. The two women then sank down and captured Candy's ankles before hauling up and stretching her out across the surface. A matching pair of fetters was secured around her ankles, and she was left lewdly spread-eagled across the water.

She laid her head back to submerge her hair as the scented

waters poured their heat into her body. The women departed and with reverence removed Toyo-tama-hiko's robe before they settled down onto their knees, holding the garment between them. Candy could see their lowered eyes locking to his departing form. Their fingers eagerly pawed at the material that had once graced the flesh of their deity.

With an indulgent groan, the Warlord stepped into the waters and sank down at Candy's left side. Once soaked, he arose again with the crystal fluids streaming down his bare physique. He towered over her and reached across her body, his erect length just brushing her side as he rummaged in a squat vase.

"Ah, here we are," he commented as one hand pulled something free. Candy turned to look and then his free hand pinched her lips and pulled her gaze back around to his torso.

The Warlord straightened with what appeared to be a pair of plain chopsticks in his hand. One end was tied tightly together with slim cord to leave the other open and resembling a pair of blunt scissors. Already fastened to one strut was more cord and Candy struggled a little as she saw what was being intended.

"I can't have you ruining my plans, or exposing what you know," he commented, and slipped the sticks into position.

Candy murmured and mewed as she looked up at him with imploring eyes. The Warlord pulled the other end of the sticks together until they met, and the two wooden bars crushed her lips between them. The flesh throbbed as it was swollen up on the other side of the pincers, and Toyo-tama-hiko quickly tied the other ends together to create a mordant and highly effective gag.

"There we are. Silent and obedient. Which is what I require from you."

The Warlord released the implement and his hands wandered up and down her slick body as she shuddered and caused ripples to roll out from her stretched physique. The disturbed waters lapped at her sides, and she murmured despairingly. As though talking to himself, he continued to casually appraise her anatomy while revealing her fate.

"The Midzhu Wani are a closely guarded secret. Normally they are kept in more discreet surroundings, but a larger exercise was required to test their mettle, and it was thought that no concubines would travel so far from the bathyspheres. It seems that an error was made."

Candy trembled as her lips pounded from being so methodically crushed but the sticks were far too tight for her to pull her assailed flesh through. Every attempt just heightened the pain.

The Warlord closed his hands to her breasts and gently caressed them. His thumbs reached up and started to flick her rings up and down, repeatedly flipping them to tickle her pierced nipples. Candy could feel him swaying slightly and she elated in the exquisite feel of his cock brushing her flanks as it dragged through the water.

"However, I cannot have you informing Hachiman as to their existence, or anyone else for that matter. You see, slave, I want them as a secret reserve force, one that I can deploy should my forces encounter trouble when they cross over."

The hands of the Warlord started to become a little rougher and he began to push down into her with a strong surge of his arms. Candy's body sank beneath the surface and her arms and legs were stretched against their bonds before he let go and allowed her to float back up.

"If the Empire knew of their existence, then, in the event of catastrophe, the Houses would demand their deployment, and to be honest, I'd rather keep them to exclusively rescue the Houses of Water from disaster or use my Water Wani to acquire a massive victory. So, now you can see my quandary. And the only solution is to hide you away and keep you silent, slave."

The Warlord pushed down harder still, and Candy's features dropped beneath the shimmering waters. She exhaled slowly to stop water entering her nose and glared up while fighting the urge to panic. He remained a distorted image as she lurked beneath the surface and then he pushed down harder. She gurgled as her limbs were infused with rending misery from being so forcefully racked. The sounds emerged as large clouds of bubbles that poured from her nostrils and stole the last of her air. As soon as the bubbles stopped, he let go and she immediately pulled on all of her limbs to yank herself back to the surface. She shook her head to fling the water from her nostrils and stole several swift pants to regulate her breathing.

"And now to make you vanish," he whispered directly into her ear before he slumped back against the side of the bath.

Footfalls sounded in the chamber and the women arose to attend the new arrival.

"I extend my hospitality to you, Oho-toshi. May prosperity be upon the Houses of Earth," said the Warlord and offered a small bow before stretching his arms out along the perimeter.

"And on the Houses of Water, Toyo-tama-hiko."

A tall and wiry male stepped into the waters on her right and looked across the form of Candy without much interest before he also lounged back. The Jacuzzi broke into immediate life and surging jets of water rushed around beneath her as bubbles poured up and tickled her back. Candy's head jumped up and she gave a stifled cry as a single and potent jet sent tight buffeting waves between her legs. The turbulence massaged her pussy and raged against her clit. With a sumptuous moan she dropped her head back into the waters and swirled it around to feel the agitated waters rush through her hair as her legs flexed and her fingers and toes wriggled.

"How goes the harvest, my friend?" asked Toyo-tama-hiko.

"A little excess in some areas, a little deficient in others. Much as always in fact."

"Balance in all things then?" quipped the Warlord.

For a short time, the two men talked of the matters of their two Houses. Oho-toshi seemed to be a master of gathering and storing food and much of the conversation centred on what the aquatic forces of the Warlord had seen of the underwater harvests. Oho-toshi, like all Kami, was a jealous guardian of his position and was not about to risk it on the word of just one House. He wanted to make sure everything was confirmed and reconfirmed from every source possible. The pursuit of perfection in everything they did was paramount to the Kami, perhaps because of habit, or upbringing, but also because success ensured the continuation of their immortality.

Candy flashed to a rigid pose as she reached climax, but the waters did not stop, and she was left howling impotently against her gag as the jets continued to pummel her loins. She threw her head aside and stared at the Warlord with utter beseeching as another orgasm was forced upon her. He failed to even notice her exquisite suffering and just kept his stare on the guest.

She screwed her eyes shut as she was goaded into another potent release. Her ability to withstand this was already gone, and she was now in an unendurable hell of ecstasy. The jets could not be denied. Their comprehensive assault between her greatly splayed thighs was constant and the stimulation was unbearable. She squealed against her gag and yanked at her bonds, fighting to get free with all her strength. Even the cane could not bring such levels of effort from her, and she found that horribly unwanted orgasm was a much more vicious weapon that any item of corporal punishment.

She stiffened her arms and tightened her legs to twist

herself and drag at her bonds so she might lift her sex up and out of the most potent stream. The Warlord responded by hoisting a leg and laying his foot to her stomach. He applied weight and pushed her down so that she was again in the full flow. Candy fought to stop him, but his strength and her awkward position meant that she had little hope of success. She shrieked against her gag as the central jets rushed against her pussy and pounded the whole region with brutal delight. Another vicious orgasm made her squeal and jerk against the limb that was serving her up to the potent flow.

"Look at those muscles flex!" commented Oho-toshi and his hand reached out to run along one of Candy's battling thighs as it bobbed up and down beneath the surface with every convulsion.

"It does indeed appear that she's having lots of fun," said Toyo-tama-hiko.

He drew his leg back and Candy tugged herself back up and managed to ease the influence of the jets. Her body was aching from the fight, and she knew she wouldn't be able to keep herself elevated for long, and yet even in her current pose she was still being subjected to the awful stimulation. All she could do was diminish it. There was no escape from continual and strength sapping climax.

"Why the gag?" asked Oho-toshi. His touch was becoming more libidinous as the sight of her turmoil began to intrigue him.

"She's new, and unruly. This one requires a lot of discipline, and its effects rarely stick for long," said the Warlord without a hint of falsehood in his words.

"And she's one of yours?" asked Oho-toshi.

"On loan from a friend, but I'm thinking of giving her away."

Candy jerked her head around as she realised what was happening. The Warlord was going to have her shipped away so she could not inform anyone as to the secrets she had discovered. He wanted his army kept covert and until he was ready to use them, she would have to vanish.

The look of absolute panic went unnoticed. Toyo-tama-hiko did not care how much she loved her master, or what being separated from him would be like, he was thinking only of the security of his House.

"Really? Won't her owner miss her?"

"No. I doubt he would even notice," replied Toyo-tama-hiko, speaking as though Candy was a trinket of absolutely no consequence to him or her owner. "Any suggestions?"

Candy fought to bellow that she was Hachiman's, that she was his personal property and not some cast off, but the pincers and yet another orgasm destroyed her efforts.

"Water concubine?" offered Oho-toshi as he saw her bounce and thrash.

"She's already experienced that facet of my world. I was thinking of a more radical shift. Come on, old friend. What would give you pleasure? What you most like to see this struggling form condemned too?" asked the Warlord.

"She would make a fine pony. Such a role would put these muscles to good use."

Candy fought afresh as one orgasm faded and another instantly began to loom, but it was fear of being taken away and hidden in the Empire that now inspired such tumult.

"How could we see to her enrolment?" asked Toyo-tama-hiko.

"Well, Hohodemi failed to make his Tyrannosaur quota a few months back. Through a little subterfuge I made it seem that Yama tsu mi had been careless and it was deforestation on his part that drove the herds further north, causing the carnivores to follow and leave Hohodemi deprived. I could see about having her placed in his best Pony Dojo. The Dojo of the Koma-gata."

The Warlord gave a discontented grumble. He let his head drop back and thereby hide his expression and any clue that this entire negotiation was an orchestrated one.

"Hohodemi would ask a great deal to enrol her, especially because he would suspect that she is important to us, so I wouldn't ask you to waste such a grand favour."

"Then how do we proceed?" asked Oho-toshi "We must find a way to surreptitiously enrol her without anyone knowing that we are interested in the outcome."

The man's imagination had been ignited. The problem of how to deposit Candy into the fate he wanted to see sentenced to was one he furiously wanted to overcome. It was the Warlord who offered him the solution, and Candy was now convinced that the whole conversation had been leading towards this moment.

"I suggest we send her to House Uka no mitama. That will get her used to being a beast while I arrange a discreet party and invite some of the Earth Kami. Yama tsu mi could make up for his supposed error by hosting it, and of course, Hohodemi will be invited to accept the apology in person."

"And while he is there, I'm sure we can draw her to his attention," said Oho-toshi with a rampant eagerness now prevailing in his voice.

"I also have a few Nakatomi in his House who owe me favours of no consequence. They can laud her attributes most effectively and then inspire his desire to possess her and train her. Hohodemi will then ask Yama tsu mi for her, and this will negate the debt that the host supposedly owes his honoured guest. Balance and peace are restored, and you have what you want—to see this elegant weeping form bound and trained as a pony, her fate determined by your desires," purred the Warlord.

The plan was now clear to Candy. By making this a secret game between them, her transfer would seem mundane. She would go unnoticed into one House before being caught up in the desires of another. It would obfuscate her tracks and make it all the harder to find her again, especially when Kami were enduring debts and favours over her acquisition. All of the Machiavellian scheming would be between Kami, and no one would suspect that anyone was even interested in her. The Warlord's secret would be safe, and as a beast she would be denied speech to ensure his secret endured. Hachiman would never find her amongst the herds. She would be lost to him forever.

"And I will owe you for this, of course. Organising a function for such Kami will not be inexpensive even if another is acting as host," said Oho-toshi and then paused in contemplation as he watched her weep and cavort against her bonds. "Still, I am eager to see if this plan works. So, I will only be indebted to you when this female is accepted into House Hohodemi."

As she writhed and fought her restraints, Candy could see that the banality of his position in the Kami of Earth was one that inspired plotting and considerable intrigue. The deities of Fire and Water dealt with absolutes such as war, invasion, and battle. The Earth Kami had a much more peaceful existence and so they devoted inordinate time and attention to the most trivial whimsies. Candy was now a pawn to amuse Oho-toshi's perverse desires. A capricious interest to see her become a pony had set a massive plot in motion, and he was anxious to see it unravel just as he intended. Like the crops his House protected, a seed had been planted and patience and care was needed to bring it to harvest.

Only Candy and the Warlord knew that the whole plot was a smoke screen, one to carry a vaulted secret into the shadows. She knew that Oho-toshi would never have agreed to be part of this trivial game if he were aware that she was Warlord Hachiman's concubine, the one he had vied for against other interested Kami, but the Warlord of Water had engineered her downfall with precision. Her one glimpse over the abyss and of a hidden army had doomed her, and it was all because she wanted mermaids to stop inflating the dildo residing in her bottom.

"Agreed. And if I fail to secure Hohodemi's interest in her, then I will owe you a great debt," said the Toyo-tama-hiko, gaining added commitment to the plan through the possibility that if it failed, then the Supreme Warlord of Water would be in the debt of a mere Earth Kami.

"Agreed," was his enthusiastic reply and Oho-toshi stood up and brushed excess water from his limbs. The jets of water stopped, and Candy went limp to float between her restraints and pant in recovery. Twitches of her thighs made more waves, and her deep breaths created steady ripples.

"Escort my guest to his chambers and bring in my Mikado," ordered Toyo-tama-hiko.

The women stood up and attended the Kami as Toyo-tama-hiko lingered in the waters. The sound of their footsteps vanished, and silence descended.

"So, Candy. This is it. Your fate is sealed. You will be lost amongst the faceless herds of beasts and shuffled from place to place until we can get you all tightly bound in a harness and bit, prancing at the end of a whip," stated the Warlord, causing fresh lines of tears to tumble from Candy's eyes. He mocked them with a dark titter and slid back so he could again lay his foot to her torso and casually torment her with repeated dunkings. She accepted the abuse with little response because her heart felt like stone. She was forced under the waters and made to hold her breath for as long as she could but there was little resentment or fight left in her. Her body was exhausted, and her thoughts were numb from the terrible knowledge that she was to be separated from Hachiman for the rest of her days. Such a crime made Toyo-tama-hiko's repeated dips seem like a paltry abuse.

"Warlord," came the voice of Hirata. "I have news."

The Mikado walked around the tub and leant down to piously offer a scroll. The Warlord unravelled it and scrutinised the contents. Hirata looked over to her and smiled when he saw her miserable expression.

"You are sure of this information?"

Toyo-tama-hiko dipped the scroll in the water and lifted it out. The delicate script instantly ran from the page and left a small dark cloud of ink floating before him.

"Yes, Warlord. It is from a significant and trusted source. The Amatsu mika hoshi are definitely bringing a new vessel through."

"So soon after the last?" quizzed the Warlord.

"Apparently, a vessel bearing some important political personages has had its navigation charts and equipment doctored. It will blunder off course and be steered into a potent confluence of Izanagi and Izanami. The loss is being prepared to further destabilise the region and other agents in various ruling bodies will proclaim sabotage, murder, and assassination. Basically all the usual provocations."

Toyo-tama-hiko screwed up the sodden page and tossed the destroyed message aside.

"A time of celebration then. And that means a festival," he muttered before he loosed a jubilant laugh. "I said that there would be a party, but promised nothing about organising it personally. With every Kami attending the great plane, I can still see about having her presented to Hohodemi, acquire Oho-tashi's debt, and dispose of this troublesome slave all in one fell swoop. Well done, Mikado, this is wonderful news indeed. You may have this slave for the night and then send her to me first thing in the morning."

"Thank you, Warlord."

Candy flinched when she saw the sudden ravenous glower

of the Mikado and then flung her stare around when she felt the end of the pincers being manipulated. The cord was untied, and the two sticks jumped apart. A moment later, her jaws were fling wide and she screamed in anguish as searing mayhem ran through her long-compressed lips. She sucked them in, pursed them tightly, and shuddered as the horrible process of recovery continued to rage in her mouth.

The Warlord dropped the item into the waters and strolled from the Jacuzzi, leaving her to the callous desires of his most trusted priest.

CHAPTER THREE

L ady Uzume could see numerous smudged streams of black rising from the mountains. Thousands of campfires were soiling the sky above the peaks with a spectral cloud that drifted off into the distance. The enemy forces were definitely mustering back into a cogent force after her second in command had broken their lines and routed them at the cost of his life.

Her mount continued to trudge onwards as the bulk of her forces followed reverently in her wake. It would take a few more days to reach the peaks and on the plains before them, destiny would be unveiled.

Uzume had bound her new toy as tightly as possible and left her in pained, demeaned isolation. The supply convoy had then been sent back to the Empire.

With a hand on her sword, she clenched to feel the reassuring presence of her most prized blade. It had served her in countless battles, but never one as important and decisive as the one she now faced. Uzume knew she might not survive this fight, and this was the very reason she was so eager to embrace it.

Warlord Hachiman was her beloved master, and yet he had sent her here to provoke war with the Eastern Provinces while he gauged the combat readiness of the Houses of Water. The invasion of Earth was being planned and to guarantee success, not only would they need to make sure they had solid naval support when they crossed over, but also that their neighbours on the home realm did not make a move on the

Empire. If the Provinces noticed the bulk of the Imperial forces vanishing over to assault the other world, they might be provoked into indulging an invasion of their own.

In addition, there were those who believed that her master had too much power over the Imperial armies and so they greatly sought to diminish this influence. Hachiman had decided to take the incentive and was intending for the Warlord of the Wani to seek her hand in joint command over that species. There was no chance that a hybrid such as Toyotamahiko would be allowed to rule his own kind, but with Hachiman's most trusted agent sharing this position, permission would be more forthcoming. The imminent battle with the Provinces would result in shame for Uzume because she was vastly outnumbered and stood no chance of success. She had been given a salvage force, one sent to retrieve a fictitious shipment of firearms that agents on Earth had sent into the vortex. As sometimes happened, the gateway between Pangaea and Earth had drifted and rather than dumping it in the heart of the Kami Empire, the cargo vessel had been deposited somewhere in the east. The Provinces had already retaliated against the recovery force once and killed a scout unit, and then their army had massacred a second wave. Now Uzume was moving in with what remained of her troops to reinforce the Wani who had dug in to protect her retreat. However, there was no shipment. It was all a lie to ensure Imperial indignation at the theft of material and the murder of its loyal soldiers, and therefore let Hachiman bring the full brunt of the Mitama and Wani against their long-time foes.

Hachiman had orchestrated everything so he could feign outrage and expel her from his service for this defeat, thereby allowing her to be recruited without anyone suspecting his involvement, and even this was all part of a greater scheme.

The Wani would sustain significant losses on Earth. They were after all, a fanatic berserker force, one that could be ambushed or tricked into rash action by rebels and brigands. With the Wani removed from his control and therefore his responsibility, Warlord Hachiman would be spared the shame of their defeats.

When these defeats became too excruciating for the rest of the Empire to tolerate in silence, then the humiliated Lady Uzume would be forgiven by her old master and offered her former post at his side.

The only variable her master had not accounted for was whether Uzume could endure being separated from the man she adored for such a duration. As Kami, she was immortal and her flesh could defy the passing centuries, but she was unsure if her heart could do the same.

If she knew inside that she could not bear it, then her skills would fail and she would not leave the battlefield alive. If her sword arm and tactics were strong, then her heart would also have the fortitude to endure divorce from his side.

The sultry submissive concubine that was Candy had gone with her master, and clearly there were plans for the nubile captive from Earth. Hachiman had not enlightened her as to what they might be, but Candy definitely had a part in the coming epoch. To once more have Candy at her beck and call, bound before her and eager to please was another factor in Uzume's desire to endure her detachment and return to her master, but it would also make the intermediate duration all the more harrowing.

There was of course Xiao, the trinket she had snatched when her initial foray into the mountains had stumbled upon a small mining village. Its destruction had been the catalyst to rouse the Provincial armies, and it had furnished Uzume with a cute feminine trophy.

The virginal girl was a delight to torment and degrade. She was untouched by the Houses that processed new slaves and made them more amiable to their lot as the playthings of the

Gods, and Uzume was finding extreme satisfaction in warping the girl's psyche all by herself. She would be trained to adore her kidnapper, and this long and ferocious process would help Uzume pass the time.

The mental image of what she would next inflict on her slave made her shiver lecherously. She smiled and drew her telescope from a saddlebag. Hoisting it to the armoured eyepieces of her grandiose helmet, she could see the hints of the Wani battalion in the extreme distance.

The Provincial forces still lurked in the mountains and were reforming after their initial defeat. A surprise Tyrannosaur charge into their flank had been an instrumental factor in routing them but they would be ready for this tactic now.

Uzume surmised that they might be waiting for the Imperial force to mount the offensive, thereby giving the Provinces the advantage of higher ground where her cavalry would have poor footing and their archers, trebuchet, cannon, and ballista could be used to maximum effect.

The Eastern Provinces were a loose alliance of various major settlements, all descended from continental Far East nationalities of Earth. Even though they were united in their hatred of the Kami Empire, it was unlikely that this unity would last. Petty squabbles amongst their leaders would soon start to crack the cohesion of their army and if Uzume kept her forces back, they could establish some defences and force the Provinces to emerge from the mountains and march on them before their own troops turned on each other. It would negate some of their advantages, diminish their strengths, and allow her to cause serious casualties before her own lines crumbled against their onslaught.

Lady Uzume lowered her telescope and grinned privately. She was eager to immerse herself in the sanguinary heat of battle. Despite the physical aspects of training a slave, there were a lot of psychological aspects to consider—tactics, contingencies, and plots. Sometimes the absolute honesty of life and death warfare was an oddly liberating diversion.

CHAPTER FOUR

Candy tensed her arms and felt the rope tighten to her body. The bright blue coils had been woven onto her torso, capturing her arms behind her with forearms pressed together and held in a single horizontal line. The diamond pattern she so often encountered when bound by the Kami ran down her front and her spine, creating a cocoon that pressed in on her from all directions and wrung her breasts between two lines. A pair of lengths rushed down from the last of the harness, emerging at her hips before they tugged into her inner thighs and rose over her buttocks to snag the weave on the other side.

It had been a swift relocation to this room. Hirata had unfastened her and ordered her out of the Jacuzzi. She had obeyed the Mikado with stolid movements and no resistance. Her grief at losing her master was still ruling her and she just didn't have any strength left to try and rebel, complain, or do anything but mindlessly accept her lot. She couldn't even focus on what had been said about a new arrival, or what this "great plane" might be and what its significance was. She just didn't care anymore.

With eyes lowered, she had followed him to a simple chamber where smooth stone walls bore some small lamps and a series of lacquered cabinets and an ornate low table in the middle of the room. Several mirrored doors led into other rooms and allowed her to see herself being bound from every angle, and despite her melancholy attitude, the process had not been an unwelcome one. The rope was soft and sensuous, and the hands of the Mikado were gentle and caring as he slowly created an intricate masterpiece of bondage upon his prisoner.

Ordinarily, she would have found her predicament exciting. To be handed over to another like a toy, especially as a reward for exemplary service, it made her feel important while also impressing upon her how owned she was. Nevertheless, all she could think of was Hachiman. She couldn't even concentrate on forming her own plots. She knew that she had her own means, her own skills that she could use to affect her fate. With time, patience, and skill at manipulation, she could find a path back to her beloved owner, but right now she was in mourning and every attempt to try and craft a stratagem just ended with miserable pining about Hachiman.

The Mikado shed his robe and grabbed the ropes that ran above and below her breasts. Closing his hand, he made the coils tighten into her already swollen assets and then he towed her towards the table. She stepped up onto the smooth surface and was steered into the middle before he let go and settled back. Candy stood to attention as the Mikado sat down crossed legged and looked up at her.

"You miss him, don't you, slave?" asked Hirata.

"Yes, master," she stated without consideration.

Hirata smiled and clapped his hands. One of the doors opened and two women strode in. The twins were gorgeous and slender. They wore their hair short, spiky, and dyed a vibrant blue that matched their makeup which included sapphire lipstick for both their full luscious lips as well as their ringed nipples. A collar embraced their throats, and the towering posture device was crafted from purple patent leather with a single large ring set at the front. Blue tinted stockings flowed up their long legs and a mauve suspender belt kept them in place. Each strode upon knee high patent boots of an identical shade to their collars. The high-heeled boots had a zip at the side over which ran a number of buckles. Each woman carried a small wooden tray and as they knelt down on either side of the Mikado, they started to present him with his meal. Small bowls were arranged before him and with eyes still fixed on Candy, he started to eat.

"I'm not surprised. Hachiman has a powerful presence, and a flawless reputation . . .in *all* things."

Candy swallowed and felt fresh tears well in her eyes. Her lips trembled and her stomach seemed to drop away. She sniffled slightly and fought back the need to weep.

"You blame Toyo-tama-hiko?" he enquired gently.

"I . . . I don't think so," she stammered.

"So who is responsible for your desolation?"

"I don't know," she said flatly, deliberately forsaking his title with view to irking him. She was not in the mood for conversation. If the Mikado wanted to torture her, beat her, or ravish her, then she hoped that he would just hurry up and get on with it. The prospect of some physical pain was a welcome one because it would distract her from her psychological wounds.

"Come now, slave. Surely you have some idea why this is happening?" he crooned.

"A stupid secret. That's all," she grumbled.

"Petulant," commented Hirata. "But I forgive you. It is unfortunate that such a thing has befallen you, but we are all here to serve the Kami. Our own pleasures and wishes must sometimes be forsaken so they may have what they want."

He helped himself to some noodles, washed them down with a sip of water, and then continued to address her.

"Don't you agree, slave?"

"No," she retorted boldly.

"The Empire has endured — unchanged — for thousands of years. The Kami have ensured our prosperity and longevity with their skill and dedication. Our lives have the duration of a finger snap when compared to theirs, and carry just as much significance. The Kami have greater obligations and duties than any mortal can fathom, so why should the infatuation of one slave successfully change their designs?"

"I only know who I truly belong to."

"He may have your heart, but *we* have your flesh, and what *you* have to learn is that sometimes, that is more than enough."

Hirata set down his chopsticks and lifted a small bowl. One of the women filled it and he gestured towards Candy. The twins arose together and stepped up onto the table on either side of her.

"My Nakatomi have desires of their own and I advise you to enjoy them because I assure you, when you are transferred to House Uka no mitama there will be no more of these encounters."

Candy turned her full attention to him but before she could speak, the woman to her left grabbed her chin and hauled her face around. Candy looked at the beautiful features of the woman and then met her cool hungry eyes. Her resistance melted and the woman's lips stretched into an excited smile.

A sudden loud clap echoed in the room as the other female dropped her palm to Candy's rear. The soft warm heat spread across her cheek and her hindquarters jolted forward into the arms of the other Nakatomi. The woman locked an arm around Candy as she bumped into her and pulled her head in to demand a kiss.

Candy parted her lips and let the woman run her organ along her lower lip before she sucked on it and then curled her tongue into Candy's mouth. She tried to reciprocate, but could not match the woman's obvious passion. The female gave a small snarl and grabbed the ropes at Candy's cleavage before tugging on them to pull her closer and then she squeezed to make the ropes dig in. Candy's mouth dropped open on a small moan and the woman dove back in to continue her feverish kiss.

"Keira is having trouble. Maybe you should offer some encouragement, Kara," announced Hirata.

A pair of fingers slid under the harness at the small of her back and gave a brief yank to pull her rear out for attention. Kara then started to throw her other hand down into the presented cheeks. She slapped from side to side and sometimes threw the back of hand into Candy's thighs. Keira hauled Candy in and fought for a more energetic response. She let go of her head and instead started to swirl her digits against Candy's breasts. Her dextrous fingers danced upon her rings and made the tips stiffen in moments. When this still failed, she dropped her attentions and began to operate her clit ring. Prancing fingers flipped and stroked, swirled and pawed while her sister continued to swell Candy's rear with a succulent internal heat. The skin started to tingle from the spanking and the occasional pinch to a rosy area made Candy mew.

"Enjoy the feel of this slave, my Nakatomi. After this, she is destined to become a beast, a pet of the Kami. Your kisses will be the last ones she feels."

A trio of stern slaps dropped onto her right cheek, making her legs wilt a little beneath her. In the aftermath of each slap, Keira gave her clit a brief pinch to make it course with sudden sensation. Bounced between the two assaults, her head began to swim with licentious glee.

A thought suddenly rushed into Candy's brain. If she were indeed as important to her master as had been implied, she had no cause for worry. If Hachiman truly wanted her, then he would have to fight for her. He had recklessly loaned her out and she had been stolen. If he could recover her, then no doubt he would have learned his lesson and not underestimate the desire of others to keep her or steal her from him. She was shedding tears and suffering because of Hachiman's foolhardy loaning. Here she was, being overwhelmed by delicious feminine kisses, caresses, and spanks, and all she was doing was moping about her former owner.

Candy vowed to disregard her affections for Hachiman. She was owned by the Houses of Water, and would soon be entering the service of other Houses. It was time to revel in and devote herself to these new roles, to suck every moment of joy from her subjugation. Perhaps her master would find her, and if so, she would welcome him with delight, but if not, then she was better off without him and his fleeting attentions. If Hachiman never appeared before her again, it meant that all of his talk and promises had been a lie, a joke to torment her, and she was not going to waste another tear on him.

Candy's passion suddenly reared and she started to kiss back with greater verve. She was a submissive creature, one who would take pleasures however she could. It was time to stop brooding on what was lost and time to start having some fun.

She thrust out her rear and rose to tiptoe to offer the best target she could. Her chest reached up and traced her hardened nipples against the breasts of Keira as her tongue swirled around and nuzzled against the woman's own eager organ.

The hand on her pussy came away and the woman embraced her. With her arms stretched out and leaning on Candy's shoulders, the woman devoted herself to libidinous kisses while her sister continued to deliver her stinging palm into Candy's rear and thighs. Each slap made Candy sway and luxuriate in the warmth that was spreading through her skin.

"Yes, that's much better," attested Hirata, and returned to his dinner while watching the provocative show.

With her eyes half closed, Candy continued to devote herself to enjoying Keira's expert oral attention and she fuelled her lust with every slap that met her bottom. When Hirata had finally finished his meal, he leaned back and decided to let his performers finish.

"Take her," he uttered forcefully.

Candy was pliant against their hands as Keira pushed down on her shoulders while Kara ducked down and gave a brief pull on her knees to make her legs fold. As Candy sank down, Kara dropped onto the table and flipped over. She reached up, grabbed the outside of Candy's thighs and pulled her loins down onto her face. Candy arched and gave a gasp as a spry tongue rushed along her lips and then cavorted against her clit. The tip poured into the ring and slid back and forth, stretching the rampant morsel with every surge.

Kara stepped forward and made use of Candy's agape jaws. Sinking one hand into the back of her hair, she clenched and used this smarting anchor to pull Candy into her own humid sex. Candy responded with jubilation and thrust her own tongue deep into Keira before lapping upward and pouring the full flat of her wet length against the female. Candy continued with a slow and measured rate, lapping diligently while the woman held tight to her hair and let her other hand roll across her torso and tease her own skin. The hand circled breasts, toyed with rings, and stretched up and down the full length of her chest while her head rolled back and she panted with delight.

When Kara's diligent tongue escorted Candy into orgasm, she gripped tightly and held on so that her target could not escape. Jolting against the brutal pleasure, Candy's own affections became more haphazard, a failing that acquired a few slaps to her cheeks to encourage a more precise rhythm. Fighting to concentrate as Kara suckled on her clit and rushed her tongue around her pussy, Candy tried to pull away, but the woman just held on and made sure she kept her face buried between Candy's thighs.

Keira's breathing deepened and she started to squeak with rapture. Candy thrashed her organ as skilfully as she could, dancing her tip to the woman in a final effort. As Keira squealed with rhapsody, Kara continued to assail Candy and make it even harder for her to continue. Only when her sister pushed Candy away did the other concubine release her hold and drop back to the table.

Kneeling and gasping for breath, Candy watched as the two women stepped from the surface and gathered up the plates. Hirata kept his eyes on her and then shuffled back a little. His cock jumped up from beneath the table.

A Mikado had once again been instrumental in shaping her desires, and her gratitude to Hirata for banishing her torpor was great. Candy lowered herself onto her front and slowly slithered across the tabletop towards him. Hirata just smiled and leaned back to prop himself up on with his arms.

The Mikado said nothing as she craned her neck off the edge and devoured his manhood. Her tongue was a little raw from all the activity, but her lips and neck were ready for action. Still raging with lust, she locked her maw to him and began a slow and methodical fellatio. Savouring every moment, she strained against her rope bondage to feel it shift against her and she pumped her head up and down, taking him as deeply as she could. It was a testament to the skill of their show that his arousal from it quickly brought him to climax. He barked with joy and his fingers clawed at the ground as he shuddered and filled her palate with the taste of him. Candy consumed with abandon and quaked on the tabletop.

"I wish to retire. Secure her here and let her think on what her future holds," he stated and moved back, pulling himself from her clamped lips.

The sound of heels clicking on stone moved closer and the sisters grabbed Candy's ankles. A few loops of rope embraced each joint and her legs were stretched out, spread wide, and tied to table legs.

Hirata stood up and the women closed in to thread rope through the coils on Candy's shoulders and stretch more lengths out to the other corners, pinning her down and leaving her head draping from the end.

He ran his fingers through hair and then marched from the room with the Nakatomi in tow. A moment later the lamps dimmed slightly to leave her pale skin glowing slightly in the remaining twilight.

CHAPTER FIVE

Candy spent a restless night spread and tied to the table. Her insomnia was not inspired by the pose, her nakedness, or the slight chill in the air, but it was from the sheer mystery of her fate. Every time she started to worry, she snarled and fought away such negative emotions, focusing instead on dreams of submission to new masters.

The eerie world of the Water Kami was a timeless void where night and day did not exist, so although every minute seemed like hours, when a door opened and someone started to enter, the banal duration suddenly seemed as though she had only been deserted a short time ago.

Candy turned her head around and saw Kara sauntering towards her. The woman wore only a pair of mesh tights and a set of leg hugging leather thighboots. Wrapped around her hindquarters was more leather and from a triangular panel at the crotch sprouted a bright blue dildo. Kara set a tube and another device down by Candy's hip and stepped out before her. She stamped a heeled foot down by Candy's head, hooking the instep on the edge of the table.

"Lick!" she snapped.

Candy cocked her head and started to pour her tongue against the warm hide and felt a distinct tremor run through it as the woman enjoyed her power over her.

"Mmmm, I just couldn't sleep with the thought of this supple body splayed across the table. I just *had* to get up and fuck it," she crooned.

Kara crouched down in front of her, grabbed the artificial

cock at the root and jerked the head up towards Candy's face.

"Suck it," she hissed. "Suck it like you took my master's cock."

Candy opened her lips and the woman thrust her pelvis up to have the toy stampede into her maw. Her eyes bulged and she gagged a little. When she tried to pull away, Kara grabbed the back of her head in both hands and held firm.

"No you don't!" she warned and lifted her hips higher. Candy watched the leather on her thighs ripple with the play of muscles as Kara swayed and while holding firm, began to ravish Candy's mouth. With lips locked to the smooth rubber toy, she caught the scent of the Nakatomi's wanton arousal, and this inspired her own libido.

"Yes, that's it. Let me fuck your face!" growled Kara and her loins jumped up and down as her fingers pawed at the back of Candy's head.

Suddenly she let go and stepped up onto the table. After prancing over Candy's bound form, she knelt down between her thighs and took up what she had been carrying when she had first entered.

In the dim reflection of a door, Candy saw her unravel wire from around a small silvery egg that she promptly stuffed down behind the crotch plate of her harness. The end of the coil bore a small plastic control with a dial, and when she spun this, a steady hum emerged from the smothered egg.

"Oooooh, yes," moaned Kara, and after tucking the control into a small sheath at her hip, she grabbed the tube of lubricant, held it over Candy's rear, and squeezed. The viscous gel dripped down from above, spattering her opening and chilling the skin. Kara giggled as she saw the opening clench.

"Oh don't fret, slave. I'll be warming up that little hole soon enough."

Kara dropped a hand into Candy's back to prop herself up and snatched the dildo with the other. She steered it into place and swirled the head against her target. Candy mewed and tried to relax so as to permit easier entry.

The woman remained poised and snatched Candy's hair. She hauled her head up whereupon the other palm clapped over her lips and held tight. With a sadistic thrust the toy opened her and rushed deep. Candy shrieked against the smothering hand and broke into spasms. Her anus reacted with searing animosity to the trespass, but Kara just laughed and jiggled her hips to churn the fully sheathed toy within her.

"Yes, that's it, slave! Suffer!" she purred and jumped back so that the toy departed in full before she stabbed back in again. The second entry was a little easier and when she pressed up against Candy's rear, she could feel the tiny vibrations of the egg through the leather and in the toy itself.

Kara started to slowly draw away and then rushed in with more celerity, and as Candy grew used to the invasion, the hand at her mouth came away and instead held tightly to her flank. The hand in her hair remained, and Kara took delight in delivering small pulls to hoist Candy's head and make her jaw drop open. Generally this came with a thrust of the dildo, and her croak of answer came all the easier.

The burning pain gave way to a luxurious heat that ran through her rear and filled her stretched channel. The slither and slide of the toy as it drilled deep into her body made Candy moan with licentious joy and the momentary tremble when she felt the egg lean to her made her envy Kara's intimate companionship with it.

"I enjoyed spanking this cute butt, but now I get to have some real fun with it," hissed Kara and remained deeply impaled so she could again squirm her pelvis and churn the toy.

"Oh thank you!" uttered Candy and gave a squeak as the woman yanked sharply on her hair.

"Mistress!" snarled Kara.

"Yes, mistress, I'm sorry, mistress," she stammered as the toy nudged deeper and pushed to the limits of what she could accept.

"That's better. I can see that your imminent devolution will be advantageous," muttered Kara and then pulled on her hair again before she spoke with harsh tones, "It'll keep this disobedient mouth shut for good!"

"I'm sorry, mistress. I'll be quiet," she croaked.

Kara cast her disdainfully away and held to her sides with both hands.

"Oh speak if you want. You'll not have that option for much longer."

"Mistress, I don't want to be a pet!" sobbed Candy, struggling against her ropes as she was reminded that her time was running out and that her transfer to another House was imminent. She may well have been resigned to it, but was still scared.

"Pet? My you've got a high opinion of yourself, don't you? You'll be an animal. A creature kept contained and servile. It'll take you a lot of hard work, commitment, and time before you can work your way up to such a vaulted position as that of mere pet," said Kara and continued her ravishment with fresh gusto.

"Mistress! This isn't fair!" gasped Candy as her body was surged forward with every drastic thrust.

"You're damn right it isn't. How did you get to be so lucky?" growled the woman. "Lift your head up and look round."

"I . . . I don't understand, mistress," muttered Candy as she obeyed the order.

Kara curled an arm up and around and delivered a backhand slap to Candy's cheek. The stern slap made her cheek swell with sorrow and the impact threw her head back down. She sobbed and let her head just dangle from the edge as the side of her face throbbed.

"Other side, slave."

"No, please, mistress. Don't!" she exclaimed, shaking her head in denial while keeping it down. Kara slammed with venom, pushing deep and making Candy whimper from accepting the length.

"Other side! Now do it!"

With a meek turn, Candy presented the target and closed her eyes. The slap struck home and dropped her face back down whereupon she wept softly.

"Much better. Now, shall I tell you why you are so fortunate, slave?"

"Y . . . yes, please, mistress," she uttered drearily.

"You are going to explore the pleasures of a completely alien House, and you are going to do so yet again. I was born into service of the Houses of Water. I adore my master, and Toyo-tama-hiko. I am loyal unto death and beyond to the Kami, but oh, to be able to see what else lies beyond this aquatic domain," said Kara and gave a long wanton groan as her voice and body quavered at the mere thought.

"You have tasted the rapture in the palace of Warlord Hachiman. You have been with the Wani daughters, and with Lady Uzume. You have been with the Warlords of Water, and Oho-tashi. And now . . ."

Her words ended as she panted and started to succumb to orgasm. The raging egg and her own lustful fantasies were proving too much to deny, and Kara launched the toy into Candy as she continued to speak in fits and starts.

" . . . now you get to be a slave in new and unexplored ways. Facets I have only dreamed of, and yet you curse this exemplary fortune."

The woman gave a spasm and eased the dildo back until it came free of her bottom.

"Cheek. Now!"

Candy jerked her features up into view and yearned for her chastisement. The slap was stronger this time, inspired by anger at Candy's resentment of what Kara regarded as a triumphant reward.

"What will they do to you, slave? What animal will you become? Who will use you? How will they use you? Will you get to come? Or will you be kept chaste? Oh, imagine it — desperate for relief, charged with arousal that you cannot satisfy. Mmmmm, I would give anything to endure your fate. You are embroiled in a game of the Gods. Failure will have me demoted or sent to Yomi, but you, you can act however you wish. You are probably the most free being in the whole Empire!"

Kara's rate started to become corrupted as flashes of bliss made her jolt and stall her molestation. Candy felt the toy fire into her and then wait before jumping back and repeating its assault. Kara threw her head back and gave an ecstatic squeal. Her thighs clamped together, and her body juddered as the egg raged against her pussy. When she had sated her desires in full, she flung herself back and fumbled for the control to end the stimulation.

Sprawled between Candy's legs, she gathered herself and once her breath was steady, she stood up.

Candy gave a whimper when a heel leaned into her rear and pushed down into the flesh. A turn brought more distress to the skin.

"Ungrateful little bitch."

Kara gave another sharp prod that made Candy squawk and then with a derisive huff she stomped from the chamber and slammed the door in her wake. Candy closed her eyes and let her head hang limp as she embraced the feel of the throbbing ache in her bottom.

CHAPTER SIX

Lady Uzume heard the sharp brittle rattle of arrows striking the armour of her steed and felt several projectiles bounce harmlessly from her shoulder plates. The great beast gave a screeching roar of irritation as several of them bit between joints and sank into its dense hide. A moment later, she was in the hectic fray.

The Wani fought on with consummate skill and unbridled fury, striking down a human soldier with every hack of their massive swords and pole arms. The crack of firearms was now a sporadic sound with most magazines having been emptied in the seconds before the two armies clashed. The terrible swathe that the Imperials had gouged into the enemy ranks with their automatic fire had quickly been filled by the overwhelming numbers gathered by the Eastern Provinces. After having feared the Empire for so long, every man who could hold a weapon was anxious to exorcise this loathing in one bloody orgy. Thinking this to be the full measure of Imperial might, they thought victory over the ancient enemy was at hand, little realising that this was a tiny fraction of what the Kami could bring to bear.

Tiny forms crumpled under the massive feet of her steed as it stomped into a flanking regiment. The Wani were occupied with the main line, and the Mitama Megalosaur cavalry were intercepting other flanking units while skirmishers to pierce the line and reach either the command group, or the war machines. The Imperial line was ailing, and so she had personally led the Tyrannosaurs into combat.

Uzume dug the butt of her assault rifle into her shoulder and opened fire with wanton spray. Spent cartridges danced across the saddle as her mount's maw dove down and snatched up clusters of enemy troops that it shredded with several grinding bites. The beast danced on the foe and was immediately joined by its brethren. The regiment unfortunate enough to be underfoot promptly broke.

With titanic armoured carnivores prancing on their number and eating them whole while the riders brutalised them with machine gun fire had proven too much for the eager unit and they were suddenly fleeing for their lives. A great roar went up as Wani acknowledged the prevention of the flank attack and gave praise to Uzume for her intervention. With a Kami in their midst and fighting with them, the savagery of the Wani visibly increased and even the most grievous wounds failed to slow them now.

Lady Uzume instantly dropped her rifle and let it dangle as she grabbed the reins in both hands and hauled as hard as she could. The Tyrannosaur was already moving after the routed troops, and she had to stop it. With bestial instincts at large, the steed took great effort to bring round and steer back towards the main fight. The enemy was gone, and the elite riders were now totally exposed. Already the whistle of clouds of arrows was rising to deafening volumes.

With head held low, her steed rushed towards where the Wani were continuing to sell every life as dearly as they could. A deep humming roar disturbed the air, and a massive projectile missed her by a few feet. The gigantic spear thudded into the chest of a Tyrannosaur, one that was more stubborn in its pursuit of the routed foe. The creature gave a pained squawk as it was thrown to the ground, crushing a dozen fleeing soldiers with its final act. It tried to get up, not realising yet that its heart was pierced, and it was in fact already dead. Its rider was up in seconds and rushing for the fight, only to be cut down by the deluge of arrows raining down on the area.

Uzume hauled to the right and redirected her mount at the culprit. The bolt thrower had been brought forward from the rear along with three others that were readying to fire. The first one exploded into splinters when her mount dipped its snout and rammed its armour-plated skull into the side of the ballista. The second and third war machines crumpled under foot, but the fourth turned at the last moment and fired. Lady Uzume wrenched at the reins to try and dodge the spear but at point blank she had little chance of success. Denied its binge meal, the Tyrannosaur was already anticipating eating this target, heedless of its inedible status.

The ten-foot spear plunged into the agape maw of the steed and punched straight through. The serrated point exploded from the back of its head and grazed Uzume's shoulder as its velocity allowed it to drill straight through armour, flesh, and bone.

The mortal trauma took valuable moments to be acknowledged, by which time the weapon was already being wrenched apart by its monstrous jaws. Uzume slipped a tanto from her belt and cut the straps of her safety harness. She didn't have time to fumble with buckles, her steed was seconds from collapse.

Leaping from the saddle as her mount started to sag, she landed heavily, and a storm of pain rolled up her legs as they supported the full weight of both her landing and her dense armour. A member of the ballista crew charged her with an axe. She flipped the tanto to its point and hurled the small blade into his throat before hoisting her firearm.

Uzume realised the jeopardy she was in but could not succumb to fear. She was distanced from her own forces. Her elite riders could not interfere lest they risk crushing her, and now a wave of screaming enraged enemy troops was coming straight for her. These troops had been deployed behind the war machines to allow the devices an open field of fire, but they now streamed over the wreckage to seek the rider responsible for such destruction. The other Tyrannosaur were now spared the lethal projectiles and were again wreaking havoc on the enemy as arrow, bolt, and handheld weapon bounced harmlessly off their armour or opened inconsequential wounds. Without heavy firepower, this process of attrition would take hours to kill them.

The rifle jumped in her grip and pummelled her shoulder as she leaned into the weapon and applied careful bursts into the approaching mob. The double drum magazine ran empty and without pause she released it and drew her katana.

With all the cold skill of her birthright, Uzume met the foe without remorse or concern. The shimmering blade flowed like a living tentacle and wove through armour, around shield, and about weapon to pierce heart or take head. Hot crimson saturated her armour and ran down her in steady lines as she continued to hold her ground and weave amidst truculent hacks and sanguinary swipes.

Her foe was mere militia, peasants with token training in holding a blade and in marching in formation. Against a centuries old battle goddess trained for decades in the art form of total war, they stood little chance. However, Uzume was still only one warrior, and although she did not age, she could still tire and be killed.

Dozens were dead, but her arms now felt like lead, and it was becoming harder to ignore the weight of her armour and evade the enemy. Stern impacts affected her balance and bruised her flesh but still she would not relent. Facing certain death, she did not regret her actions. Hachiman wanted war with the Provinces and Uzume was pledged to this, even if it meant transgressing his will and perishing in the process. The defeat of an expedition force might not be enough to promote war, especially with conflict with Earth looming. The death of Masuda, the destruction of the force, and perhaps even her own death were certain to see the Provinces razed.

Uzume sheathed her blade in an enemy chest as he readied to stab at her side. A flash of light caught the edge of her vision and she glanced to see a claymore coming down on an overhead arc. She was too exhausted to leap away, and the massive blade slammed down into her chest. The already much pummelled ceramic plates fractured, and the impetus of the blow threw her down and to the ground. The wind vanished from her lungs and the grip on her sword was lost to leave the heirloom lodged in an enemy casualty.

Landing on her back, Uzume's wakisashi appeared in her hand and skimmed along the ground to take feet off at the ankles. In the momentary lull she fought to rise only to have a warhammer catch the side of her helm. A pulse of white rushed across her eyes and she was thrown aside. A trio of brutal blows assailed her back, trying to get through her armour and then a fourth snagged her shoulder and spun her over.

Supine and with senses reeling, she watched another claymore rise up in paired hands and ready to drop its point into her heart. The integrity of her armour was gone, and she couldn't even roll in her current dazed state.

The point wavered in the air and then dropped to land beside her as a Megalosaur snatched up the bearer and barged onwards to scatter the soldiers. Three Mitama leapt from the saddle and landed around her to hurl their weapons into the mob and then beat them back. A forth Mitama grabbed her and helped her to her feet. With a submachine gun in his other hand, he sprayed freely into the nearest enemy forces.

"You have to retreat, Lady Uzume!" he bellowed as the din of steel landing on steel and ripping of flesh joined roars and screams of pain and fury.

"Never!" she hissed.

The warrior ejected a spend clip, slapped in a new one, and continued to hold back the enemy as his comrades used their swords to assist him.

"The Empire must be told of this threat. You are the only one who can relay the message and not have it dismissed. You are Kami!" he implored.

"Your name will be honoured, and this defeat will be avenged a thousand-fold," she snarled and offered him a small bow.

Rewarded beyond measure by this act of reverence from his deity, the soldier jerked round as his weapon ran out of ammunition. His eyes flashed with joy, and he threw down the spend firearm before drawing his sword.

"I conquer!" he roared, and charged towards the battle line.

Elated and filled with purpose, he ploughed into the battle as a berserk whirlwind of destruction.

Lady Uzume shook off her weakness and clambered into the saddle of the nearby mount. The rescue party had given her a route out and as she kicked the steed into a full gallop, a pair of Tyrannosaurs fell in behind her. Their vast backs gave her a shelter from enemy fire, and she could already hear the dizzying rattle as clouds of arrows pelted their backs. The Provincial army had seen who she was and were desperate to bring her down, but in seconds she was out of their range.

The protecting riders instantly turned their mounts and thundered back into the fight, intending to hold the army as long as possible.

The adrenaline of battle was starting to fade and the extent of her injuries and fatigue were making themselves known. Uzume stiffly reapplied the saddle harness and hoped that if she lost consciousness, the steed was well trained enough to make it back to the supply line on its own.

CHAPTER SEVEN

With her rear hot from its invasion and her cheeks raw from punishment, Candy relaxed into the ropes and breathed softly. Kara's words had inspired her, and now she was mulling over what had been said. Another uncertain duration trailed lazily past until the lamps increased in potency and a door opened to allow people entry.

The sisters were still dressed as before and again they carried trays that they set aside. She was freed and brought back up onto her knees, whereupon they skilfully removed the full harness. Candy swayed as the tight clinch of the rope vanished and offered small purrs of delight when she was pushed back down onto her front.

Lying along one side of the table, the women then began to arrange food upon her back. The small packages were warm on her skin, and she remained as still as she could to let the women work. Once the array was completed, they knelt back in their former positions to await the arrival of the Mikado.

Hirata entered at a casual rate and yawned. He stretched, slid up to the table, and accepted chopsticks. As though she were any other inanimate object, he began to pick items from Candy and devour them, occasionally offering one to Kara or Keira who accepted it with hands clasping to their thighs.

The odd affair was a definite pleasure. There was something so sensual about feeling the slight slip of a piece as it moved against her skin and then vanished, leaving behind a fleeting area of warmth. A small measure of hot fluid was tipped into the small of her back, making her arch her chest with a gasp of shock. The pose helped hold the small reservoir in place and Hirata dipped items into the sauce while Candy felt the heat siphoning into her skin. A piece moved up by shoulder blade and fled and when she sagged a little, a brief trickle escaped the well and ran towards her hip. The succulent feel of the hot line traversing her flank made her mewl softly. Hirata acted quickly, snatched a new morsel, and caught the stream before it dropped onto the table. With small swirls he mopped up the spill and carried the roll back up to the sauce before eating it.

When breakfast was completed, a cloth was run down her back and the Mikado gave a contended sigh.

"You were a delight, slave, but it is time to deliver you back to my master," he said and there was a small hint of regret in his voice. "Nakatomi. Bring her."

Candy was hoisted back to her feet and with the women holding her hands, she was brought behind Hirata and back into the labyrinthine tunnels. It was a fairly long walk, but she was glad of the exercise after her long captivity.

A robed priest pulled open a heavy door and she was brought into a dark room. The inadequate lighting revealed hints of furniture and other items, but concealed the true purpose of the room from her. Candy was delivered into the middle and a spotlight came on.

Kara and Keira retreated to stand in the gloom behind Hirata as he loitered in the periphery of the spotlight and new figures emerged from the darkness. The Imbe were threatening apparitions with leather masks that depicted fearsome demonic countenances. The snarling black skin was adorned with small horns and extended as hoods down to their shoulders where a cross-shaped harness emphasised their brawny chests.

The Imbe stepped to a metal strut that descended from the ceiling and stopped at shoulder height whereupon it spread out into a horizontal crosspiece. The smooth rounded steel had several thick straps already riveted into place as did the lower area of the supporting beam. Set out under the shadow of the crosspiece were thick fetters with steel cable attached to them. The cable sprawled on the floor and entered two stern winches a short distance away.

Candy was turned around and pushed back against the item. The cool metal calmed her skin, and her arms were lifted up and set to the pole. Straps were drawn over her wrists, above and below her elbows and a final set hugged her upper biceps. The belts were hauled tight so that they drew her ferociously to the steel. Another strap was established across her forehead, and it was yanked back to pin the back of her head against the metal. Another strap was grabbed and brought over her mouth where a stout phallus was already established upon it.

Upon seeing the broad dimensions of the toy, Candy tried to move her head aside but the belt across her forehead greatly hampered her motions.

"Wait, don't, I . . ."

Hands grabbed her ankles and pulled outward a moment before fingers sank into her cheeks and squeezed until with a groan of protest she was forced to open up and let the toy in. The rounded head nudged her teeth apart and started to push harder. The slick, slightly pliant material stretched her jaws wider and wider until she had formed a rictus that brought them to the verge of dislocation.

The tightening of the oral belt caused the leather to dig into the sides of her mouth and the bloated dildo gag to brush the back of her throat. She jerked but could not defeat the holds on her legs as she kicked and struggled to break free. The belt was pulled in another notch and the gag voyaged deeper to make her retch and gurgle.

The fetters were abruptly buckled into place and the

winches were manned a moment later. The handles were cranked round and round and the spool quickly gobbled up the slack. Her soles slid against the floor and then left the ground as her legs were stretched apart. Her body weight fell onto the supporting restraints and Candy gave a croaking whimper against the stifling phallic gag.

Almost choking on the oral intruder, she thrashed against the impossible impositions on her body. The winches clicked on another notch and her legs were drawn even tighter. Tendons and muscles throbbed with distress, and another click of the winches made her joints thunder with internal mayhem.

The snap of latex gloves being dragged into place and then released caught her ears and she felt hands pulling her buttocks apart. A pair of fingers stole entry as the lubricant that covered them assisted swift access. Candy cried out and fought to flex and expel them as the cool gel was worked into her anus. She knew this was a precursor to defilement and the brutality with which she had been secured suggested it would not be an easy intrusion to take. The slithering fingers jumped in and worked the lubricant around before they fled, having encountered no trouble against her attempts to resist.

A rigid strut touched her rear and started to slip into place. Candy fought to wriggle and deny it a target but her stretched legs allowed her hips virtually no movement. The rigid tube reached her sphincter and began to pour into her. The size of the intruder was not as bad as she surmised but then some sort of wide flange met her opening. The disc was slightly malleable, but was still of a dimension that she could not easily accept. The Imbe pivoted the device and started to push it into her until she cried out from the stress.

The disc slipped back, and she was allowed a moment to recover before they again solicited entry. Candy tried to relax but it was not easy because the Imbe were working with little patience. She was given only seconds between lessons in dilation and each time they pushed it until she gave a genuine howl. The Imbe were well versed in the tunes of a slave being processed here and were never once tricked by her faked squeals.

Wider and wider she was stretched until amidst her gurgling holler the disc slipped through and popped into place. She thrashed against the straps as her insides reviled the sudden distending presence. Her sphincter had been acclimatised to the flange, but her channel had not. She strained desperately to try and force it out and ease her misery as she felt the pipe reaching into her body and the great circular plug inside her. The security of this dam was further enforced when a matching disc on the outside was pushed into place. Fingers dug into her buttocks and drew her open so that the second disc could be pushed in as tightly as possible.

With her orifice now crushed between two brutal flanges, there was no way for her to defy the introduction of anything into her body.

Another device was brought forth, and at first it appeared to be some sort of strap-on harness save that this item was destined to fit the other way round. The phallus that they inserted into her was peppered with holes and stemmed from an overlarge base in which she could see valves and other considerations to allow technology to control and tend her in her captivity.

Candy groaned as the long wide trespasser rushed into her, choking her pussy until the base pressed against her. A small key was taken up and slipped into place before she felt it closing a pair of metallic clamps. The two fanged pincers grabbed her clit beneath her ring and squeezed until it was held firmly between them. The fleshy tunnel was coursing with sensation as the morsel sought to retreat back but the clamps kept it stretched and held tight between them. The straps were then set around the tips of her thighs, over her hips, and around her waist to ensure that this item was kept irrevocably in place.

Two metal soles were gathered and brought to her feet. Her toes were grabbed, and her writhing feet delivered to the items. Each toe was slid into a small, ratcheted metal band. These adjustable rings were then tightened until the root of each toe was held tightly in place. Straps were then set over her foot and a pair reached over her ankles before connecting back to the sole to keep the full measure of the metal plate pressed to her skin.

A pair of mittens was collected, and the tight leather gloves drawn onto her hands. With forceful motions they steered her fingers into the individual interior sleeves and consequently onto the ranks of wicked barbs awaiting them. Even the slightest movement of her fingers was now going to be punished by them. The Imbe then opened her wrist straps, and each glove was buckled into place so she could not shed it.

The true nature of her predicament was then revealed to Candy when she saw the manner in which she was to be transported.

The close fibreglass sarcophagus was moulded to perfectly fit her contours and keep her held in a ridiculously tight stem. Clasps along the sides were already open and two of the men separated the coffin into two halves.

Candy screamed and struggled afresh as she bore witness to her new home. A terrible sense of claustrophobia overcame her, and she fought to get away from the approaching tomb with all her might.

The container was placed beneath her and the head portion lifted up behind her. Her feet were untied and her valiant fight to break free was ruthlessly countered by the brawny arms of the priests. Candy shrieked and continued to resist as they brought her legs together and slipped them inside. Sockets in the base met the bottom of her metal soles and locked into place, attaching her to her carrying case.

Interior belts were drawn up from between her legs and reached over before they were buckled to the interior walls and wrenched tighter. Brutal straps ran over ankle, above and below her knees, and across her thighs. She felt the anal tube snap into place against some sort of internal connection and then more belts encircled her waist, travelled below her breasts, and then another ran above them.

While one Imbe held her sarcophagus, the others unfastened her arms and pushed them down before a new series of belts inside the container replaced those that had been fixed to the bar.

Her head was untied, and as she thrashed and fought madly to get away, she was pushed into the accommodating slot before a belt was drawn over her forehead.

"How goes her preparation," said Toyo-tama-hiko.

"She is nearly complete, Warlord."

The impassive features of the ruler appeared over her case. Candy thrashed as fiercely as she could but almost no motion was visible.

"Enjoying yourself, Candy? Quite snug, isn't it?"

"Pleeeease, master. Don't seal me in this thing. I'll do anything you want! Anything!"

"Well, Candy. It seems that Warlord Hachiman is seeking you quite diligently. In fact, one might say that he is being more than a little fanatical over one Kami-tsu-ko. What do you say to that?" he asked coolly.

Candy closed her eyes and smiled as she realised that her master was actively seeking her.

"Well?" said Toyo-tama-hiko, adding more gravity this time.

"I . . . I have pleased him, and . . . he . . . spent a great deal to purchase me, master," she said, hoping that if she could convince him of her worth then negotiations to have her returned would follow. The ferocity of her containment was already overwhelming her and the hope that she could be returned to Hachiman made it even more unendurable.

"And yet he loaned you to me with such alacrity."

"Because of my worth to him it must have been a show of how much he values your alliance, master," she said. The hidden conversation she had seen between the two men had suggested that they were allies, and if she reminded Toyo-tama-hiko of this, he would be less likely to condemn his friend's favoured concubine to this crushing hell.

"And then you go and accidentally find my secret army? Quite a coincidence."

"I don't . . . I . . . what do you mean, master?"

Candy could feel her world slipping through her fingers as she discerned what the Warlord suspected. Desperately she fought to find something to convince him otherwise.

"Spy!" he barked.

"No! No I'm not!"

"The only thing quicker than his lending of you to me was the speed with which you discovered my army. And at the one time they were visible. I am becoming more and more convinced that you are a spy for him. Is this so?" he growled.

"No, master, I swear. It was an accident. I wasn't spying, I promise. Just let me return to my master. I'll not tell him. You have my word."

"The word of a slave or the word of a spy. I find both unacceptable and this is too great a matter to trust to such a flimsy protestation. I can't have one little concubine detract from all the glory that will bequeathed to my Water Wani when they are unveiled in combat."

"Please, oh please Warlord Toyo-tama-hiko. Please, spare me. I will never tell my master. Never ever! All I've ever wanted to do is serve."

"As I spy?"

"No! No! I'm no spy!" she cried and lurched against the straps. Her fingers were pricked by the spines and the coffin rattled on the floor from the savagery of her efforts to escape.

"Well we'll find out soon enough. Well, perhaps not *soon*, but eventually. This method has broken even the most recalcitrant of slaves, so I'm sure it will be adequate to coax the truth from your lips."

A glass container was brought over. The metal base hummed softly to itself as tiny jets of water were pushed out against the inside walls to create a slow but steady whirlpool.

"Wh . . . what the hell is that thing?" she whispered in terror.

"Hell is exactly what this is, slave. The creature in here is so delicate that should it even bump against the glass it would be destroyed."

Candy's heart began to race as possibilities of dreadful encounters with monsters sprung into her mind.

"They are called Irukandji, and they are a form of box jellyfish."

"No! No! Don't sting me! Pleeease!" she wailed, fearing the horrible scars that such a beast would leave behind.

An Imbe lifted the lid as Toyo-tama-hiko looked inside and was handed a pair of pincers.

"The individual stingers of a jellyfish are like tiny harpoons. They fire and unravel, and if you imagine that all the rope of the harpoon is covered in poison then you can see how they deliver their sting. This little fiend is different. The nematocysts of Irukandji are like syringes. They pierce and pour their poison out at the tip. And that venom is well . . ."

The Warlord snagged his prey and hoisted it from the container. Candy could barely see anything. Whatever it was, it was smaller even than the tip of her little finger.

"I'll ask you again, slave. Are you a spy?" he asked gravely as he held the pincers over her.

"I sweeear! I'm not! Oh God I'm not! Please believe me! Please!"

"We are going to the great plane of Izanagi, Candy. A journey of several weeks. You will be transported in this container, and in here, you will know what torment is. I will ask you again when you emerge, and I am sure that when you do, your words will be honest."

"Noooooooooo!" she roared as the pincers drew close.

Candy gave a croak as she felt a sharp sensation nip her breast. It was of little consequence, and she almost felt like laughing because it was so trivial. After all of the Warlords threats, was that it? She had endured far more demonic pain from mere Kamube.

Toyo-tama-hiko carefully dropped the creature back in the container and it was taken away.

"Not very painful is it, slave. Well the clock is ticking," he warned and turned to the other Imbe. "Continue."

The tiniest touch to her breast had left a tingling presence but little else. Candy wondered if perhaps she had been exceedingly lucky and the creature had been defective. Perhaps its poison was stunted, or it was already dead. However, now her attention was fixed on what was heading towards her. A moulded face mask was gathered up and brought over to her and she could see that the interior released three tubes. The two for her nostrils were fairly short, but the one beneath them was much longer. The end of the slightly corrugated item was snatched, and she sucked in her lips to stop its application.

Again, fingers grabbed her helpless cheeks and her jaws were forced apart. Candy gave a cry of resignation as the Imbe acted with celerity. The tube plunged into her mouth and started to thread down her throat. Her eyes bulged and she lurched against her bonds as she felt the awful thing entering her body and bouncing her channel on its ridges and trenches.

The face mask continued to move towards her, and the tubes entered her nostrils. Retching and gurgling, she was plunged into darkness as the item secured to the sides of the sarcophagus to keep her head pinned down and her body subjugated. Every part of her was now immobilised and her body was invaded by devices to sustain and nurture her in her terrible bondage.

The form-fitting lid was taken up and placed atop her. The clasps were set in place and Candy was left wheezing through her nose, pressed in on all sides with an irritating pain dwelling in her breast.

Her coffin was taken up and carried away, the Imbe becoming her pallbearers as she was no doubt being loaded up for the journey.

Lost in the void of her cell she dwelt on what else was going to be done to her, and after about half an hour she realised why this tactic was so good at breaking a slave. The sting had taken effect.

Excruciating muscle cramps started to thunder up and down her arms and legs and then rule her stomach muscles. She quivered and her world turned over and rolled from dizziness. She sweated and twitched, her skin and face feeling as though they were aflame from within. Every single particle of her body throbbed as though battered and bruised and the pain did not diminish, it just kept persevering and never for one instant did it fade in intensity.

Candy jolted against her prison as dazzling light thundered against her clenched eyelids and poured through them. As her sight cleared, she saw that the container actually allowed her to see out. The face mask had glass lenses and the upper section of the container also had two glass panels. The caps had been removed and she could now see the face of the Warlord over her. He saw the tears in her eyes and the anguish written in them and simply smiled before he again disappeared out of her limited view.

Candy sobbed and writhed, the terrible pain of the sting coursing through her entire body. She could not believe that such a tiny beast could carry such a sting. It was ludicrous. The jellyfish could not even bump glass and survive, so why did it need venom of such potency?

Cursing nature and delirious from pain, Candy watched the cave ceilings passing by. The banality of the view was a terrible curse for it offered her absolutely no distraction from the impossible misery rushing through her physique.

An unknown duration elapsed as she was carried away and then she saw a great domed ceiling that revealed the ocean above them. The sound of the coffin being secured managed to filter through the dense walls and then she found her breathing becoming a little harder to acquire. It was clear that her nostril tubes had been attached to an oxygen tank and were providing her with breath while as she was shipped back to the surface world.

There was a brief hint of Toyo-tama-hiko walking past in his diving armour and then the world dropped away. Water closed over her sight, and she was thrust into the deep. The docks drifted overhead and suddenly she was streaking through the water at a ridiculous rate.

Candy realised that she was tied to the back of a Kronosaur and that the Warlord himself was taking her back to dry land.

The water realm streaked past as she sobbed and prayed for the pain to end. In only a few minutes she started to see hints of the sun again and the glorious dazzling orb was a treat to her eyes. She could not believe just how much she had missed it.

The ocean broke over her eyepieces and her stomach sank as she was flung high into the sky. The great beast arched over after having launched from the waves and like a whale it crashed back against the water. The slam of her body against the insides of the sarcophagus went unnoticed because of her anguish, and as the monster started to swim away, she squinted to bear witness to a cloud speckled blue sky. The sound of waves hitting her prison created a steady drum roll as the great sea beast swam relentlessly towards the coast.

Gibbering from the ordeal, she later felt their rate slow and then she felt herself being unfastened. Unable to do anything save suffer and watch, she was carried away whereupon she saw the towering flanks of a dinosaur. A small crane grabbed her skin-tight cell and hoisted her up before she was drawn inside a luxurious howdah and strapped up against one wall.

The pipe in her throat suddenly swelled and stretched outward to fully choke her throat. It was then that she felt the pipe shiver as sustenance was pumped directly into her. The act of feeding had been taken away, and the machines connected to her would control her body and keep her alive as she suffered unspeakably in the hellish coffin.

Candy mewled and gurgled as she felt fluid being introduced into her rear. The forced enema continued to slither into her before it started to swell her channel. She shuddered in her tight cell but even this pain was nothing compared to the choler of the sting. The automated systems pumped her up to a most distressing level and as she lay there, crying out against her confines, they slowly siphoned away the douche.

She was trussed and being controlled more than she ever thought possible. She was completely dependent on the mechanism and could do nothing to defy it. The Warlord has sealed her up alive and she would suffer until he deemed her worthy of freedom again.

Candy was distracted from her duress when a small group of gorgeous concubines sauntered in and began to take up positions throughout the carriage. Dressed in provocative lingerie, each was adorned with metal bands that caught wrist, ankle, upper arm, and thigh, and also enclosed their throats. All of the items had several D rings already fastened in place and the nylon and lace bore small and deliberate holes that allowed these rings to emerge.

Toyo-tama-hiko entered the howdah and appraised the area as the women doted on him with utter reverence. He gave Candy's prison a minor glance and proceeded up into the higher floors.

Whimpering and screaming for deliverance, she continued to just loiter in her tight container and suffer for the amusement of her tormentor. No doubt the thought of her desperate situation was a significant source of arousal, and this was soon proved to her. The Warlord would often bring slaves and then restrain, punish, and pleasure them right before her, and many times he regarded her tear-filled orbs through the tiny vents that accessed her stare.

As the great beast began to plod across the land and make for the central plains of the Empire, Candy became aware of the full diabolic powers of thus unholy form of transport.

A minor torment came from the random charges that wandered through the metal soles. The flash floods of goading power left her skin riddled with an aggravated loathing. She would fight to screw up her toes and lift the soles away to ease her situation, but the bands and straps were too tight. It was a spiteful and annoying abuse, one that frustrated because of her inability to get rid of it. She fought on and tried to slip her toes free, but there was nothing she could do save endure the regular vexing assault that plagued her feet and added greatly to her ordeal. Nevertheless, these episodes of devilish maltreatment were soon replaced and almost went unnoticed when the true evil of the sarcophagus began.

Small electrical pulses were passed between the pincers that were currently holding her clit captive. They made the nubbin flex and continued to command it with steady and dedicated efforts. The whole length of the inserted dildo also began to tremble as machines at its base passed vibrations down the length. The pain of the sting was vaguely mitigated as she was pleasured but because of its scathing nature, it took some time for her to focus sufficiently on the bliss to begin an ascent towards climax. With her breath racing in and out of the nostril tubes, Candy began to quake against her bonds as the warm succulent joy of relief started to spread through her choked pudenda. She tried to flex and roll her belly and hind-quarters but was far too comprehensively restrained to have any effect on the process. She could clench her pussy to smother and concentrate the feeling of the restless dildo, but that was all.

Candy gritted her teeth against the oral invader, closed her eyes, and stalled her breathing in expectation. The orgasm would be a delight to embrace because for just a moment, in those seconds of unbridled ecstasy, the pain of the Ikrudkanji sting would be eclipsed. Even a moment without it would be heaven.

Everything stopped.

Candy's eyes jerked open, and she flew into a panic as her pleasure hung at a steady level and refused to grow. The glo-rious explosion of rhapsody was just a few pulses away and the pain of the sting was already starting to erode it.

Screaming her hatred of this abuse, she tried to roll her channel and grind herself up against the devices to earn those last few touches and swirls that would grant her relief. She filled her mind with every delicious fantasy she could, focus-ing on the most powerful moments with Lady Uzume and Warlord Hachiman, but no matter what she did, she was too tightly bound and couldn't get anywhere near enough input to even maintain her current level. Relief started to slither away, retreating and leaving behind the constant cramping pains of the sting.

Candy soon learned that this was going to be the worst part

of her ordeal. She would be teased to the very brink of release and was then deserted so she might feel it dissipate and remind her of just how potent the anguish of the sting was. By almost removing its power with the promise of orgasm, she was endlessly introduced to the agony. The process almost seemed to regenerate her virginity to an Irkundji sting, restoring it via teasing and denial.

As her absolute need for relief grew and grew, her dark rapture from this most brutal form of containment and the endless misery of the sting found fresh fare. Her masochism started to germinate within her again, even though this was well beyond anything she had previously managed to find pleasure in. Every thwarted orgasm offered this monster within her more strength, allowing it to grow stronger and make her yearn to feel the terrible return to the unfettered power of the sting. The last moments before the machines cut off were now the most sought after because in those seconds she wailed against her coffin and readied to hurl aside orgasm and revel in the plunge back into pain.

Against such deviant sexual cravings, the machine was soon having trouble stopping her. Candy was now so aroused by her diabolic torment that she was getting closer and closer to orgasm. Every distraught flick and twitch of her pussy now served as another step up towards bliss.

Sodden with arousal, she squirmed and hollered, and the more she was teased, the slower orgasm withdrew. She would teeter on the verge now for long minutes, every tiny insignificant shuffle of her loins being more than enough to stimulate her hypersensitive and long starved pussy. It was taking longer and longer for the sting to work its dreadful effects and erode her pleasure, but Candy was not the first fanatic masochist to have been fed to this sarcophagus and precautions were in place for a debauched creature such as she.

Her clitoris now felt as though it was aflame. Heated,

roused, flushed with excitement, every tiny electrical flick of the prongs made her spasm and jolt against her bonds. Every shudder of the dildo made her squawk from the impossible levels of reaction it gained.

The ascent towards ever denied orgasm commenced as usual and she rocketed up towards it in her super-aroused state. The machines then stopped as they always did, and Candy floated in a debauched haze of pleasure. Her flexing loins continued to waft her upwards and she could feel this long and lethargic climb into pleasure finally gaining success. There was nothing they could do to stop her. Climax would be hers and she had earned it all on her own. The devices they had locked onto and within her were body were powerless against her skills at absorbing pain and pleasure. By ferociously committing herself to her status as a sex slave, she could even overcome the malicious imagination and intentions of even the greatest Kami.

Ice cold water suddenly poured out of the holes in the dildo. The arctic geysers instantly stole all warmth from her pussy and swelled it upon a sudden churning tide of excruciating cold. Candy screeched against her bondage as the brutal douche shattered her climax and made every muscle in her body strain to sudden astonishing degrees. The surprise was more than enough to remove her pleasure, and as the waters were quickly sucked free, Candy was left twitching and fazed, all hint of orgasm gone.

Candy sobbed as the pain of the sting returned and took hold of her entire body, but it was not just a sense of sorrow and grief for a slain orgasm that coaxed out her tears. Candy was now weeping with a sense of complete abandonment to the control of the Kami. No matter what she did, no matter how diligently she tried to eke a meagre victory in her slavery to them, they would always win. They were centuries old, they had seen everything, experienced all, and committed an equally comprehensive encyclopaedia of excess on all manner of concubines. She was utterly theirs and strangely, this absolute ownership was a most satisfying and reassuring thing. Candy now knew just how flawless their dominion over her was. She sank into the stringent pain of her tomb and readied to continue her infernal suffering for the amusement of her master.

CHAPTER EIGHT

Lady Uzume's mount was tiring but she could not slow down, not while there was the possibility of the Provinces organising a pursuit. It was unlikely that they would be able to catch up with her, but there was always the chance that a Stray aircraft may have ended up in their hands and might be deployed to intercept her. It was a remote possibility, but she hadn't just survived such a one-sided battle to permit any risks on her life through carelessness.

The dust cloud created by the main column grew closer with every bounding step of her mount. Soon she was able to make out the reassuring contours of her howdah. At last she was safe. The firepower of the convoy would ensure that any pursuit was shredded before it could do any harm.

With a great sigh of relief she allowed her steed to finally slow. As its charge dropped to a slow trot, she could feel its titanic breaths between her legs as the massive carnivore fought to steady its pounding heart rate. A trio of elite Mitama outriders galloped up with weapons at the ready so they could defend their deity.

"Lady Uzume! What happened?" gasped one of them. He had seen the damage wrought to her armour for it indicated the unthinkable, that their deity had actually been attacked. Whether they believed that she could actually be killed or harmed was inconsequential, the fact that others had raised a hand to her was just as abhorrent to the Mitama.

"The Wani have been defeated. A great dishonour has been inflicted upon the Empire," she hissed.

"Your orders, Lady Uzume?" growled the officer. He was obviously eager to mount a retaliatory strike as soon as possible, but the mission was complete. War would come soon enough and the Mitama would have all the blood they wished when they moved on the Provinces en masse and with the full support of the Houses of Fire.

"We head home. This information is too valuable to be entrusted to messengers and must be delivered to the assembled Kami by one of their own."

"At once, Lady Uzume. I will have the column improve its pace."

She pulled on the reins and turned her mount towards her howdah where she could see that the ramp was already being lowered. Uzume opened her harness and started to dismount. She scowled inside her helmet as she felt her physique protest at being used. She had been in the saddle for long enough that her body had stiffened up and her many pulled muscles and contusions now made themselves known with even the slightest movement.

Landing on the extended platform, she straightened and refused to fall even as her whole body seemed to swell against the armour. She opened the door and strolled casually in before securing it and hiding any possible display of weakness from her subjects.

Aching and injured, she began to strip off her armour. She slipped into a simple satin robe and wandered upstairs barefoot to find Xiao still bound and in distress. The girl was in the exact same place she had left her, and it was reassuring to have such ruthlessly enforced stability around her.

Uzume knelt down and embraced the tightly contained form. She nuzzled into her collar and kissed the girl's cheek. She was now committed to Xiao because she had survived the battle and escaped the conflict intact. With her mistress returned to her with her future secured, it made Uzume wonder what she could do next with the hapless slave girl.

"Would you like to be my pet? My little feline companion that cuddles up at my feet?"

The look of abject horror on the girl's face made Uzume laugh aloud. No matter what mental turmoil she might personally be in, Xaio's distress always cheered her up.

"I think so. But before I turn you into my pussy, I'm going to give you the honour of attending mine," she crooned, and started to unfasten the gag plate so she might make use of the girls trembling angst-riddled tongue.

CHAPTER NINE

Time became meaningless in the nightmare trial of the transport container, and everything revolved around the minor torment of her feet, the agony coursing through her veins, and the brutality being visited upon her pussy. Candy became a simple creature of response to whatever was being done to her. She no longer fought it, no longer tried to find a way to defeat or trick her way around the impositions, she was utterly surrendered to the automated will of the devices that embraced, sustained, and abused her.

From the passage of night and day, she assessed that perhaps twenty days had elapsed before the endless and relentless pain of the sting started to dwindle. The potency of the venom was such that even a slight diminishing of its power brought no small measure of elation.

Candy dared not hope that the pain was ending. It had been her companion for so long that she could scarily remember what it felt like not to be continuing barbarous agony.

The misery retreated further, and Candy sobbed with joy. She was finally being purged of the dreadful sting of that mordant little demon of the deep.

The toys within her were now forced to employ the savage chilling douche with more regularity and often had to add the rending assault of the metal soles to push Candy back from orgasm. They were utterly dedicated to ferrying her to the very brink of release and then deserting her, but now Candy was free of the excruciating poison and could throw her full conscious efforts to attaining climax. The voltage in her feet got more intense and the temperature of the vaginal enema lowered and grew in volume, matching her efforts and then overcoming them. It was a war being fought over pleasure and neither side would tolerate failure or show restraint.

Sounds came through her sarcophagus and it moved. Delirious from the lengthy trial, she flashed open her eyes and peered around as best she could. She found that she was in a different place. Her tomb had been taken off the howdah and she had been too embroiled in her ordeal to even notice. The coffin dropped back, and she was staring once again at a stone ceiling.

The sounds of the locks being opened were the most glorious sounds she had ever heard. The lid was hoisted up, set aside, and Toyo-tama-hiko loomed over her as two women began to unfasten and extract the face mask.

The swollen tube was not deflated and rolled from her throat, bouncing her oesophagus on the various ridges. The tips fell free of her nostrils and mouth and Candy sucked in her first oral gasp of air in more than two weeks. She broke into racking coughs and flexed against the straps as warm light again caressed her body.

She strained against her bonds as though to illustrate how desperately she wanted to be free of them. The Warlord seemed to notice this act.

"No, not yet, Candy. First, we have some unfinished business."

"Wh . . . what do you want of me? Haven't you done enough?" she managed to weakly mumble. Ordinarily she would never speak thus to a Kami, but her time in the box had eroded her perception of reality. Thoughts were aired immediately, and she was having trouble severing the link to her mouth.

"I have to know whether you are a spy for Hachiman."

"I'm not. I never was. I'm just his slave. He wanted

someone from Earth and so he bought me. That's all. I swear," she whispered, licking her lips during the reply as the dryness of her parched mouth revealed itself.

"You understand that I have to be sure, slave," he warned.

"I'm not involved in your plotting. I just want to serve," she stated.

"I want the truth, Candy. Tell me and I will spare you a return to your isolation," he stated.

Candy gave a mortified scream when she saw him lift a pair of pincers and expose another tiny gelatinous entity between them.

"Dear God, no! Not again! Please, not again! I'm not a spy! Never was! Never! No! Don't sting me! I'll go insane!" she squealed. Her eyes were full of tears and were locked to the terrible creature.

"I want the truth!" growled Toyo-tama-hiko and the pincers began to lower towards her breast.

Candy flew into berserk paroxysms as she fought to get free. She screamed her innocence as her mind reeled from the prospect of another sting. For two weeks she had been in absolute anguish. There was no way to endure it again because she now knew how long the effects were, and every second would be a hell she could not bear to repeat.

The beast hovered just above her nipple and Candy just started to scream in fright. She shrieked for Hachiman to save her, crying out to him as though her were truly her deity and she sought salvation.

Toyo-tama-hiko turned and dropped the beast back in the container. One of his servants closed the lid and carried it away.

"Ssssh, slave. I believe you," he said soothingly, and stroked her forehead and cheek.

Candy broke into a weeping fit of jubilation and relief. She nuzzled into his hand as best she could and muttered adoring thanks to him for believing her and not subjecting her to a repeat of the torture of the Irukandji.

The many straps that had for so long kept her subdued were opened and her feet were finally separated from the mordant electrified soles. When she was hoisted upright, she gave a deep mumbling croak. Her struggles against the pain and stalled pleasure had kept her body from wasting, but she was still very much used to one position. Her entire physique thundered with new aches from changing position after all this time, but to be free again made it all worthwhile.

Candy was pulled from her tomb and the inserts into her body were opened and extracted. The clamps let go and the dildo slithered from her pussy. The anal barrier was parted and with a twist and a haul the women started to pull on it. Candy jerked and unleashed a howl.

"No, leave it installed in her," said Toyo-tama-hiko.

The women let complete go of her, and Candy fell from their hands and collapsed on the floor. The sudden vicious drag had hauled her sphincter open, and the item had almost escaped from her. Her rear had erupted with the starkest woe and as she landed on her the ground she instantly rolled onto her front and grabbed the brutalised orifice with both hands. She mewled and shuddered on the floor, and while she recovered from the sadistic extraction, her sarcophagus was taken away.

"Now what do we say, slave?" came the impassive tones of Toyo-tama-hiko.

Ruled by her subservience to the Warlord, Candy managed to lift herself up.

"Th . . . thank you, Warlord," she stammered, and began to crawl over towards him.

Every limb was tardy in its response, but she managed to lower her face to the ground and kiss the toes of his boots.

"Pleasure me."

Candy looked up and saw his cock jutting proudly from his garb. She pushed with her arms and managed to propel herself into a kneeling position. She then reverently reached up and embraced the solid manhood.

With her hands working at the base of his shaft and his balls, Candy opened her lips and took him as deep as she could. Locking lips to the warm phallus, her cheeks hollowed, and she started to draw back before plunging back down. Her tongue spiralled around him and frolicked on his tip while she shuddered with delight. This man had condemned her to the most diabolic trial she had ever encountered and had done so on some trivial suspicion that she was an agent for someone he considered both rival and ally. The fact that he had been so merciless made her fellatio all the more devoted and passionate. When ruled ruthlessly, Candy could not help herself from succumbing to fierce adoration.

"You may reward yourself while you're at it, slave," he casually announced.

Her hands let go and dropped to her sides before they reached between her legs. Her fingers were still a little weak, but she had been waiting for this moment for far too long to be denied by something as trivial as fatigue. Straps, freezing enemas, bitter charges of energy, and a skin-tight coffin may have succeeded, but exhaustion stood no chance.

Candy arched upward and her moan of rapture hummed against Toyo-tama-hiko's cock. One hand continued to stroke her pussy, running along the length and pausing only to offer a few prompt whirls against her engorged clitoris. The ring danced under her touch and spread succulent warm joy inside the pierced morsel to vastly escalate her pleasure. Her clit ring could be the most baleful companion when used to castigate her, but when serving her pleasures, it was one of her greatest treasures.

Her head darted down and hauled slowly back as her

hands worked feverishly. She reached up and turned her nipple rings, flipping them up and down and tickling the tips as she continued to suck and masturbate.

Candy started to quake as she felt the tightening of her physique and the spread of heat in her loins. Her eyes rolled and like a starved woman stood before a feast, she readied to devour this climax.

"Don't you dare come without my permission, slave!" warned Toyo-tama-hiko.

Her eyes widened in horror, and she looked up along his torso to meet his wicked glower. With hands on his sides, he grinned and seemed to take as much pleasure from her chagrin expression as he was from her oral dedication.

Candy blinked rapidly as she slowed her rate. She was already almost there, and it would be impossible to stop herself. She had been tortured and teased for weeks. Countless denied orgasms were leaving her livid with need whereas Toyo-tama-hiko was not so frustrated and would no doubt deliberately hold himself in check.

A slap stung her cheek.

"No slowing down either, slave," he warned.

Candy gave a whimper and restored her previous efforts. She tried to avoid her now throbbing clitoris, but every touch between her legs only brought her closer. She had succeeded in delaying the inevitable, but she needed to ensure she did not fail the Warlord.

She instantly became a dervish of oral gratification. Her head plunged, her maw ached from the suction she established, and her tongue burned from over exertion as it became a serpent of spry devotion. She released her nipples and restored the extremity to its previous task. Her fingers teased and tickled, employing every trick and technique she knew to try and make the Warlord come before she did.

Candy recalled the bite of the Irukandji. She dredged up

fell nightmare memories and poured disturbed fantasies through her mind's eye. She draped herself in repugnant images, but nothing helped. Her body had waited too long and suffered too much to let her mind stop it now.

Candy almost gave a cry of joy when she felt the cock swell against her serpentine tongue.

Fingers closed into the back of her hair and tightened. The rear of her scalp flashed with discomfort, and she sucked even harder as the anchor was used to pull her away. As though addicted to his cock, she strained and fought to stay in place but Toyo-tama-hiko was in no mood to be denied.

The tip of his penis came away and hung right before her maw. She stretched her tongue forth and managed to take one lap before he moved her back the final measure that left her tongue tip fluttering against air. Candy stared at the poised organ as she continued to masturbate and prayed that she be allowed to once again devour it.

"That's it. Keep going, slave!" he purred.

His hand truculently connected with her cheek and then returned to deliver its back to the other side. The Warlord gave a small dark chuckle and repeated the attack three more times with greater speed. Candy shook and swayed as she released ever-louder cantankerous pips. Each slap imparted heat to her face and every subsequent smack added more until she gave a series of alarmed cries at this spiteful abuse.

The hand remained poised, and Candy strained against the hold to her head. Her neck muscles stood up against her skin and her maw dropped open to let her tongue spill forth and beckon towards the awaiting manhood. Her thighs twitched as she neared orgasm and sweat trickled down her flushed form.

The Warlord moved her a little closer and her tongue spiralled around his tip. She gasped and made her scalp burn from her attempts to get back onto him.

"Close your mouth, slave."

Candy complied instantly and glared with anguish riddled eyes as he moved his hips forward and traced the erect cock around the perimeter of her maw, tickling the soft skin and making Candy mewl with despair. The feel of him so close was intoxicating but she dared not disobey. She was already going to suffer terribly for coming without permission, and was tempted to just drown herself in succulent images and delight in her orgasm, heedless of the consequences. She was going to fail so she might as well get it over with, but there was still hope. If she could just hold out a little longer, perhaps she would succeed. Candy knew that she would be defeated as she always was when she faced a Kami, but she still had to try.

"Open!" snapped Toyo-tama-hiko.

No sooner had her mouth opened into a perfectly accommodating "o" than he sheathed himself into the eager orifice. Candy shook with elation as she used her head in the manner *he* desired, attending him at the rate he wanted and in the manner he wished.

Her tongue returned to its previous efforts and Candy became dizzy with bliss as she started to ascend into long overdue relief. Toyo-tama-hiko's cock twitched and she felt the rush of her reward pour down and enter her throat.

"Now, slave. You may come," he hissed.

The Warlord thrust deep and threw her head back and forth on drastic moves that stole her breath and left her possessed by the wondrous feeling of successful service and absolute abandonment to his usage.

Her face became a tight grimace of monstrous strain as she fought to maintain some shade of effective performance. Her body convulsed and jerked as her hands danced, her body now being operated by chaotic flashes of rapture charged motion. In moments she was squawking against his cock for mercy, even though it was her own hand responsible for this unendurable sensation.

The hand in her hair drew her from his shaft and shoved her aside. Candy collapsed as an otiose heap on the floor. Her hands now held tightly to her pussy as though to contain the eruption of ecstasy. With eyes tightly closed, mouth stretched wide, and thighs clenched to her palms, she muttered prayers for strength as she endured the aftereffects of such powerful release.

"Now. We have made good time to the central lands and not all of the guests have arrived, so as promised, I am going to loan you to House Uka no mitama until the time of the celebration, whereupon you will be restored to my side. Should the festival be cancelled because they become a stray arrival, you will remain with them until such time as the festival for recovery is held."

Candy's head jolted up and she regarded him with a mortified stare. He barely even registered it.

"Take her to the temple of House Uka no mitama."

Hands grabbed her shoulders and forearms. Her hands were pulled from between her legs and she was tugged up onto her feet. Having been so occupied with the Warlord, she finally checked her surroundings and found that she was in a small chamber with several elegant banners hanging from the walls.

She was spun around to face an open door and with feet slipping beneath her she was marched out of the room. Candy looked over her shoulder and tried to find something to say.

"Warlord, I . . . please . . . I . . ." she stuttered, but he was already turning away and discarding her to her destiny.

CHAPTER TEN

Warlord Hachiman stood before the gates of the great wall with his Mikado poised one step back and to his right. Both he and Ame-waka-hiko were in full battle armour with copious blades and firearms adorning them. A dry and tardy breeze scudded along the massive courtyard and made their cloaks flap and slither upon the stone.

The gigantic portal had been opened in welcoming and ranks of Mitama stood to attention on either side of the Kami. Each was as still as a statue from being in the proximity of their Gods.

The burly and alien form of Toyotama-hiko marched over, bowed deeply, and joined his superior on the other side to the Mikado. He seemed to be in a fair mood, for which Hachiman was glad because it would temper his response to the imminent bad news.

The ground was beginning to quake as the multiple footfalls of hundreds of tons of reptilian mount grew closer and closer. Take-mika-dzuchi emerged from the shield wall with a trio of lieutenants in his wake. The master of the artillery regiments bowed to the other Fire Warlords and then spoke with staid evenness.

"My spotters see no sign of pursuit, but we will keep the long-range batteries trained on the convoy just to be safe."

"Why such precaution?" asked Hachiman. "It was merely a routine salvage mission."

He knew precisely what had happened, and his only concerns now revolved on the variables. He had planned everything as well as anyone could, but sometimes fate intervened and warped the plots of even the mightiest and meticulous Kami.

"There are signs of conflict," reported the Warlord of Thunder.

"Signs?"

"The Wani are gone. As are most of the Mitama. There is no hint of them anywhere on the horizon so we must assume that they have been defeated."

"How can this be!" hissed Toyotama-hiko, his great clawed hands furling into fists as he became aware of the seriousness of the situation.

"Patience. We will have out answers shortly."

The assembled leaders remained where they were and watched as the convoy entered the gates and came to a halt. The command Howdah turned around and lowered its access ramp to the ground. Standing boldly at the forefront was Lady Uzume. Her armour was riddled with dents and scratches, and a number of deep cracks opened several of the plates. Behind her were four officers who each held the end of a najinata. Held between the two polearms was a body and it was wrapped in the battle banner of the Mitama.

Uzume dropped to her knees, interlocked her ankles, and pressed her forehead to the floor.

"Revered and blessed Warlords, your humble servant returns to you with grave and most sorrowful tidings. The Eastern Provinces attacked our forces and beloved Masuda was slain. I personally led our troops to save the Wani for they were surrounded by the enemy army and vastly outnumbered. We fought with honour, but could not prevail. I have returned to bring you the news of the uprising, to bring a great hero of the Empire back for a funeral befitting such a great warrior, and to face my punishment. Permit me to end my life."

Hachiman left Uzume where she was and walked over to the body. He opened the banner and regarded the calm features of Masuda. With a vexed flick of his wrist he closed the shroud and stomped towards his agent. When his boots appeared before her, she arose a little but remained on her knees. Hachiman hoisted her chin and then delivered a ferocious backhanded slap across her cheek. The blow wrenched her to one side and deposited her on her flank.

"Disgrace! You have shamed us all with this defeat. You will not take your life because that erases your crime far too easily, and I want you to live with this dishonour, and you will do so without letting it slur me, or the Mitama you so ineptly led."

Hachiman turned his back on her and took three steps before he addressed her again with callous words that dripped with loathing. He had to make sure that everyone believed this scenario. Uzume's dismissal had to seem genuine and as much as it pained him to do so, a larger scheme was at stake here and for their prosperous and content future, pain had to be endured in the present.

"The Mitama and the Wani have fought with honour. The disgraceful failings of their leader should not be permitted to reflect on their reputation. So, in the name of the Sun-Goddess, I eject you from House Hachiman. May you live many years with this weight hanging on your soul."

Hachiman started to march from the courtyard, leaving Uzume cowering on the floor. His aids fell in behind him, but not before Toyotama-hiko glanced over his shoulder and gave a small almost imperceptible hiss of excitement. Hachiman pondered how the ancient quotation was proving so true when it stated that all warfare was based on deception. Through his deceits and schemes he was ensuring levels of unparalleled victory.

CHAPTER ELEVEN

Candy was shown through the various passages and was delivered through a guard room and into open air. She now saw that she had been transported into a great mountain range where cruel cold peaks clawed upward at the sky. About the snow-capped spires of rock were a number of elegant palaces, each of which bore the beautiful flowing flags of various Imperial Houses.

A small wagon was parked outside of the palace of Toyotama-hiko, although it looked more like a cage on wheels rather than any normal transport. The three-yard by three-yard cube had an open rear door and two women in severe ponygirl outfits were already harnessed to the "T" shaped yoke that reached out from the front. Each pony had a brilliant mane of brightly coloured hair, and their every movement caused the many small bells that hung both from their tack and their exposed nipple rings to chime and jingle. Perched atop high-heeled hoofboots, their hands clasped to the beam that was presented before them and their leather cuffs were locked to rings on either side of the malleable handgrips. From the base of the rigid corsets that crushed their waists and served as the basis for the entire harness sprung a swaying tail of hair that was dyed to match their own vivid manes. Fitted with blinkers, they chewed upon their bits and shuffled nervously from foot to foot as though anxious to commence their journey.

Candy noticed them with new eyes for she had been told that this might well be her fate. She found that it was not altogether objectionable and considered the delight she might find in being able to run and trot about the land. There was the other benefit in that a ponygirl would not be expected to enter civilised society, would not be expected to have secrets that could be torn from her, and so she would finally be free of Kami subterfuge.

Perhaps this was the full measure of what Toyo-tama-hiko wanted. His sly comments had been a means to remove her from the world, to hide her behind a bit so that Hachiman could not find her, reclaim her, and be informed as to what the Supreme Warlord of Water was breeding in that abyssal trench. But was it even more than that? Did he expect the secret to not only be lost, but be erased? Even if Hachiman found her, would her humanity be too eroded to expose what she had once known? Would life as a pony eventually strip away Candy and leave only a happy prancing filly in its place? The Empire had stripped away Candice to create the voluptuous Candy, so she had no doubts as to their ability to perform this act again.

She was shown up into the back of the cage and her hands were entered into a set of dense manacles that hung from a foot of chain fixed in the middle of the roof. She settled onto the wooden floor and looked around as the door was locked behind her.

A single slap to the rear of a ponygirl had the trained women leaning into the yoke and then gathering speed until they were galloping along the smooth winding roads that travelled from palace to palace.

Candy merely sat and held to the chains as she watched this strange land pass before her. Sometimes her gaze strayed to the rippling bodies of the ponygirls, and this stoked a lewd intent. There was something so alluring about the stamp of their hoofs, the huff of their deep breaths, the flick of their hair, and the sparkle as gems of perspiration welled on smooth sun kissed skin or trekked across their leather tack in chaotic trickles.

Kara's envy was now understandable. The woman may have been Nakatomi, but she was destined to dwell only in the undersea realm of her masters. Kara's exploration of perversity and indulgence was limited to that realm alone, and although Candy never really got to experience dominance, whole other arenas of learning were open to her.

The ponies knew the route home and were trusted to deliver her. They negotiated the lofty passes, trundled through deep valleys, and bolted through dark mountainous tunnels when the peaks above proved too treacherous or were occupied by another sprawling Imperial palace. The plane of Izanagi seemed to be a sacred one and so each House maintained a representative around it. If this were truly the case then it meant that the Moon-God and Sun-Goddess might also be close by, holding court amidst this grand settlement of the elite Kami.

The other traffic on the road was formed from female slaves and their passengers. Other ornate gigs allowed Kami or priest to recline in splendour and savour the sights about them. Wagons and carts hauled merchandise and shipments, and splendid coaches with teams of fillies towed groups of travellers.

They turned from the main road and began to approach a squat palace. It lurked on the sun-drenched side of a stubby mountain and the building sat amidst gardens far larger than any others she had seen. A small but effective perimeter wall offered battlements that were laden with Wani, and it also sported the flags of the Great House of the Earth Kami known as Uka no mitama.

The wagon raced towards a small gatehouse where a squad of armoured Wani stood to attention with miniguns trained on the land. The monstrous cluster barrelled machines seemed trivial in their grasp as did the vast metal magazines worn on their backs. The wagon rocketed through unmolested and almost undetected, and Candy found herself in an eerie realm where the slaves of the Empire were devolved through the imposition of strict animal costumes.

There were several courtyards with marvellous stables situated about them and paddocks placed amidst the neighbouring fields. Beyond this domain of human equines were other pastures in which could be seen a variety of other beasts that were the true fare of this house. The distant creatures were clearly not designed to mimic horses, but she could not secure any more details because there were numerous trees and bushes in the way, as well as barns and other buildings that arose amidst these fields.

There was a large contingent of human horses stationed here, so it seemed that there was a close relationship between House Uka no mitama and House Hohodemi, and therefore her transition from one to the other would be exceptionally easy in this palace. No doubt this was another intended part of Toyo-tama-hiko's plan to subjugate and hide her.

Staring at the distant strange shapes that could be spied moving through the few gaps between tree and building, Candy wondered what other depraved machinations this House had to offer her.

As the cage moved through the main courtyard, she saw another reason why Hohodemi had stationed so many of his House's products here. Amidst the stables were also kennels, and in these squat prisons she could see dozens of men and women in the process of being trained as hunting dogs. Their trainers were dressed in mockery of riding outfits save that they were generally formed from a fetishist fabric to inspire lust and thus further torment their adoring charges, none of whom were free of some mode of stern chastity device.

Hidden behind muzzles or artificial snouts, the hounds

clambered over each other for the attention of their regal masters and mistresses who chastised a wayward performance with cane, whip, or crop.

The cage continued through the courtyards and was delivered to the main gates were several people had already gathered. Standing boldly at the forefront was a tall and monstrously built male with intoxicating emerald eyes. His head was shaven, and he wore a great fur coat that trailed to the ground all around him and hid everything save his arms. These were bare, and his huge muscles bore entwined tattoos of strange mythological beasts rampaging amidst exquisite patterns and delicate flowing symbols.

Standing at his side was a smaller individual with a more streamlined physique. His arms and pectorals were coated with the same extravagant bestial tattoos, and he had a wild mane of black hair that fell about his features and hung to his shoulders. Wearing leather trousers and tall form-fitting boots, his arms were crossed over his chest and a slender stalk of black plastic jutted from one fist. The two silvery prongs on the end instantly revealed what this was, and Candy immediately committed herself to obedience rather than taste of its ministrations.

Four women stood in a line behind the two men. Each was dressed identically and other than hair colour it was difficult to differentiate between them. Each salacious beauty wore a slim belt with a leather pouch at the side, and a pair of tight leather riding chaps that poured down their legs and entered knee high riding boots. Silver struts emerged at their ankles and reached back to hold a brutally fanged wheel. Candy hoped the cruel impression of these spurs was just to intimidate, and if so, then it was a function that was having the desired effect.

The upper bodies of these equerries were completely naked save for the rings that transfixed their nipples and the silver collar that encompassed their throat and presented a ubiquitous ring at the front. Candy assumed that these women were all Kamube because their hair was still worn in the facet of their former life as a steed—shaven away at the sides. Each cascading mane was fastened into a high ponytail that tumbled down to the base of their spine and each woman bore a riding crop and stared blankly forward while they stood to rigid attention.

For a brief moment, Candy's focus slipped past the entourage and caught a glimpse inside the palace. Through the large doors she saw a great reception hall and was momentarily startled when she spied a woman in majestic regal attire wander through holding a pair of silver bowls. Her corseted body, bow shaped bustle, and trailing voluminous skirts were all formed from shimmering vinyl and her long hair was wound up into a bun that lurked beneath the rear of a small top hat. What was just as startling was what followed her—a small pack of slender female forms. Each was lost within a comprehensive costume that kept them on all fours and presented them with a feline countenance and swaying tail. The human cats scuttled after her with eyes that anxiously looked up at the bowls she carried. The strange procession left her field of vision and Candy realised just how absolute the services of this House were. House Hohodemi focused only on steeds, but this House handled the massive menagerie of other roles available should one wish to train or force a human into a depreciated animal role.

The cage slowed to a halt and a pair of the Kamube immediately strode around and opened the door before removing her cuffs and drawing Candy free. They held her by her arms and brought her before the fur swathed male. She kept her gaze lowered but this was corrected when a crop nudged under her chin and hoisted it high into the air. The other woman used her crop to tap at Candy's thighs and make her spread her legs.

"Imbe. Identity," flatly ordered the fur-clad priest.

"This is the kami-tsu-ko from House Toyo-tama-hiko. She is to enjoy the efforts of our House for the Supreme Warlord's amusement," replied the Imbe.

"Grazing sheep," was the deep impassive command of the male.

"Yes, Nakatomi," announced his Imbe. "Stable the ponies and bring the specimen."

The other two women moved around to the ponies and began to gently stroke their manes and faces as well as to soothe their breasts with some delicate tickles. The women offered equally approving words, telling them that they were good ponies and asking if they wanted to be hosed down after their long run. The ponies whinnied and stamped their hoofs with delight and Candy felt an even greater envy of their status. All they had to do was run and obey, and for this they received the most sublime treatment. The ponygirls enhanced Candy's jealously further because it was obvious that she was to be offered no such gentleness.

The equerries opened their pouches, and one produced a pair of handcuffs that brought and locked Candy's hands behind her back. The other dropped a choke chain over her head before offering the leash to the Imbe. He grabbed the lead and strode onwards to let the Kamube fall in behind them. The chain rattled and offered a gentle squeeze that made her stumble forward and shake her head to loosen the minor crimp it had applied. The noose of steel links loosened, and Candy gave a cry when a lucent streak crossed her buttocks. A capricious swat had chastised her delay and Candy quickened her step to keep up as the steady boot falls of the women and chime of their spurs continued to sound warningly behind her.

The strong bare back of the Imbe occupied her vision and

she watched with growing prurience as the leather on his form shimmered and flexed with his bold stride. The prod hung in one hand and her leash in the other to offer him total command, and his assistants were poised to offer arbitrary correction as they wished. Several times they struck her rear or thighs for no reason, simply to enjoy punishing a slave just as they had been once disciplined before they had gained their promotions.

The group left the areas where the ponies pranced and played, and Candy's legs started to tremble beneath her as she saw what the operatives of this House were truly capable of. It was a terribly demeaning place, where slaves were dragged down by stringent uniforms that turned them into mere herd creatures. Yet, it also seemed to be a place of liberation from humanity, of shedding civilisation and etiquette to embrace animal instinct, drives, and passions.

Before she had a chance to gauge the full measure of what was being done to the slaves here, Candy was suddenly shown down a small path and brought to a long barn.

A corridor ran down the centre of the building and featureless doors were situated along either side before reaching a barred gate at the other end. Beyond this all she could see was tall grass and hints of dark forms moving within it.

The Imbe paused before a door and turned around. One of the kamube opened it for him and Candy was brought to a small chamber where the next phase of her ordeal was to be implemented.

A single light revealed that this was a room with a singular purpose, a changing room that would turn her into a mere grazing animal. The Imbe removed her lead and opened her cuffs as the women grabbed the first chapter of her initiation.

A stern leather catsuit appeared in their arms. The polished dense hide had various rings riveted into place upon it, and the garment extended into mittens and socks, both of which had a padded palm and sole.

Knowing that to resist would just mean being forced and probably punished as well, Candy allowed them to steer her limbs into the sheaths and then zip up the back of her new skin. She was pushed down into a squat and her hands delivered to the floor. Slim lengths of chain were employed to connect the rings at her ankles to those of her wrists. Shorter ones then connected the middle of her shin to the middle of her forearm and a pair of clips irrevocably connected her knees to her elbows.

Before she could try to rise, a sculpted metal strut was set to her back so that it covered the zip. The strut followed her contours and revealed a monstrous posture collar at one end with rings set along the bottom. The hinges at the back had allowed it to part at the front and her throat was encompassed by a towering wall of meagrely padded steel that set her chin up to such a degree that it made it hard to open her mouth against its demands. She also felt the presence of two familiar solid nodules against either side of her throat. Any option to plead for mercy was now gone.

The collar was locked, and the jaws of the waistband were also closed. This tight steel corset grabbed her sides and dragged in before it too was locked at her stomach. She now had no way to rise up from this awkward four-legged stoop.

An open-faced leather hood was pulled down so that it covered her collar. The ranks of clips that were fixed to the neckline snatched the anchors on her collar and Candy was left with no way to draw it free.

A box was opened, and she gave a whimper as she saw the final part of her transformation appear. Ordinarily she would have laughed because it seemed so ridiculous, but crushed down onto all fours, she found it less jovial.

The billowing white cloud of wild wool was brought around her body and locked into place, leaving only a black leather head and four legs emerging from its massive folds. The capability of this wild cocoon to protect was shown to be negligible when the prod dug in through it and reached her rear. Candy gave a squawk as a snap of pain charged into her rear and made her lurch away towards the door. The collar gave her a vindictive blast that caused her to stifle her complaints and simply obey.

She strained against the demands of her uniform but could not escape its strict control. She had to fight just to waddle, and she felt terribly demeaned as she was made to awkwardly amble before the feet of those who had done this to her. She could scarily even achieve motion, every shuffle of a foot or hand made her muscles burn, but another jab of the prod and few swats of the crops to the backs of the shins soon committed her to complying. The words to implore them to let her get used to the position were not easy to keep in check, but she was having enough trouble as it was without adding shocks of her control collar to the ordeal.

Drearily, Candy very slowly made for the door and another jab of the infernal prod turned her and steered her towards the gate. Huffing and panting for breath, she shuffled onwards, her body aching from having to try and trek onwards against this absurd imprisonment.

A kamube opened the simple barrier and another jab into her rear caused her to scuttle forth into the grass. The gate was locked, and she was deserted to her lot.

No word had been exchanged; no command given. They regarded her as a beast and treated her as such.

Candy tried to collapse into the green stalks but the chains connecting her hands and feet would not let her stretch her exterminates apart enough to let her settle down. She tried pulling them in but the strut along her spine would not let her torso curl up and permit this. The only way she could lay down would be to adopt a most savage splits, and she just was not flexible enough to accomplish this. Candy sobbed and strained as hard as she could, trying to break a chain free of its mooring so she might find some meagre solace in this terrible pose. It was useless. This evil house had done its work flawlessly. She was doomed to perching herself on her four feet and not be able to settle down. How could she be expected to exist like this? She would not be able to sleep, to rest, to do anything at all. There had to be more to this lot, there just had to be.

Candy swallowed for strength and started to push on into the tall grass in search of answers, all the while fearing that this was it, that she would be trapped in this ferocious pose for her whole sentence here.

Brushing through the grasses she came across another female sheep and realised that each of them bore a number that was stencilled on the forehead of their hood, which easily identified them.

The impossibly hobbled woman was diligently munching on the greenery, closing her teeth on a bushel, wrenching it free, and then hastily devouring it. She barely even registered the new arrival's presence and merely continued eating with alacrity.

Wondering what was expected of her, Candy continued to wander onwards. She moved through the grasses as best she could, slowly gaining familiarity with being able to move. She had to rest often because the demands of the uniform were not small and despite her physical fitness it was not easy to operate within it.

All she found were other women in sheep uniforms, eating as quickly as they could. Finally, she reached the low wooden fence that surrounded their grazing field. Scarcely a yard high, ordinarily she could just step over it, but in this terrible costume it was an insurmountable obstacle. Candy peered through and saw the stables with their beautiful ponies and anxious hounds, sultry trainers, and adoring servants. Tears welled in her eyes as she dreamed of being sent there. Her trial in House Uka no mitama was going to be a stringent one, but she was sure it would make her transfer to Hohodemi all the more succulent when she finally earned it. It at least gave her something to look forward to, and she stared longingly at the elegant curves and tight uniforms of the trainers as they tacked up, hosed down, fed, trained, and led the ponygirls around.

Candy started to follow the fence as best she could, hoping to find something other than grass and sheep in this infernal paddock.

Finally, she broke through onto an area of stone that existed on the other side of the barn in which she had been created. The preparation chambers were on one side and the grasses between the gate that accessed the field and this side of the barn had hidden this place from her when she had first been introduced.

The side of the barn had a panel upon it with a large lever and a small gallows holding a bell and striker.

Riveted to the ground in ordered rows were ranks of low platforms. A padded table was moulded to fit the contours of their horizontal torsos and a single wooden stem supported them. Fastened along the sides were straps that draped onto the ground. Behind each was a wooden rack, and on each side hung curls of rubber piping that connected to handles with either a hose or a large bulbous head attached to them. On top of each rack was a small control panel with several gauges, a couple of dials, and some switches in addition to a small lever. In all, it appeared to be some sort of archaic industrial gas pump.

Candy decided to take a closer look but as soon as she stepped out, she felt the collar started to tingle. She tried to halt her passage, but her momentum was not easy to counter.

The two prongs started to pass a higher charge between each other, and she gritted her teeth and started to stumble backwards as best she could. The punishment lessened.

Confused as to what was going to be expected of her, she lurked in the grasses and merely watched the ponies with lecherous eyes.

The sun was starting to vanish behind the peaks and spread long angular shadows across the mountainous terrain. Suddenly, several men dressed identically to the Imbe but with very few tattoos emerged. One of them rang out some deep booming notes on the bell and then lifted the lever halfway so that it stood out horizontally from the barn. Moments later Candy heard movement all around her as the sheep congregated and started to shuffle into position about the pads. With soft relishing sighs they sank down and rested their weary limbs.

The priests moved amongst them and brought up the straps to thread the buckles and then tighten them over the backs of the women. The Imbe appeared and walked around the women as they were being restrained.

Candy feared what would be done to them overnight, but she needed to rest, and this was the only way she would manage it.

Having seen that the electronic perimeter was deactivated she moved out from the grass and moved towards a vacant spot where she settled into place. Straps were drawn over her body and she was hauled into the cushioned top of the platform.

"Invert the field," ordered the Imbe.

Candy guessed what that meant and when the lever was lifted all the way up, she flinched when she heard an agonised squawk from the grass. Two of the priests turned and headed into the vegetation, homing in on the howls of a woman who had refused to accept the call or been too far away to make it back in time.

The woman cried out and wailed as she was hoisted up and brought to the open area whereupon her responses dropped to disorientated murmurs and gurgles when her belt ceased functioning.

"Fill the herd," announced the Imbe, and brought immediate action from his subordinates.

The men moved amongst the captive women. They took up one of the handles and paid out the hose before simply inserting the end into the rear of each woman. The same plug that Candy still wore was not doubt in place and each woman shuddered and wriggled as a switch was flicked and the hose shuddered and gurgled as an enema was administered.

Candy gave a spasm when she felt a hose suddenly slip between her buttocks and slide into place on the anal plug before locking to it. Unable to regurgitate the hose she gave a shocked gasp as she felt warm fluid being forced into her rear. If she tensed, the influx suddenly swelled and stretched at her channel, so she instantly relaxed and let the flow negotiate the twists and turns of her body and fill her completely. It was not an unpleasant sensation and coupled with the chance to relax her limbs, she simply hung in her bonds and savoured the feel of being washed internally. Candy started to hiss and huff as the process continued and she started to feel her insides protesting against the amount being forced into her. A brief attempt to try and eject some of the measure again made the reservoir immediately beyond her sphincter swell suddenly and bring discouraging pain. Candy panted for breath and strove to relax as the internal ocean continued to grow and grow.

Just as she was reaching the limits of what she could accept without crying out, the pump stopped for a few minutes, during which time she could hear the deep grumbling moans of the other sheep. Candy's voice joined them when then pump began to siphon away what it had bequeathed. The feeling of deflation made her shiver and whimper as the pressure eased and vanished from inside her body.

"Assess the harvest," added the Imbe.

The priests again started to work through the ranks. They would twist the pumps to unlock them and then hung them back up before checking the gauges on each frame. Candy could hear an assortment of deep purring moans, wanton groans, and despairing whimpers. One by one the women were attended, and the sounds of their varied responses grew closer and closer until it was Candy's turn.

She felt the haul at her captive sphincter as the hose was extracted and then put away and then the priest appeared at her side with tubing in hand. She looked at him with an imploring expression that was utterly lost beneath her uniform.

"Six units short. Very unacceptable," he muttered to himself.

Candy could now see that the hose connected to a solid stool that he set down right before her so that she was staring down a nozzle that emerged from the top. The priest vanished and Candy fought against her posture collar to try and find out what was going on. Clearly, she had erred but had no idea how or why or what her punishment was to be.

The hose started to spray her face with water and Candy gave a brief squeak of shock and struggled against her bonds. The priest manoeuvred the stool so that the jet was striking just beneath her nose and then moved to the woman ahead of her.

Candy spluttered and tried to access air as water entered her nose and poured over her mouth in a near comprehensive sheet. Gurgling and sobbing, she instinctively tried to avoid it but there was no way to acquire the inch or so that would grant her a reprieve.

The flow cut off and she coughed and gasped for breath.

Peering up, she saw the priest assess the gauges for the woman in front of her. He smiled and nodded with approval before removing the bulbous headed hose. He reached under and slotted it into the underside of the platform where it locked into position. The priest flicked a control and the woman quivered as the toy vibrated and poured her reward into her pussy. The priest moved to the neighbour, found the gauges inadequate, but not a degree to warrant punishment, and simply deserted the next girl who gave a despairing whimper of regret that she had failed to earn her prize.

Candy's attention was summarily returned to the small stool as the jet was switched on again and hurled water onto her face. She thrashed madly as her air was cut off or she was forced to capture inadequate hints of a breath through the flow. It was incredibly frustrating. The simple stream was stupidly easy to avoid, but her bondage was leaving her helpless to achieve even the slightest motion. When the cascade stopped, she was left retching and hacking from the small amount she had accidentally inhaled in her rash efforts to find precious air.

The woman before her was now lying slack and was also panting, save that her response was due to a long and much deserved orgasm. The toy was now silent, and the slave was resting comfortably, whereas Candy knew that she was in for a long night of chastisement. If only they had told her what to do when they had entered her here, but then, why would they tell a sheep how to be a sheep. She had to learn the hard way, and indeed it was a very hard lesson.

As she hung in vulnerable misery, being smothered with water at sporadic intervals while those slaves who had complied with the demands of the field earned equally sporadic episodes of ecstasy from their shivering toys, Candy tried to figure out what to do.

The enema that each of them were subjected to had have

been measured when it was taken away, and the amount of extra material used to judge what they had done for the day. A slave who had eaten well was permitted to rest. Those who had gorged themselves were given an orgasmic reward, and the acutely lazy were punished. From listening to the sated purrs of delight from the woman in front of her, Candy knew what she wanted for tomorrow evening, but first she had to survive the night.

CHAPTER TWELVE

U zume stroked the velvet head of her pet. Xiao was curled beside her, resting after she had been given a vigorous over-the-knee spanking that had been applied just to amuse her mistress. The purple velvet catsuit covered her entirely, and a leather harness reached around her body to accentuate her curves and bestow a flowing elegant tail. Leather paws removed her fingers and left her feet smooth and featureless. Her features were hidden behind a simple mask with a feline countenance and small pricked ears.

Uzume extended her other hand and poured some more sake into the small dish. She had chosen to come and sit in the garden and relax on a large leather cushion while her Mikado saw to packing her possessions as well as her other concubines. To improve the image of her dismissal she had given orders that all, including her Imbe, be installed in the most brutal of bondage sarcophagi. With electrical toys locked to them, they would be screaming impotently against their gags in isolated personal anguish. Their hellish containment would impress upon them how bitter their mistress was. Her spiteful retaliation against her own possessions might help word spread and it would add extra legitimacy to Hachiman's plot.

She listened to the soft sounds of the garden and tried to look morose. If she were not approached soon, she would have to actually leave the palace and try and find somewhere to relocate to. She was owed a few favours from some Earth lords, but she would prefer to remain in this region.

Undeserving of being shown the courtesy of being

introduced to him, she was caught by surprise when Toyo-tama-hiko walked past her. She was a pariah in the palace, disgraced, and ejected. To the priests and concubines of the house she did not exist.

"Taking in a last look of the House?"

"I doubt I even deserve that," she said meekly and took a sip of her drink.

"Nonsense," he rebuked.

"I failed my master. I don't deserve life, but I also don't deserve death."

"Death is a subject that also concerns me, for I lost many Wani."

"They were a credit to you, Warlord."

"And yet you have been disgraced and ejected from House Hachiman because you went back to help them. Any other power in the Empire would have just left them to cover a withdrawal, but you took the Mitama into the battle to save them, and it cost you everything."

"My gratitude for pointing out the utterly obvious, War-lord. If you have finished reminding me of my miserable fate, I'll bid you farewell as I have to try and find somewhere to sleep tonight."

"Hachiman was a fool to dismiss you," he said evenly.

"Careful with your words, Warlord. You will end up join-ing me in vagrancy should such a tone reach the ears of your leader."

"But what if he were not my leader. What if he were my equal. What if he were *our* equal."

"You speak as you did when you were thrusting into Candy in the playroom."

"And I stand by those words, even now, just as you stood by my Wani. Your name is already vaulted in their ranks for this. But you are in disfavour with all others, especially be-cause Masuda was well liked. Some are saying you deliberately allowed him to be killed lest he grow in popularity and threaten the strength of your position as Hachiman's agent."

"Preposterous," she snapped and yanked on Xiao's tail to make her jerk and hiss as the butt plug that entered her bottom stretched her suddenly.

"Indeed. But whispers have a way of echoing upon each other until they gain strength. You are in disgrace now, but I fear unless you do something to mitigate the damage to your standing, your lot will worsen. You may be stripped of Kami status."

Uzume paused for a moment as though to steady herself in the face of such a threat.

"I cannot act, Warlord. None will allow me to sit at their table. I will have to call upon every favour I have just to find a bed."

"I already have the backing of the other Great Houses. The Warlords of Water have taken this matter to the Houses of Earth and Air and have found receptive ears. Hachiman has too much power. Taking the Wani from his authority was universally agreed upon as the solution, but they still do not want one with their blood leading them. Dividing power with you is assured of success."

"I agree."

"Then come with me as my guest to the festival. When we arrive, the matter will be brought before Sun-Goddess and Moon-God. House Wani will be established, and we will stand as Warlord and Warlady of that force, and we will carve a name of honour and victory in the blood of those of Earth when battle begins."

"You are most gracious, Toyotama-hiko. How could I ever repay this boon?" she answered with a genuinely joyous edge to her voice. It was not happiness that she had been saved from disgrace and further retaliation over Masuda, but that her master's plan was occurring precisely as he intended. Another milestone had been reached on the road that would carry her back into his arms.

"Let me pound that feline's pert bottom to start with, and then perhaps later we can see what else can be done to satisfy me," he purred as his eyes wandered up and down Uzume's reclining form. Uzume just grinned and began to unfasten the straps that held tail and plug to her pet.

CHAPTER THIRTEEN

It was a long and arduous night of water torture for Candy. When she managed to nod off, she would be awoken by the sudden flow of her punishment. Sometimes this caught her at the end of an exhale and thus left her livid with panic as her tolerances were pushed to the limit by each instance of liquid castigation.

The dull glow of a new sunrise began to warm the sky, and this was the hardest part of the night for Candy. As the sounds of activity across the palace began to grow in volume, as ponies were tacked up, and pets walked, she continued to suffer. Praying for the priests to arrive and set her free, every new instance of abuse was even more maddening than the last.

Finally the small group of men returned and the Imbe oversaw their actions. The whole electronic field was again switched off and toys were removed and hung up, straps were set free, and her infernal torture device was switched off and placed in the frame. The straps let go and she rapidly shuffled for the grass.

"Arm the field!" announced the Imbe and a couple of sheep gave an anguished squeal as they were caught at the perimeter when the invisible barrier was re-established.

Candy threw herself into her task and found that this was not like any grass she had ever encountered. It was soft, and had a strange tang to it. Clearly it had to be nourishing enough to sustain them and so she ripped free tufts and ate as vigorously as she could. The day was long and tiring, but

Candy desperately wanted to avoid another night of watery abuse and pushed her body on and on until she thought she was going to collapse or her jaw fall off from overt use.

That evening, when she finally took her position, she veritably collapsed onto the platform. Weary as she was, she managed a murmur of happiness when the priest behind her merely moved on, her quantities having been judged sufficient for the day.

As the days trailed by, Candy noticed that those sheep who were consistently earning a reward at night were being taken to the gate and escorted out of the field. After seeing this occur a couple of times, she scuttled to the fence and looked out to see where they were being taken. She saw that it was a large three storey building a short distance away but there were no more clues as to their fate.

Other women were introduced to the replace the extracted, and Candy herself repeated what she had seen on arrival when a fresh face appeared and looked at her with aghast horror before simply moving on. As expected, the new arrivals often earned punishment that night and many of them bellowed and hollered for mercy, adding the discipline of their collars to their ordeal.

Candy finally managed to earn a reward after eight days in the field and the orgasm the machine bequeathed was ample reward for all the hours of ferocious digestion. Each night now she acquired the toy. It was pushed up into a slot in the underside so that the rounded head nudged into a gap in the padding and leant tightly to her imprisoned loins. It threw succulent vibrations through the catsuit and dragged her through several savage orgasms before it finally stopped. Several times throughout the night she was rewarded again, and each time she was left elated and overjoyed at her role in this field. She was succeeding, she was excelling, and perhaps soon she would be taken to the next building and therefore another step closer to a transfer to ponygirl status.

It was during this time that she started to notice a change in her body. Her breasts, while trapped within the catsuit were starting to feel tight within their cups and possessed of a rippling itchy feeling that she could not discern the cause of.

In many ways, she missed being a normal slave. Although there were far more demands upon her, she was at least able to speak, to converse, to have some modicum of self-determination. There were no options for disobedience with this House, she was trapped and would serve her function. Only reward or discipline was possible against the impossible confines they imparted upon those handed to them. The names of the priests were also lost to her. They never employed identity, just rank. It made them seem even more beyond her bestial understanding.

The grasses beside her suddenly parted and a priest appeared. Candy's heart leaped with joy that she was going to earn a path out of this dismal and pointless servitude. He stepped before her, checked the identification on her forehead and then moved on. Candy was flabbergasted.

A shock of raging fire crossed the back of her thigh and made her shriek. The collar retaliated and made the cry rise upwards into a squall before she managed to check her failing and stop making noise.

The cane struck the other thigh, and she accepted the encouragement and started to head forward towards the barn. Finally, she was going to be freed of this accursed uniform. Candy loved to serve, to be owned, to sate the desires of those about her. This facet served no clear purpose. She was almost here out of spite. Was that the real purpose of House Uka no mitama? Their mundane duties in rearing herds for the Empire were augmented by being the last stop for recalcitrant slaves. A slave who continually failed even against the brutal demands of this House would only know condemnation to

Yomi.

The gate was opened, and Candy was shown to one of the changing rooms where a trio of kamube quickly stripped away her uniform. The fleece and the leather all left her body as did the steel backbone that had kept her close to the ground. The anal plug remained however, and Candy realised that while she may have escaped the field of the sheep, her lot as a human beast was not yet over.

She was brought to her feet and cuffs were set to her wrists and feet to pin them behind her back and to greatly hobble every step.

"This one is coming along nicely," commented the Imbe and reached up to squeeze one of her breasts.

Candy gave a squawk as unexpected pressure caused a flare of pain within the flesh. She jerked away but the short hobble chain caused her to lose her balance. She fell aside into the arms of a kamube who yanked her back upright with an irritated huff before grabbing her tightly. Candy was pinned to the woman's naked chest and could feel the warm nipple rings digging into her back as hands reached under her armpits and the woman's forearms stretched out to rack Candy's arms and establish a fierce grapple. Candy rose to tiptoe and arched her chest up as she tried to ease the force being applied to her.

The Imbe stepped forward and grabbed her chin before he squeezed the other breast. This time he employed more strength and Candy cried out from the maltreatment. She jiggled on her feet and the kamube tightened her grapple to keep Candy subdued.

"What have you done to me!" she barked suddenly.

"The grass that has sustained you is laden with other ingredients. Hormones to be precise. You are now ready to be transferred to the milking barns."

"What!?!" she blurted.

"You will be turned into a human cow, and will serve House Uka no mitama as such until you are deemed worthy of further elevation."

"This is insane!" she snapped.

A stern slap caught her cheek and jerked her head aside.

"Keep your disrespectful words to yourself, slave! Or we will send you to Yomi!" he snarled.

Candy let her head loll back around and hang limp. The heat of the chastisement still possessed her cheek, but in truth it was fear of the underworld that had subjugated her.

"Bring her," spat the Imbe and started to march from the barn.

One of the kamube stayed to put away the uniform in preparation for the next hapless slave who would have to wear it, and the other two held her arms in strict holds while frog marched her in the wake of the priest. They pushed and tugged with vindictive regularity, obviously greatly irked by the contempt she had shown the House that they now served. The kamube of House Uka no mitama had to have been the most fanatic devotees because in any other House, elevation from sex slave, maid, or bondage subject was only a minor elevation. Escape from the fields and to a bipedal and intelligence state was a much more drastic promotion and their featly was correspondingly heightened.

Inside the barn were long slender corridors of stone. Along each wall were equally spaced door sized mirrors with a small switch set beside them.

A switch was thrown and one of the sliver panels slid aside into the wall. Candy was roughly yanked into a small featureless chamber.

A single light hung overhead, and this spotlight poured a dim radiance down onto what she would be calling home from now on. The walls bore several hooks upon which resided a whip, a flogger, a cane, and a large broad leather paddle. Large, corrugated hoses were also set on each wall and were compiled in curled hoops.

The stone plinth that arose from the floor looked like a large "X" with a rectangular hub serving as the apex. The upper surfaces were with padded with cushions of leather but this consideration for comfort was offset by the thick leather straps that had been fastened to the stone and which hung in readiness. As she was brought towards the item, she could see a pair of holes to one end, and a single, smaller pit towards the other.

With rough movements she was brought to the side of the plinth and then simply thrown down face first onto it so that she was staring at the left wall and the pipe that was poised there. Candy gave a croak of distress from the rough landing on her already distended breasts and flashed a look of loathing at the kamube. The women just grinned and released her ankles before hauling them out onto the wide lower *V* of the device. Candy struggled, but the Imbe merely stomped forward after grabbing the cane and then rained a trio of strokes into her exposed rear. She squealed and writhed but the women merely laid a knee to her calves and pushed down. The flesh throbbed from their brutality, and she shouted for them to stop. The Imbe turned her demand into a wail as he started to thrash her rear with fierce and uncompromising strokes.

A strap caught her ankle, and another replaced the female knees in the backs of her legs. A third crossed the tips of her thighs and as one kamube grabbed the chains between her cuffs and tugged upward, the other started to fasten her waist band. Candy's upper body was forced into the table and her breasts dropped into the two holes. Her shoulders coursed with mayhem, and she gave a keening mew of distress as the hold was hoisted upward to improve her pain.

With her lower body captive, the kamube released her

cuffs and dragged her arms up and around. Candy again fought to stop them but once more, the cane of the Imbe returned to her burning rear and started to etch effulgent lines of woe across the quaking mounds.

Her wrists were secured, and then so too were her forearms and biceps. The caning stopped and Candy sagged in resignation. Wheezing for breath, she just lay in her bonds and continued to feel the awful pound in her rear.

The Imbe stood poised with his cane and Candy just lay where she was. Suddenly, her head was pulled up by her hair to a degree that caused her mouth to drop open. The kamube then crudely thrust the end of the hose into Candy's maw before she could react. The item erupted into automated life that caused Candy to test the effectiveness of her bondage to the full. The straps groaned as a keening muted wail fought the inflating bladders that stretched out into her mouth. Her jaws were hauled open, her tongue was barged into the bottom of her mouth, and her cheeks then started to swell outward. Candy hurled herself against her bonds as her mouth seemed to explode with terrible distress. The stretched skin coursed with mayhem and the corners of her jaws raged with ghastly havoc.

"Nothing more to say, slave?" crooned the Imbe as Candy threw her head around and tried to spit the item free, but it had swelled to such dimensions that it effectively stopped up her maw. The corrugated pipe swayed from side to side as it reached forth and vanished into the wall, but she could not disconnect herself.

Candy's eyes bulged as the piping on the other side of the room was delivered to her rear and locked into position to leave her again surrendered to the automated processes of these infernal locations. A final strap was pulled over her upper back and yanked to pull her into the surface.

"You'll learn obedience here, slave. If you don't? Well, back to the grazing field you go," warned the Imbe and with his assistants in tow he left Candy to her fate.

The door slid shut and she saw that it was formed from one way material. She could see everything that occurred out on the corridor, but no one could see in. She now processed her trip to this room with horror. Every panel she had passed had seen a woman's despairing eyes fixating on her as they lay spread and invaded in this demeaned isolation.

As the door locked into position Candy snorted and sent a deep humming howl against her terrible gag. Some sort of suction had been established in the holes in which her breasts now resided. Thick rubber with raised internal bands clamped to each hanging mound and squeezed. Her nipples were free of these internal sheaths but then they were afflicted by their own even fiercer haul.

Candy lurched and shrieked as the bands formed a strange form of fist that rolled from the base towards the tip, crushing the flesh before a second and even more vicious suction snatched and hauled at her nipples. Candy could not believe what was happening to her, but was helpless to defeat the process. All she wanted to do was go back to her master, but his rival was making sure she stayed out of his reach until she posed no further threat.

Candy's concerns about the future were momentarily forgotten when a wet phallic rod rushed forward and buried itself in her pussy. She jerked and then fought afresh as it started to draw back and reveal its own collection of ridges before it again pistoned into her.

The automated ravishing continued with mechanical efficiency, driving deep, pulling back, and repeating. Her pussy was bounced upon the pliant but drastic series of ridges and troughs and her clit ring danced and rattled upon them as she was molested by machines. The pleasure of the assault was actually quite satisfying but the rending hauls at her breasts were not making it easy to enjoy herself.

Suddenly Candy felt the meagre and almost pleasant sensation of pressure draining from her breasts. The machine continued to tug and wring her breasts, but the internal swell was vanishing from her and despite the abuse, Candy started to succumb to the rhapsody.

Laying her head down so that she was watching the upper face of the plinth, she shuddered as the dildo again rampaged into her and the pressure in her breasts continued to vanish. The steady charge of the toy brought her to orgasm, but the machine did not stop. Her fight to get free increased as the pleasure started to become more than she could bear and again she was reduced to a maenad of effort when she could give the breast cups no more but regardless, they continued their efforts. Roaring onto her gag and struggling as much as she could, she feared that the machine had broken and would continue to suck at her until she went mad, but it was just being thorough. When the vacuum and dildo stopped and the sheath let go of her tormented assets, Candy collapsed onto her bed and wheezed softly for breath.

The dildo was now curled back into its housing, leaving the lubricant that it had oozed during its rhythmic efforts to drool from her and into the waste pit beneath her loins. Candy retched and found new animation when she felt water being eased into her rear and nourishment into her mouth. Unable to let it go anywhere, she was forced to gulp down the offered sludge as hastily as she could because any excess caused her mouth to stretch wider and her cheeks to bulge to a terrible degree that forced her into instant compliance.

A terrible and yet sumptuous thought struck her. During her time in the Empire, she had seen no cows, and yet she had seen milk and also drunk it herself on several occasions. Had it been dragged from women such as her? When she had sipped at a serving of milk, had it originated from the breast of another human female? One locked and alone in a small room, strapped down, and squealing in pain as she was fucked and sucked dry by this nightmarish production facility?

She laid her head down and closed her eyes, fighting to relax as the image of all those who had been forced to donate so painfully to her continued to creep through her mind.

CHAPTER FOURTEEN

The sound of the door opening roused Candy from her phased torpor. Her exhaustion and the banal existence in the room offered her no clues as to the passage of the time and because there were no windows and the light was always on, even the passage of days was removed.

She lifted her weary head to see the same two kamube marching in. The door slithered shut behind them and they immediately began to strip off their meagre clothing. She stared at them with bemusement as they shed their garb and then stepped out before her. They were now naked save for nipple rings and collar.

The taller of the women had a slightly more slender build and had dark hair that was almost black. Her features were slightly angular, bestowing a more gaunt and vicious countenance. Her breasts were small, but they were very pert. The woman closed her hand about the flogger and ran her fingers through the thick suede-lined leather strands.

"I am kamube Ivy."

The other crouched down before Candy and hoisted her chin in one hand before the other slapped Candy's swollen cheek. The woman was shorter and more curvaceous than her partner, with ample breasts and enticing curves. She had brown hair and hazel eyes that glittered with malevolence.

"And I am Kamube Petal," she snarled and added another couple of slaps to make Candy cringe and whimper as she tried to get away from the abuse. The woman grabbed her feeding hose and pulled up to make the prisoner cry against her gag and snort for breath as the huge oral anchor sought to emerge but could not fit through her pained maw.

"You dared to slander this great and devoted House? I cannot even begin to comprehend such dishonour," said Petal.

"But what can one expect from a barbarian?" commented Ivy.

Candy gave a startled look to the woman before her. The kamube read the expression and simply grinned before letting go of the pipe. Candy sucked in to bring the gag back the tiny measure it had moved and ease her sorrow a little.

"Yes, we know who you are, you slut. You're Hachiman's little imported whore from Earth," snarled Petal.

"We hate people from the other side, don't we, Petal?"

Candy gave a wail against her gag as her anal pipe was snatched and pulled to make the capturing plug drag against her sphincter. Her hands clawed against the cushions, and she thrashed her head from side to side.

"Indeed we do. Especially stuck up little privileged bitches who don't know their place," said Petal and stepped to the wall to arm herself with the broad paddle. Her partner let go of the pipe and Candy wilted within her straps.

"Just because you have been honoured beyond equal to have been in the presence of the Kami . . ." said Ivy, and then after a pause brought the flogger down in an overhead arc that had it lay its thick strands across Candy's back.

" . . . does not mean you are no longer kami-tsu-ko," she continued and then commenced with a slow and weighty beating. The leather tendrils slammed to her back and filled the room with their stark signal as a struggling heat started to swell within Candy's back. Every swipe escalated the distress, and as the woman continued to growl her words between swipes, Candy started to find the weapon less easy to endure.

"You are a slave. We are kamube. Our master is Imbe Yeng, and you are subservient to us! Understand! You are our plaything!"

Candy flinched with every stroke and bitterly regretted her earlier words. She had caused great offence and these women were now going to avail themselves of the chance to punish her for it. Candy was actually frightened. She had never before been so abandoned. There were always Kami around to study her, use her, protect her. Now she was alone and defenceless. These former slaves could do anything they wanted to her with impunity, and this made her scared.

"And this ungrateful barbarian has been blessed to be used by Lady Uzume, Warlord Hachiman, and even the Supreme Warlord of Water no less. How can someone who has been given such treasures be so disrespectful!" added kamube Petal and Candy flew to attention as the paddle swung around and clapped to the sole of her foot. The tender skin exploded with turmoil, and she tried to curl her toes in and protect the region. The woman flung the weapon overhead and laid it to Candy's rear. Her cheek rippled and lucid heat swelled within the assailed skin. The other buttock was attacked, and the flogger began to again rain down on her back.

"Toyo-tama-hiko lent you to our House," said Ivy. " . . .and you should be grateful to experience what we offer."

Petal grabbed Candy's big toe and pulled down. She tried to stop her but the severity with which the woman was treating her intimidated her into giving up. She closed her eyes and relaxed her foot to give the woman the target she wanted.

"You will be released when Toyo-tama-hiko desires you returned to him," said Petal and started to lay the paddle to the bared sole. Each stroke made Candy spasm as she tried to scrunch up her toes and defend herself, but the woman now had her target and was not letting go. Candy's shriek wafted through the gag in the form of feeble murmurs. She cast her head around in torment while instinctively fighting to get away from this infernal monsoon of discipline.

"Whereas *we* suffered long and hard in the fields and barns, in the kennels and cages before we were elevated, and yet you dare to slur our beloved Imbe with your words and show us no respect?" growled Ivy.

"Well we're going to pay you lots of visits, cowgirl. We'll make sure you get all the attention you believe you are due."

"We are kamube of House Uka no mitama, and if you cannot respect the House, then oh by the Sun-Goddess you'll learn to fear it!"

Petal jumped forward and started to energetically alternate from cheek to cheek with occasional hateful swings into Candy's inner thighs. Her partner continued to drop the broad tentacles of the flogger onto Candy's back, and she was lost in a tornado of anguish.

She jolted and felt her sanity being carried away on a tide of desolation. The fright caused by these harridans with their derision and scornful comments made it impossible for her to find any pleasure in this abuse and when they finally stopped, it took Candy a few moments to realise that fact. Her swimming sight cleared to see them getting dressed and Candy was left with throbbing back, feet and rear. Again, she dropped down onto the plinth and just let her mind drift on indistinct half-thoughts and vague recollections of her past.

She had no idea how long it was between their departure and the next time she was milked, given an enema, and force-fed, but when had just finished her next session of brutal milking, forced pleasure, and feeding, the door shuffled aside and the two women entered, this time both wearing curling elegant cowboy hats and bearing bullwhips in their hands.

Ivy dropped her whip and grabbed the feeding hose as her partner marched over and took up the enema pipe. Candy was mortified to see the woman offer a malignant smirk and then bend the hose over several times to crimp it. She could guess that Petal was doing the same.

The hose started to chug quietly to itself and then began to shudder as the build-up started to cause more distress to the machine.

"Ready for a binge, cowgirl?" hissed Ivy and simply dropped the hose.

Candy's eyes bulged as a huge measure of backed up food was forced into her maw. It thundered down her throat, swelling it and making her snort in apathy. As the massive flow decreased to a more stolid level, she jerked to attention as another swollen influx rushed into her rear and made the area just beyond the tightly fastened plug swell to horrible levels. The bloated douche stretched her channel and made her cavort against her bonds as she fought to operate her canals and ingest the sudden excess.

"Ready for another?" asked Ivy and reached down to slowly take up the deserted hose. Candy threw her head around and tried to keep the item out of the woman's hands, hoping to avoid her long enough so that the feeding would finish before she could bend the hose.

Ivy stepped over the hose and settled down. Her rear pushed down and snapped the line taut to make Candy mew as the gag was pulled on. Her mouth could not allow the swollen item free and so it strained at her features to engineer a cruel anguish.

"Hmmm, that gives me an idea for tomorrow," came Petal's sultry voice and then Candy felt the flow of the enema suddenly stop.

Ivy grabbed the hose, stepped back off the pipe, and bent it over.

"I can't wait to see it," said Ivy, her eyes locked to Candy's imploring stare as she again cut off the flow. Candy sobbed and watched as the hose started to quake from the accumulating backup.

"Here we go, cowgirl. Enjoy!" she snarled, and both of the

villainesses dropped the hoses.

Candy flexed and struggled as a sudden massive wall of fluid and food slammed to her rear and mouth. Her channel thundered with engorged misery as she was forced to process more than she could ordinarily bear and as she suffered and offered keening whimpers, the women just laughed.

"What a silly beast," accused Petal.

"And she smells like a filthy one," said Ivy.

"Well let's correct that shall we?" laughed Petal and strolled to the wall opposite the door upon which hung the weapons and the only unused hose. She paid out the length and turned the valve at the tip. Cold water trundled forth and poured over Candy's body. The heat in her skin from the fight to get free was instantly stolen and she jerked as it continued to roll over her, numbing her skin and making her cry out from shock.

Candy gave a squeal of resentment when the tardy flow was turned onto her pussy. She was still hot after the fucking the machine had given her and the water felt freezing from the contrast. She fought to close her legs and the drastic drop in temperature made her hurl her head from side to side in a bid to get free. She stared up at Ivy with utter imploring, but the woman stood aloof and disdainful, merely mocking Candy's expression with another detached chuckle.

The nozzle closed in, and the flow started to pour into her recently ravished sex. Candy's entire physique launched to a tensed and rigid stance. Her squeal of dismay even managed to hum over the gag as the cleansing continued and stripped her humid pussy of all its previous warmth.

"There we go. Nice and clean. Fresh and ready to serve," attested Petal.

She switched off the flow and hung up the hose. Candy could not relax even though the abuse had finished. Shivering, her body flinched and flicked as the cold continued to haunt her hide. The inserted flow dribbled from her pussy and into the waste hole and she let her head hang limp down the front the plinth.

"We had best get a move on, Petal. We don't have much time to get to the breeding pens," whispered Ivy, and without any more consideration for the hapless female they were so thoroughly tormenting, the pair of vixens sauntered cheerfully from her stall.

Candy just lay where she was and tried to stay calm and recover some body warmth. She barely noticed a priest open the door and enter, look around and check her hoses before finding all in order and departing. The backup in flow had caused someone to investigate, but without the capability for speech, she could not inform about her abusers. Besides, why would a priest ask a mere cowgirl what had happened. It would probably be considered beneath her intellect.

Candy loathed this role. She did not mind being regarded as a sex slave, as a toy for the amusement of others, or in being humiliated, degraded, and insulted, but to be utterly ignored was most infuriating. She found herself reminiscing about previous exploits, and even the stern encounters with sadists such as the Wani daughters were now a most welcome memory. Even though they had treated her horribly, they had still acknowledged her existence and had used her for their own grim purposes.

Yet another banal period of time passed and was marked with another milking and another session of feeding and internal cleansing. As she expected, the two cruel kamube again entered her stall and again started to strip off their token attire.

"Time for me to remind you of your place, cowgirl" hissed Ivy, and this time she availed herself of the cane. Candy whimpered when she heard the spiteful women test the weapon with a few broad hacks at the air.

"As I remind myself of how much more elevated I am than you," added Petal.

The woman turned her back to Candy and stepped over the feeding hose. She lowered herself a little until the hose was taut and then rolled her hips forward. The corrugated ridges rolled through her pussy and caused the gag to drag at Candy's face. The woman moaned wantonly and swayed, her ponytail flopping from side to side as she shifted her hindquarters against the pipe. Candy stretched her neck forward to try and ease her lot, but Petal lowered further to ensure that the ridges bounced firmly against her sex. Lines of moisture appeared on the hose as she obviously exalted in her masturbation, and Candy was left to stare with utter envy at the sultry curves and inviting rear of the nude woman as her knuckles went white against her own thighs and her grunting moans started to echo through the room.

"See how we can do whatever we want with you?" said Ivy. "And as you watch Kamube Petal ride your feeding hose, I'll take my pleasure from your backside."

Candy cried out as the bamboo sceptre started to hum against the air and strike her rear. Every time it fell, she could not help but jolt, and this drew the pipe up between Petal's legs and made the woman arch over and groan with glee.

"Harder, Ivy! Harder! I want to feel her pain between my legs!" bellowed Petal. Her thighs were trembling as every vicious swipe translated into a pull that further delighted her.

The rhythm of the cane remained constant but now it started to land on the upper regions of Candy's thighs to make her responses all the more drastic. Candy shrieked and fought to get free as she was brutalised for her ill-chosen words.

"That's it! I'm almost there! Oh! Cane her, Ivy! Cane her harder!" screamed Petal.

Tears flowed down Candy's cheeks, and she stared wide

eyed and frozen at the image of the gorgeous woman before her taking all she wanted from her captive without any consideration for her wellbeing or sanity.

Petal suddenly stumbled forward, her steps awkward as she kept herself pressed to the pipe and made Candy's maw thunder with pain from having to keep it tightly drawn between the woman's pussy. The steps caused the ridges to course against her clit and the woman squealed with ecstasy as she climaxed. She stole a great breath, threw her arms around herself and held tightly and then started to take a few steps back. This took her rapture further and she had barely taken three small steps before she could take no more and flung herself from the pipe. The naked curvaceous form collapsed on the floor and shuddered as Candy managed to pull her gag back in a little and ease the suffering in her face. She could see the moisture on her pipe and was torn with jealously and regret for what she had done.

Ivy stopped her attack and hung up her weapon before she moved to comfort her partner. She knelt down beside her and held her close while the woman quaked and slowly composed herself.

With their play at an end, they again dressed and simply deserted Candy to the ongoing process of her new role.

If only she had kept herself fixed to the role of a beast, then this would not be happening to her. The milking was a ghastly imposition, but the pleasure the dildo dragged from her bound and spread body was a definite compensation. However, by daring to anger these women, she was earning herself an unwanted deluge of additional duress.

Candy dropped her head down and wept tears of self-pity for her lot. She just wanted to be returned to the care of a Kami and not left to this lowly and desperate fate. Candy knew that she was being softened up for transfer to House Hohodemi and the process was working perfectly. After having served as sheep and cow, she would do or say anything to have a bit pressed between her teeth and to gallop at the end of some reins. Hated though this imprisonment was, it was making her appreciate her former duties, and making her greatly hunger to finally get away from these fell barns and fields. However, the day of her freedom was unknown and until then she had to patiently endure the abuse of these irked kamube.

Another milking passed and a short time after, the two women again entered her stall. Candy just hung her head and mewed in despondent woe as they chuckled and started to strip off.

"This time, cowgirl, it is you who will do the pleasuring!" said Ivy and stepped over the pipe, but this time facing Candy. She stepped back and stood with legs flexed and parted.

Candy whimpered as she felt cord being tied around her big toes. She was familiar with what this might entail, and when she felt the slack being drawn in to bend her feet forward, she was not entirely surprised when a pair of pegs were clamped to her earlobes.

"Well. Get going. I'm getting bored!" growled Ivy.

Petal revealed that she had selected the whip but with such a small target she instead crouched down and simply took the very tip of the weapon. With this foot of single tail, she started to thwack Candy's soles.

Candy squealed and her head jerked back to draw the hose between Ivy's legs. The wicked women shuddered, and her hands tensed against her sides.

"That's it. Keep going!"

Candy's head dropped back, and she managed to haul upward again and continue to draw the ridged length against Ivy's pussy. She stared with aghast despair as the dark pipe rippled through the parted wet lips of the woman, who just glared down at her with contempt even as Candy desperately fought to pleasure her.

Petal busied herself with the most terrible swipes across Candy's feet, thrashing them with callous disdain and making every attempt to shield them haul at her earlobes and add to her tribulations.

Candy's neck was aching terribly but when Ivy complained about a flagging rate, her partner increased the speed and strength of the brutal swipes to restore a decent rate. Candy sobbed and continued to throw her head up with all her might, trying to please the woman before she did herself serious harm.

"Come on cowgirl! Pleasure me!" snarled Ivy, and Candy gave a squall as the whip crossed a particularly vibrant intersection of welts.

Candy improved her efforts as her entire neck burned and the muscles throbbed because of her exertions.

"Haul up and stay still! Now!" roared Ivy as her thighs shivered.

Candy cast her head up and pulled the pipe tight to the woman's sex. The black length slid through her lips and leant itself to her swollen clit. The woman answered the entry with a cry and started to jiggle against the pipe as she rushed into the arms of a potent climax.

Ivy settled down even more and this tested Candy's ability to stay where she was. The back of her neck coursed with anguish and tears welled in her eyes as she chewed on her gag and fought to keep the position.

Ivy shifted forward until her belly was pressed to Candy's face. The view of the twitching stomach smothered Candy's breath and the woman held tightly to Candy's head as her hindquarters skipped back and forth in tiny shuffles while she shrieked and savoured every instance of her pleasure.

Ivy stepped off and Candy's head dropped down. The scent of arousal plagued her nostrils, and Candy barely responded when the pegs were removed and her toes freed. The women just deserted her again, and she just continued to whimper and pray for an end to her ordeal.

On their next visit, they settled their naked loins onto her toes and demanded that she pleasure them. By wiggling her toes she could dance them upon their clitoris" as they crouched over each foot, and they made sure she did as each wished by raining cane and crop down into her thighs and rear.

Candy swore that she could withstand no more. The women were destroying her mind with their callous use of her bound body. How much longer was it until the celebration was to be thrown? How much longer until she was reclaimed? She hoped that she had not been forgotten, because the mere thought of being condemned to this demeaning life was too nightmarish to entertain even for a moment.

CHAPTER FIFTEEN

Candy sobbed and struggled with elation when she saw the elegant and handsome form of Toyo-tama-hiko appear in the mirrored portal. It slithered aside and he smiled as he recognised her.

"Well, Candy. Have you been enjoying what this House has to offer?"

He stepped in and the door slithered shut behind him.

"Perhaps you would like to stay longer. It looks like you have made some friends," he blithely commented and let a finger trace across the welts that now coated her rear. Candy jolted and bellowed her denial against the terribly effective gag.

"Have you endured enough of being an animal, slave? Domestic pets are very neglected are they not? Would you like to take a step back towards some attention and become my puppy?"

Candy threw herself against her bonds and the hose whipped up and down as she tried to confirm her assent. Anything would be better than a domesticated caste, even puppygirl was preferable, and it would mean that once more she would be at the side of a Kami and away from the petty spite and diabolic ministrations of the kamube caste.

"Then I will free you of this role," he announced.

Candy sobbed with joy as his hand trailed along the feeding hose before it reached her face and caressed her swollen cheeks.

The Warlord continued onwards and reached her rear,

whereupon he unfastened the hose and then opened the two flanges of her anal plug. Candy pushed her bonds to their tolerances one more time as he suddenly pivoted and drew on the terrible item. Her sphincter was stretched to intolerable levels in an instant, but the item did not come free.

Toyo-tama-hiko let go and she sucked the disc back in, her anus now pulsating with a keen ache. He gave her a moment to recover and then repeated his haul, drawing the disc until Candy was squealing against her gag. This time he did not let go and merely held it where it was, educating her flesh to stretch before he allowed her to devour it.

"We're getting there, slave. Endure this, if you want to leave this place. My puppies are toilet trained, and there will be no need for this particular item."

Candy instantly strengthened her resolve but as her orifice was pulled open to a hideous degree she again hollered and writhed before the Warlord let go.

"This time it's coming out, slave," he warned.

Candy bellowed against her gag for him not to do this, that she needed just a few more pulls to loosen her bottom.

"No slave, it's coming out. Right now. So get ready."

Candy lowered her head and readied for the agony. The disc started to emerge and on a steady and lethargic pull, it hauled her open and as she thrashed and wailed as much as she could, it finally popped free. She immediately dropped into an exhausted heap as the pain in her rear started to ease and then vanish. She had done it. She was finally rid of the item that marked her as a controlled and utterly helpless beast. She quivered as the oral gag deflated of its own accord and slipped from her lips. Then she mewed pitifully as her long-stretched cheeks and jaws finally managed to close and the skin raged with misery from the process of withdrawal.

The straps began to release her body and she was finally able to move her long contained limbs. They responded meekly and she had to shuffle aside before she flopped reck-lessly onto the floor. She instantly lavished kisses to the boots of the Warlord.

He accepted them for a brief time and then leaned down to help her back onto her unsteady feet. A collar awaited her and after buckling the slim leather item about her throat, he snapped a leash to it.

"Come with me, slave," he said, and started to walk away. Candy was giddy with excitement. She had forgotten just how delicious it was to be collared and to walk at the end of a lead behind her master. She writhed with lust as she ambled in his wake, recovering use of her limbs while her eyes feasted on the enticing curves and fetching physique of the Warlord. He had put her through hell, but now she was back at his side, and she felt all the more admiring of him because of what he had done to her. She had suffered greatly in the field and barn, and it was all for him, whether he had seen her distress personally or not, he knew what this House did to its captives. Candy entertained notions of him, with a slave impaled on his cock, or even better, his hand upon his own shaft and im-ages of Candy, weeping and imprisoned as a cow or sheep running through his mind's eye as he played with himself.

She was taken to the main palace, and it felt as though she had been given the greatest of gifts as she walked up the steps and entered the reception hall.

Stumbling in his wake, she was taken aside and up a flow-ing staircase that delivered them to the upper floors. As soon as she entered the corridor, she gave a croak of shock upon seeing a row of female heads emerging from wooden mount-ings. Each prisoner stared blankly forward and wore a leather hood that bestowed her with a pair of moulded antlers. Candy's horror turned to wonderment when she saw one of the women look round a little and regard her.

The Warlord continued to lead her into the palace and

Candy was astonished to see even more rows of captive females, all mounted inside the wall with their heads being the only portion that emerged. Some were brutally gagged; others were not impeded in any way. The House had been training the women as deer and she wondered if they had either eluded capture long enough to merit this fate, or as was more likely, they had been caught and served to this bondage to punish them for their lack of skill. The hounds in the courtyard suddenly made a lot more sense and Candy was greatly aroused at the thought of a team of Kami with their bondage hounds, hunting down and pursuing this luscious female prey.

She was brought into a circular chamber where a trio of kamube awaited her with her next uniform. Unfortunately, Ivy and Petal were also present amongst them.

Candy was grabbed and her body inserted into a fishnet catsuit. The form-fitting garment covered everything save her breasts and her loins. Next came a shimmering leotard of polished rubber with holes in the crotch and at the chest along with a spry slender tail that jutted up just beneath the area where the base of the spine would soon be. She stepped into the high cut leg holes and gave a tremble as it was brought up over her shoulders. Her breasts were eased through the two openings at the front and the back zip was hauled up so that the whole garment embraced her with a close fondness. The high collar of the garment reached her jawline, and a small padlock was established to run through the zipper and the two small rings that existed on either side of it.

Tall gloves and stockings appeared and each bristled with moulded straps. Each also had a pad that resembled paw halfway along them. Each latex item was drawn up her limbs until it could be buckled tightly to upper arm and thigh so that her feet were sealed within tight socks and her hands were lost within tight featureless mittens. The three slim straps created a firm hold that clearly would not let her wriggle free of the items.

The artificial paws now covered her knees and elbows and Candy realised that she was to be a four-legged pet to her master.

She was summarily forced down onto her knees and her devolution continued when they bent her arms up so that her hands touched the front of her shoulders. The clusters of straps were drawn around her folded limbs and wrenched tight before being buckled. Her calves were hauled fiercely into the backs of her thighs and her forearms were similarly hauled against her biceps.

Before proceeding with any other additions, they decided to silence her with an animal countenance. An open-faced rubber hood was pulled down over her head and dropped into place over the collar of her leotard. The hood had two perky ears jutting up on either side of her head, but they were not open, so the hood muffled her hearing somewhat.

Next came a sculpted snout in which she could see an interior stalk that sported a swollen pliant ball of translucent purple jelly.

"Open wide, slave."

She stretched her jaws wide, but clearly, the item was still too big for her to accept.

"Wider!"

Candy strained her jaws until they throbbed and she could accept the orb. It slipped over her lips and nudged to her teeth. The Imbe pushed harder, and she gave a keening whimper as her jaws were parted more than she could happily endure. A brief flash of pain afflicted the corners of her maw and the enormous gag popped into her mouth. Such was its size that her teeth were still kept far apart as they chewed impotently on the mouth-swelling sphere.

The padded rim of the snout nestled against her face.

Straps reached up over her head and were drawn around the base her skull before they were hauled tight and sealed. The final pulls caused the ball to be pressed deeper into her mouth and she gave a gurgle of response as it pushed almost to the back of her throat.

Perched on her knees, she was embraced from behind and a grapple was established around her neck and waist. Her folded arms were drawn apart and two harnesses of latex were brought towards her. Candy struggled against the priests holding her when she spotted the rows upon rows of tiny studs that flecked the inner surface of each collection.

Candy gave a mewling howl as the first straps were tightened around the base of her breasts. The small fangs pressed against her skin and created struggling waves of misery. As she gasped for breath, every inhale made the tiny and wicked fangs more distinct. The interior of the snout grew hot and humid as she gurgled against the gag and fought to get free. The snout had only a few airholes, and these were not very large, making it hard for her to even gasp or pant.

Equally spaced around the garrotting breast strap were four more belts, and each was similarly armed with interior walls of spines, and each reached forth to fasten to the perimeter of a metal hoop.

The ring was placed to the tip of each breast so that it ran around the mamilla and then they started to draw on the straps. The rings pulled her breasts into her chest and the spines made the skin rush with discomfort as they dug in. Her assets were compressed to her and swelled impotently against their tight cocoon. Every breath now caused each brutal ensemble to pulse with new sensation. She jiggled to seek some slack or a way out, but this only made matters worse. Any movement made the inward facing arsenal of spines escalate their effects. Her concerns were heightened by the fact that her ringed nipples were still very much accessible in this format and were already throbbing from the strangling hold that had been set around the root of each breast.

The grapples came away and Candy dropped onto what had once been arms but was now effectively forelegs. She snorted into her animal face and cringed as she continued to feel the effects of the breast harnesses grow in potency.

Giddy from the restraint, she looked up and saw Toyo-tama-hiko gloating at her degradation.

"Quite an attractive pup," he commented.

The Warlord reached up with the toe of a boot. Distracted by her efforts to come to terms with her latest role, Candy paid the extremity little attention until it nudged her swollen breast. She gave a cry and scampered aside. Her limbs tangled beneath her, and she collapsed onto her side. The impact further aggravated her breasts, and she gave a squawk against the gag.

"But a little awkward," said Toyo-tama-hiko with a chuckle.

He crouched down and placed a knee to her side to keep her in position. Her folded limbs flailed, and she looked up at him with a beseeching expression. The Warlord ignored it and reached down between her legs so he might casually massage her loins.

The openings in catsuit and leotard offered him complete access and he used this to stroke the lips of her sex. His fingers rushed along her pussy and Candy quaked with glee as she was roughly masturbated. His other hand groped her mesh-smothered flanks and ran along the smooth contours of her latex-clad torso and legs.

"Will you be a good girl? Or must I put you on a leash," he pondered.

Candy's eyes drifted shut and she laid her head against the floor. Panting, she felt him start to paw his fingers against her clit and she gave a series of whimpering barks of response.

A hand moved to an exposed breast and his fingertips grazed her nipple. She knew that this tenderness would not last and so she savoured every second as he teased and tweaked the stiffening peak. His fingers traced the metal hoop that was pressed down around the teat and then he began to knead her flushed flesh. Candy groaned and shuddered as the points shifted against her and dug in more acutely, but the savage groping of her pussy made his spiteful grope a delicious woe. He squeezed harder and Candy surged against her uniform when his fingers slid into her channel.

Toyo-tama-hiko's stretched out his fingers and placed his palm to her nipple. The digits closed in and squeezed fiercely to create a strong grasp that kept her on her side. His other hand curled back, and he curled in his index finger and then flicked her exposed and vulnerable clitoris. The shocking and spiteful slap of his finger to her intimate regions made her release a shout of shock, but then the finger laid to what it had smacked and swirled round and round. He flicked her again, making Candy convulse and pain her own breast as her body tried to pull away from his uncompromising hold.

Grinding her teeth to the soft but resilient dimensions of the gag, Candy stared up at her abuser as he alternated between the most sterling rubbing of her clit and infuriating and startling flicks to the same defenceless target.

His hands fled, grabbed her tail, pulled it down between her legs, and fed the smooth rounded tip into her eager sex. Candy moaned wantonly as she felt the cool rigid strut being used to penetrate her and then withdraw so that it could tickle her clitoris and vulva before it stole entry into her rear. Armed with her own wetness, the tip breached her sphincter and was fed deeper and deeper until the Warlord simply let go.

Hands once more snatched her pussy and breast and Candy juddered on the floor as the curled stem pressed against her canals. The spry tail started to emerge and as her innards twitched and assisted in ejecting it, the feeling of its passage pouring from her body made her cry out from startled amusement. The tip popped free and snapped back up to attention.

Toyo-tama-hiko arose.

"We shall see," he said calmly. "Heel."

The Warlord turned and began to stroll towards the door. Candy shook off the debauched haze and clamped her thighs together. She desperately wanted to continue the task herself, but there was clearly no way to do so. Resigned to her lot, she rolled and flipped herself back onto her fake paws.

Waddling after him with as much speed as she could gain, she found the demands of the uniform very taxing to meet. The sway of her torso was one of the most loathed aspects because each swing made her breasts lurch against one rank of spines and then the lean against the other. In addition, when her forelegs bumped the strangled orbs, this further caused bothersome aches.

The Warlord paused and turned to her.

"Keep up, girl. Or it's a leash to the nipple rings!" he warned.

Candy gave a jerk of sudden alarm at the prospect and instantly threw herself into the role to offset this punishment. She scampered with all her might and soon she was no longer fighting the uniform but rather working with it. If she swayed correctly, if she timed her steps properly, the pain diminished and she could actually acquire a decent rate of travel.

Trotting a few paces behind Toyo-tama-hiko, Candy barely registered her surroundings. The uniform sought all her awareness, and any distraction threw off her rhythm and slowed her. When she saw the Warlord increasing the distance between them, she had to concentrate even harder and fight all the more diligently to catch up. The process of recovering lost ground was not easy, but the threat of a lead to her rings was not one she intended to encounter.

Corridors and chambers passed by. The sounds of other slaves was diminished by the hood and then completely lost because of the sound of her scuttling paws and the panting breaths that flowed down her hollow snout. Her pained gurgles and mews of distress further helped drown out all other audio input. Candy briefly detected daylight and with a sudden scudding rush of her folded limbs she sought to catch up with her master.

The Warlord stopped and laid his hands to the handrail of a barrier. The fence had curling metal struts that reached up to support the leather padded rail and sunlight poured down onto the scene. Candy trotted over and settled at his side. She tried to catch her breath, but when she looked up and through the bars, it was stolen by total awe.

The plane was vast, flat, and would be barren in its natural state. It appeared that it might have once been a lake that had long ago dried up to leave this smooth mountain-enclosed field.

The scorched earth was pockmarked with countless raw craters and was surrounded by a wall of stone that had been reinforced and augmented for destruction. Set along the base of the mountains around the whole plane, the barrier was least two hundred yards in height and had countless weapon emplacements aiming a seemingly infinite variety of weapons inward. Cannons, catapults, howitzers, ballistas, flamethrowers, trebuchets, missile and rocket launchers, mortars, miniguns—there were heavy weapons from every time period all amassed and situated in hardened locations and manned by Wani and human warriors.

From the ranges of battlements that rolled around the wall were more warriors, all with an equal array of modern and primitive missile weapons at the ready. Whether the projectile was bullet, grenade, rocket, arrow, or quarrel, they were all trained on the vast open landscape.

There was one huge doorway that reached almost to the top of the wall, and this monstrous gate was still slightly obscured by dozens of stories of scaffolding that hinted that this titanic entrance was a recent addition. Other, much smaller portals existed and these great gates with their spike encrusted portcullises could be seen spaced along the base of the wall.

Further areas poured forth great rivers of cables and piping. The tight bundles wove out through the devastation and reached into rocky mounds that she immediately recognised as the last few remnants of a stripped submarine or ship. The stranded nuclear reactors had been reinforced with their own defences and then connected to the Empire's power grid.

The wrecks of other craft could also be detected across the plane. They were not easily seen because they had been subjected to a stripping that left only the most basic components behind. The skeletal remains of aeroplane and ocean vessel lay contorted and broken where they had been deserted.

Candy and her master were located close to the uppermost reaches and along the wall at the same height she could see other such balconies and hints of regal forms emerging onto them.

"Hmmm. It should be here by now," muttered Toyo-tama-hiko with a sense of concern.

Candy gave a cry when klaxons tore through the hesitant quiet and roared across the whole region. She dropped down and huddled to the Warlord's feet as the unearthly bellow continued to resound and thousands of troops hoisted their weapons and drew aim.

With a grim sense of foreboding and an intrigued fascination, Candy hid within her tight uniform and just watched.

The alarms cut off and were replaced by a scratching sound. The grinding developed into a crackle that suddenly exploded into a brilliant circus of electrical arcs.

"Ah. Here we go. I was worried that this was going to end up being another stray," said the Warlord. He reached down to absently pet Candy's smooth head and continued to peer around and see where the arrival would materialise.

The jagged forks exploded from the air and gouged at soil and atmosphere. Candy was mesmerised as the sight of the very same phenomenon that had delivered her to this realm was repeated. She did not notice the thousands of observers, including Toyo-tama-hiko all turn their heads and close their eyes.

There was a sudden brilliant pulse of light that filled Candy's gaze with white. Everything went quiet for just a few seconds and then a deafening crunching boom poured out.

The impact made the walls quake and Candy released another frightened wail as she feared that the ground would give way beneath her. Blinded by the savagery of the lightning pulse, she pressed her snout to the Warlord and screamed as the land rolled and bucked beneath her.

The Warlord merely held tightly to the rail and did not even flinch. He had seen this many times and was not fazed by it. This was the only thing helping keep Candy calm because in her blinded state she was now suddenly terrified of what was going on.

She told herself that everything was normal. She was safe and in no danger. Her master was untroubled, and this meant there was nothing to fear.

"The generosity of Izanami and Izanagi be praised. May this offering strengthen the Empire and replenish us. May our gratitude be great," whispered Toyo-tama-hiko and Candy vaguely detected the voices of countless multitudes all offering a similar uttered prayer. Their unified voices engineered a sibilant dirge that faded behind the sound of the reverberating impact, and as the sounds eased, another chorus of various metallic cries ruled the air.

Candy blinked and managed to peek out again. Still a little dazzled, she gave another pip of shock when she saw the warship dominating her vision. The huge grey metal beast was leaning to port and was still crackling with a few residual arcs of power.

"This is my favourite part," hissed Toyo-tama-hiko as he brushed her from his legs and stepped back. Candy's eyes remained locked on the vessel. The whole situation was unnatural—a ship, stranded in the middle of the mountains, separated from its waters and even its own world.

A terrible and uncompromising voice roared through the various amplifiers to fill the air with its stern decree.

"Warriors of Earth. Surrender or perish!"

The words were punctuated with the roar of artillery. Shells arced in and grabbed great areas of earth all around the ship's cracked hull and hurled it into the air amidst belching clouds of fire and smoke. Chunks of burned rock rained down and created a xylophone tune as they pelted the stranded vessel. While the shells were still on their approach, Toyo-tama-hiko had dropped behind her, grabbed her mesh covered haunches, and thrust into her. Candy's holler of answer merged with the explosions and her eyes bulged as he sheathed himself to the fullest extent.

"Now for the encore!" growled Toyo-tama-hiko and as he drew back and plunged into her, he reached forward and captured her strangled breasts in his hands. Kneading them with callous disdain, he made Candy whimper and squeal as she was ravished.

A hundred bestial shrieks rose up and from the numerous smaller gates galloped the Mitama. The armoured Tyrannosaurs charged at great speed and in rigid formation. The effect on the crew of the ship was immediate. Many had taken the option of surrender by default because they simply stood and screamed or dropped to gibber and rock as their minds were snapped by what was occurring. Some even hurled themselves overboard rather than continue to bear witness to this scene.

"Such terror! Such victory!" snarled the Warlord as he watched the battle unfold while thrusting into a puppygirl and punishing her bound breasts.

After the Tyrannosaurs had emerged, legions of Wani stormed forth in their wake. They drew their blades, threw them high, and roared praise to the Empire.

As the terrifying cavalry charge continued, several batteries on the stranded craft began to move.

"Unwise," chuckled Toyo-tama-hiko and she felt him swell within her as arousal and anticipation caused him to squeeze tighter to her assets. His hips slammed to hers and Candy sobbed with delight as she was taken.

The turrets awkwardly started to turn and were seeking to try and aim on the monsters that were closing in on them, but the batteries on the walls were already poised to meet this expected response.

Thunderclaps sounded and the turrets disappeared amidst plumes of acrid smoke. The fireballs rolled up into the sky to unveil charred twisted pits of wreckage. Hands immediately started to go up from the crew that were still visible on deck as hatches started to open and others emerged, also with arms held high.

The sight of such mass defeat caused the Warlord to groan with added desire. He slowed his rate so he could let his cock slither back almost to the point of departure before he dove back in, choking her pussy with his length and making Candy shudder beneath him. Her arms and legs wobbled as the rapture of such molestation overwhelmed her.

Rope ladders started to fall down the side of the vessels and the crew began to humbly descend as the towering dinosaur cavalry formed a cordon.

"Now they are ours," uttered Toyo-tama-hiko.

His hands released her breasts, and one snatched her hips for steadiness while the other reached under and started to paw at her loins. His fingers groped and pawed at her clit as his manhood continued to rush into her on energetic and lust charged drives. Such expert attention caused her to instantly orgasm and she jolted and shuddered, every thrust making her cry against her gag.

The Wani streaked through between the cavalry and began to subdue the new arrivals. Those who resisted were immediately cut down. Resistance on board from small arms did little to the metal and ceramic plated monsters and the chatter of rifles and machine guns savaged the areas where snipers were trying to fight back.

The sight of the devastating assault made the Warlord sway and gasp with relish. The Wani hurled grappling irons up and began swift ascents while the humans continued to climb down on their own ladders. Screams and cries joined the roar of the merciless beasts and the angry snarl of assault weapons as the interior of the craft was scoured and pacified.

Candy let her arms slip from beneath her and she dropped to the floor. With her rear still hoisted into the air, she pressed her breasts to the cool stone and savoured the angry streams of pain that were engineered by the spines. Her arms flopped beside her, and she kept her cheek to the ground as she climaxed a second time. Staring out through the guard-rail, she felt Toyo-tama-hiko swelling within her. Her gaze was distorted from tears and the uniform slithered on her from the sweat that now saturated both her skin and the catsuit. She was incoherently begging for him to stop but her body refused to move. The intensity of the pleasure was too much, but her body had suffered greatly under the ministrations of the Supreme Warlord of Water, and it wanted the pleasure it had been denied for so long. Shrieking in terrible bliss, Candy floundered beneath him as she felt a third and even more potent orgasm swelling in her cock-stuffed loins.

A small squad of Mitama dismounted and followed the Wani into the ship. They emerged shortly after with several civilians and a handful of officers. These were bound and then handed down for transport back to the walls.

Candy was dumbstruck at the swift and vicious subjugation she had just witnessed. From what she had viewed, just the sight of the Empire's forces would have as profound an effect on the forces of Earth as their weapons.

Such notions vanished when Toyo-tama-hiko threw himself into her. The savagery of his thrusts lifted her knees from the ground, and he crushed his hands to her sides while he bellowed with delight. Candy screwed her eyes shut and wailed as her body was submerged in rapture and the feel of molten heat being deposited within her carried her mind on a velvet curtain of satiation.

The Warlord slowed and merely threw her hindquarters aside. She dropped onto her side and lay where she was, panting, twitching from residual flashes of rhapsody that tightened her physique.

As the crew were formed into a single column and marched for the wall, great carts started to emerge from other portals. Pulled by massive quadrupeds, the wagons delivered legions of salvagers to the wreck. Sparks started to fly and the clank and cry of metal on metal sounded as the meticulous stripping of the ship commenced with dutiful frenzy.

Chapter Sixteen

A priest applied a lead and towed her groggy devolved form out and down through the many floors of the fortress. Possessed by the cosy afterglow of the coupling and dazed by what she had seen, Candy paid little heed to her environment until she once again emerged onto open land. There she found the other Warlords of Water being shown to sumptuous litters, each of which was borne by six muscular females who were strictly restrained and held to their allotted posts by force.

Her muzzle was unfastened and the gag drawn from her lips. It was unscrewed from its internal fixture and then the emptied muzzle was restored to her.

Licking her lips, she watched the women hoist the ornate wooden carriages with ease, and Candy was surprised when her lead was used to pull her into one of the interiors. The gossamer curtains were drawn apart by servants and she found that her current master was lounged upon the soft pillows within and was reeling her in. She settled at his side in a proper canine pose and savoured his attention as he started to pet and stroke her. His mood became more licentious, and Candy quivered when he started to grope and fondle her contained form.

The women broke into a steady and perfectly timed trot that ensured that the litter did not bump or jolt, only gently rock as though it floated on a calm lake.

The extent of this new journey was lost on Candy. Perhaps it was because of the shock of the outrageous sights she had seen on the plane of Izanagi, but it was more likely that she was again sinking into the mentality of a pet. Her chameleonic sexual vices were again running wild within her, re-sculpting her thoughts and turning her into exactly what she needed to be in order to please those above her and thus allow her to gain the most intense personal satisfaction from her experiences.

The scent of flowers reached through the curtains and intrigued her. She shuffled aside and brushed a curtain with the tip of her snout so she might see.

They were being carried across wide open fields where clusters of trees offered token shade. In the distance she could see a large hill that was bathed in golden sunlight. Perched atop the emerald mound was a massive pavilion. Various pastel panels were arranged on the slopes to create a loose maze that helped to break down the gentle evening breeze. The tent was easily the size of a significant hall, and she could see a steady flow of people wandering into its various openings.

The Warlord yanked on her lead and dropped her back at his side. Unwilling to disobey, she merely curled up, closed her eyes, and fell into a contended and idle snooze.

A short time later, the litter came to a halt and without word he drew her out when it settled on the grass. The bearers hoisted it once they had left and continued on to some prearranged location. Scuttling at Toyo-tama-hiko's side, Candy was slowly led up towards a pair of green curtains that were embroidered with the symbol of the Houses of Water.

Courtesans in flowing silken robes parted the curtains and withdrew with heads lowered. The smell of luscious foods immediately poured out and caught Candy's nose, even through the muzzle. She had never smelled anything like it. The scents were sublime, and they led her onwards more effectively than the leash did. So luscious were the scents that it took her a moment to detect the sounds of raucous merriment and when she did, she looked into the hall and saw the celebration that awaited them.

Toyo-tama-hiko gave her leash a small tug and started to march forward. Another pair of scantily clad servants appeared and reverently showed him to his allotted position.

A low wooden table was divided into four sections to create a circle in the middle of the room. Each curved section was carved with detailed emblems and symbols relevant to the element of the Great House seated at it.

Clearly this was a peaceful gathering because the great powers were clad in simple comfortable robes that while exquisitely decorated and formed from the most extravagant fabrics, were clearly worn to allow the concubines access to them. Another indication was the complete lack of guards. Rarely had she seen the primary forces of the Empire gather without there being squads of heavily armed Wani or equally lethal Mitama present nearby.

In the area within the divided table was a gratuitous display of sexual gymnastics. A dozen men and women writhed and flowed. Their bodies were slick with oils that were tinted with the same pastel colours that influenced the pavilion. The subtle rainbow hues helped them seem even more unnatural because of the positions they could twist and contort themselves and each other into. Such was their flexibility that she considered if there were perhaps hints of Wani blood in them, but she could see none of the reptilian traits or influences that might indicate such a vaulted heritage.

Toyo-tama-hiko sat cross legged between the burly form of Naka-tsu-wata-dzu-mi. and the bearded form of Soko-tsu-wata-dzu-mi. He drew Candy close, and she knelt with her arms held straight to keep her back arched and her head up and proud. Naka-tsu-wata-dzu-mi stroked her back and she shivered before Toyo-tama-hiko took up a small piece of food and popped it into the hole in her muzzle. She flipped her head back and devoured the nugget. The taste was divine and was easily the equal of the grope. Candy rolled her eyes, savoured the flavour, and continued to watch the erotic show.

The various leaders of the houses were chatting and conversing freely, sometimes drawing a concubine down so they might avail themselves of her services or simply appraise her attributes on a whim.

Again, the text of the conversation became a unified background chatter. Even the talk that occurred right beside her was indistinct. It was as though she had forgotten or rather just did not care to interpret the language. Gesturing, simple command, and leash was her language at present, and she stubbornly refused to acknowledge any other.

The only thing to break her from this state of complete subservience was when she saw Hachiman enter and take the head place amongst the Kami of Fire. His countenance was a delight to her senses, and it took all her resolve to refrain from rushing over to him. Candy was aware that she was besotted with him, and indeed fantasised about him and what he had done to her many times, but until she saw him in the flesh, she had not realised just how fanatically she adored him. Every muscular curve, every subtle expression on his handsome features, every movement, every breath, they were hypnotic, and she found the efforts of the performers tedious when compared to the act of just staring dreamily at her true owner.

Toyo-tama-hiko snapped his fingers and gestured to the ongoing display. When three of the performers began to slither towards him, this caught Candy's attention and drew it away from Hachiman.

To her surprise, the Warlord nodded towards her, and the slippery players moved towards the right-hand side of their table. He handed her leash to Naka-tsu-wata-dzu-mi, who passed it to his neighbour Midzu-chi, who unfastened it just as the performers reached her.

Their warm wet hands closed upon her body and started to draw her out into the middle of the room. She was reluctant at first because it was intimidating be so brutally exposed to the assembled mighty Kami. When she had been before them before, she was usually tightly bound and helpless and although the pup uniform was highly restrictive and kept her subjugated with ease, she had grown used to and even fond of the uniform, so it was hard to process it as bondage.

The delicate perfume of the oil had an almost euphoric effect on her and swallowing for strength, Candy gave in to their touches and allowed them to draw her into the midst of the throng.

The crowd briefly parted and formed into a swaying circle of lascivious flesh. Candy trembled a little as she knelt in the middle and looked from side to side to see what was going to happen next. The performers were staring at her with eyes that glittered with frenzied lust. The degree of arousal being expressed on their lust-contorted faces was intimidating and Candy actually started to grow worried as she questioned whether she could handle this.

Suddenly, like a pack of starved animals they launched forward, and she found herself imprisoned within an ever-changing mesh of limbs. Extremities coiled around her, trapping her as fingers started to caress and tease. Candy felt herself roll over, invert, and spiral as the mound of bodies continued to manipulate her. She tried to move but could not. She fought to slither free but could find no avenue of escape. She could barely even gain a glimpse of the rest of the hall because a body, face, or extremity always rolled past her vision and hid it.

Against the sensuous riot, Candy was dragged screaming through orgasm after orgasm. The slithering body wide tickle engineered such a level of heightened arousal that climax could not diminish it, and each time she came, she was given only seconds before she was being ferried back towards a repeat.

At some command that she could not see, she was ejected from the mass of gymnasts. Her slick form was squeezed from the group, and she collapsed before the Warlord. Giddy and utterly exhausted, she just lay where she was and let her senses recover from the extreme demands that had been placed on them.

"What do you think of her, Hohodemi?" asked Toyo-tama-hiko.

"Who? The bitch?" he replied with an almost derisive snort. Candy lifted her head a little and saw that a tall and regal male had been stopped in mid stride by the question. He had strong features and a shaven head that revealed a smooth field of blonde stubble.

The Warlord gave a murmur of affirmation.

"She's passable. Is she yours?"

"No. She was acquired her from Hachiman and she's on loan as a favour."

The fact that she was important enough to warrant being passed around as a favour alerted Hohodemi's interest. Toyo-tama-hiko leaned back and gave a small sigh of satisfaction as he regarded Candy. Hohodemi settled in beside the Warlord and gave her a closer look.

"Yes. I can see why Hachiman is so smitten with her."

"Smitten? With that?"

The derisive tones were riling. Candy liked being a precious commodity, even when she was devolved. She liked to lose herself in the simple roles, but there was always the reassurance in the back of her thoughts that she would be promoted or returned to her owner soon enough. Perhaps it was because Hohodemi was such a purveyor of bestial roles. Did normal slaves bore him? Only when they were trained and harnessed, turned into ponies did he become interested. If he and his House were obsessed with the creation of ponies, all else must seem like a distraction, especially to the perfection obsessed Kami.

"Oh she is quite wild . . .sometimes. But she's crafty. She can be the most satisfying submissive one moment, but the next, well, you never know what she'll do."

"A substandard training," grumbled Hohodemi. Clearly the thought of such ineptitude made him exceedingly angry, and Candy saw him flick a scathing glower her way.

"Not at all, rather it's the product of an unusual background. She's an elite from Earth."

Hohodemi turned from regarding Candy and watched as Toyo-tama-hiko folded his arms and continued to stare licentiously at her. The man's eyebrows perked as he solicited an answer or more explanation but Toyo-tama-hiko played his hand well and left him in suspense. The silence was speaking volumes as to her worth, and the fact that she was wild was like a code phrase to activate Hohodemi's fervour.

"Earth?"

"You heard correctly. Uzume brought her in from the Wastelands. It seems that she has had quite an effect on her, and Hachiman himself was similarly beguiled with her attributes. As a favour to me, he offered her to me at my palace. It's a debt that I had not realised the significance of until I started placing her in new roles. She's already dazzled the Uka no mitama."

"Experienced and yet still recalcitrant?"

"More accurately she's eager and with a lust for rebellion just so it can be ruthlessly crushed."

"Quite the filly then," uttered Hohodemi.

"I suppose so. I don't think she has been introduced to such a role as of yet. Why, do you think you would enjoy an opportunity to try and break her to harness?"

The deliberate use of the word "try" was not lost on Candy. The mere implication that her training was not a certainty made Hohodemi all the more committed to ensuring his reputation was reinforced.

"I have not undertaken the task of training an Earth woman in many years. And she was a power you say?"

"Held the fate and fortune of millions in her hands and on her whims from a hidden throne."

"Crafty and sly."

"Indeed."

Hohodemi paused and regarded her again.

"What would you ask of me?"

"To borrow her? Well, she's not mine to give away, but I could definitely loan her to you for a while. It would be a challenge to get her used to a bit in such a limited time."

"I relish a challenge," hissed Hohodemi.

"Then I hope you will accept her then."

"You have my gratitude, Warlord," he stated with a snarling smile of intense eagerness.

Chapter Seventeen

It was morning by the time they reached the stables of House Hohodemi. The land had been covered with a gentle blanket of mist that crept through the tall grass and the sporadic trees that covered the land. Birds cawed gently and the hum of insects caught her ears as they continued along a cobblestone road towards a silhouetted structure.

The sun had peeked over a distant mountain range and was ineffectually attacking the swirling morning mist, making it glow like a blank and yet incandescent canvas. The soft heat was melting the dew, and this made the air crisp and every breath an absolute pleasure to draw. Candy drew deeply and exhaled slowly to watch her breath add more steam to the shifting folds.

She had been extracted from her pup costume and then ushered into a close bamboo cage that rocked and swayed upon four sturdy wheels. A pair of draft ponygirls had been fastened to the yoke and the muscular women stomped forward with precise heavy beats, drawing her ever onwards towards the indistinct bastion of House Hohodemi.

Candy shifted across the straw covered floor and took hold of the bars so she might steady herself and peek through. As she watched, the sun gathered more might and started to strip away the mist, and by degrees illuminate the landscape and reveal the details of their destination.

A series of great ranches were situated around a sprawling palace and everywhere she could see discreet pens and paddocks in which the forms of groom and pony could be spied.

Forks in the road led to various locations, but the one she was shown down escorted her to a great cathedral like structure.

A pair of priests in leather riding attire stopped the ponies and another pair opened the cage to bring her out and show her towards the building.

The doors were massive wooden affairs and like the walls, they were extensively carved with myriad patterns and symbols, all heavily influenced with equestrian styles. As she approached, they slowly swung open and exposed a massive hall which resounded with the clop of hooves and the whinnies of trained concubines.

The domed roof bore several long skylights that allowed great beams of golden radiance to stream in and make the flagstones glow. Huge pillars reached up to the roof and merged into it. Their heights bore iron sconces that were shaped like rearing horses and bore the hall's illumination at night. The lower reaches bore a circle of dense iron rings that could be used to quickly secure a slave.

The walls were lined with numerous individual stables, each fully equipped with all the accoutrements for its resident. Candy could see arrays of exquisite brushes, spare tack, and the means to restrain and subdue those of a more frisky temperament.

The tools of the House were virtually identical, however, there were as many different examples of human equine as there were of the four-legged genus.

Some of the women were slender and lithe, others were minute, almost midgets. Some were elegant salacious beauties with physiques that would shame even the most fastidious model or dancer and also there were muscular titans and towering amazons. Each was as varied in costuming as they were in physique. Some of the ponies had only token adornment, with only the most necessary trappings, and in some cases, a simple bit was all that remained upon their nude bodies.

Others were permitted applications of lingerie, and a number of these were impeded by simple restraints such as cuffs and perhaps a hobble chain.

The most common variety of outfit involved a torso-encompassing harness, cuffs, and a plexus of straps that embraced their heads to keep bit and sometimes a muzzle in place.

There were those who were kept in catsuits of nylon, fishnet, vinyl, leather, or in the most extreme cases, latex figure-hugging cocoons. She could see that some of the women had been treated to the most diabolic levels of restraint, and in some cases, it seemed almost impossible for them to serve their role because their bondage was so intense. Inhibitor bars that restricted them to the meekest steps on ballet boots that would no doubt be a hellish affair for their feet to endure for any length of time. She could also see that others were mounted upon their bars, meaning that rear, pussy, or both orifices were equally abused. Their every curtailed step and any other attempt at greater motion was intimately chastised by these impeding devices.

Many of these women had seen their arms held prisoner within sleeve or restraining harness and more often than not they were twisted up behind them and tied tightly down to deprive them of any hope of manual dexterity. Hoods sealed them away from the outside world, and in the more extreme cases, inflatable versions that stole all sight were applied. This meant that they had to surrender complete trust to whoever it was that was currently leading them, not that they would ever know who these people were in their intensely deaf, dumb, and blind state.

As usual, Candy's eyes quickly glazed over the more delicate versions and soon found solace in regarding the infernal and ingenious ensembles that would have an occupant crying out in loathing against them. It was a sense of obligation to her master and to her own desires that motivated this obsessive need for the extreme. Any concubine, whether novice or experienced veteran could handle and master the average pony girl costume, but these most brutal examples would require skill, patience, calm, and above all a great deal of endurance to be able to wear them, operate within them, and still be able to satisfy whatever demands the grooms and equerries of the House might demand.

Perhaps her opinions were also jaded by some measure of pride. A concubine who could gallop and prance in a standard costume was not exactly that impressive, however, one who could even maintain a small shuffle and not fall over in the most savage examples had shown a degree of exemplary skill.

So with all these considerations in mind, she was almost disappointed when she drawn away from the dark brooding cells in which the most doomed steeds lurked and instead found herself approaching a nearby area with less brutally contained females. When she cast an eye over those ponies adjacent to her stall, her disappointment faded a little because the outfits were still fairly demanding. Besides, Candy knew she had an appetite that sometimes far exceeded what her body could handle, and perhaps throwing herself to the most severe end of the equine spectrum might not be the wisest move. As titillating as she found the fantasy, she had to consider whether she could survive the reality with sanity and physique intact.

A vacant stable beckoned and she could see that the various provisions for her new caste were already hanging up in readiness. With a soft sigh, she readied to again accept the process of transformation from one mode of beast to yet another.

It seemed that the priests were accustomed to kami-tsu-ko being somewhat reluctant to surrender their evolved status.

Probably because the concubines of the great houses sought advancement and eventual acquisition of kamube status, something that a pony would be very unlikely to be able to even conceive off. Kami-tsu-ko of the Empire also dreamed of being used by the higher powers, of coupling or satisfying Mikado, perhaps even a Kami themselves, and again, when bound and kept on reins, there would be very little ability to actively saturate themselves in the joy of the experience. Candy could understand the frustration, to be so near to a living God and not be able to touch, or feel, just bear them and dwell on the end of their reins, goaded by whip or rope, perhaps even blinkered so that the sight of the elevated deities would not confuse or distract them. However, Candy had been with many of the powers, and was devoted to absolute service. If she was to be a mere pony, then she would dedicate herself to it without regret, remorse, or reservation.

A single metal pole was taken down from its hook and the square bar was quickly slotted into the middle of the floor. The hole accepted a full foot of the shaft and left a yard or so standing vertical before her. Near to the base was a set of leather cuffs with a pair of buckles to help seal them, and at the summit was another strap. The priests bent her over and it was swiftly buckled about her throat. Each forearm was then dragged down and similarly taken captive to leave her hunched over and trapped by neck and hands. Her hindquarters swayed in the air and she tugged at her bonds to verify their power.

The sounds of activity started to rise in volume as grooms began to file in and start to select various steeds to be taken out for exercise, training, or discipline. Candy pulled at her bondage and tried to turn around because she wanted to see what has happening. Unfortunately, the square design refused to let the pole pivot and so she was left staring impotently at the poised collection of anonymous leather garments. The details were hard to discern in the gloom and with a lowered gaze, but the wink of refracted light on the buckles, rivets, and straps could not be mistaken.

The priests turned to her legs, and working together, they hoisted a limb and slid a tall leather thighboot onto it. Her feet met an interior that resembled that of a set of towering stiletto heels, but the outside of the item was sculpted to accurately resemble a hoof.

Bands were riveted to the thighboots, and the buckles allowed them to be tightened forcefully about her ankles, above and below her knees, and about her upper thighs. Once these fierce belts were established, she had no hope of sloughing off the wickedly tight garments.

With her body now arched downward because she was perched on her hooves, she watched as they acquired the next portion of her uniform.

A pair of priests grabbed her by the flanks and hoisted her into the air as another duo slapped hands to her hooves and leaned back to stretch her lower half. With her legs level with her body, a fifth priest appeared and enclosed her waist within the dense sheath of a corset. The thick leather ran from her hips to just below her breasts and the substantial metal boning ensured that there was no way for her to bend once it was in place. Three *D* rings were spaced down either side of the laced rear, and the smooth front was set straight before the suede interior leaned into her skin as the laces at the back started to vanish with energetic tugs and hauls. The slack continued to diminish, and Candy groaned aloud as she was squeezed ever tighter by the mighty fist of leather. The two jaws continued to head towards each other and when they finally met, her ribs felt ready to collapse inwards. Every inhale now had to battle the waist cinching shell and when she tried to take a deep breath, she found it cut short.

When her legs were set down, she found herself in a most

awkward pose because now she couldn't wilt in the slightest. Her spine was set level by the corset, and she wobbled on her heels and pawed at the pole as she tried to accept this level of impediment as amiably as she could.

Each arm was released from its cuffs and adorned with a long leather sleeve of a similar design to her boots. Her hands were cupped together by a close mitten that removed all manual dexterity and sets of belts at wrists, about her elbows, and at her upper arm made sure that she could not slither free of them. The reason for the *D* rings located on the inner side of each belt was immediately explained when small locks were used to gobble up the ring and lock it to the corresponding one on the corset. Her arms were now locked to her back and there was no way for her to get free.

A plexus of thin straps appeared, and they reminded Candy of the variety usually employed to sport a strap-on, save this one clutched to her sides and ran down over the crease of her upper thighs to merge just beneath her pussy before it ran up across her rear and parted again to run over her hips. At the base of her spine, the harness presented a small cone of metal from which poured a great plume of delicate hair. The locks tumbled down and tickled the backs of her thigh before culminating at her knees.

The final portion of her transformation appeared and was carried towards her face. The leather harness cupped her chin and pressed to her cheeks and forehead. The numerous delicate straps were drawn across and tightened so that the whole ensemble closed inward and took hold of her skull. A pair of artificial pricked ears jumped up over her own, and finally her bit made an appearance.

The thick solid rubber strut had a large ring set through each end and she eagerly allowed it to slip over her teeth and nudge into the corners of her mouth. She clamped her teeth to the item and watched as a muzzle was brought over. The hollow snout had a pair of air holes at the far end that resembled nostrils and when she breathed down the snout the scent of leather washed through her senses and made her shiver licentiously.

A small strap was buckled to a fixture on her forehead and two more straps reached along her jaw line to snag anchors near her earlobes. Two semi-circular grooves in the leading edge cradled the bit and kept it held into her maw. She now saw that unless her snout were removed, she was powerless spit out the bit.

Candy chewed on the rubber and watched as a pair of blinkers appeared and a trio of snap fasteners allowed them to be pressed to the sides of her head and lock them down. Her periphery vision was lost and all she could see was the area immediately before her. It was a little unnerving, but she was sure that she would get used to it. It was strange to have something that was ordinarily taken for granted deprived. She had been blindfolded before and had numerous senses eradicated, but this minor impediment was unusual and all the more aggravating because it was not one thing or the other. She wasn't left in darkness, nor was she able to look wherever she pleased. Her lust for absolutes had stumbled into an annoying grey area.

The collar was opened and she was tugged upright. She tottered a little as she fought to accustom herself to the hooves, and as soon as her equilibrium strengthened, a set of reins were clipped to the exposed rings on either side of her bit.

Walking on the end of a set of reins, Candy followed obediently, if awkwardly, out of the stall and across the stables to a set of doors opposite to those that had brought her in. It was marvellous to sashay and swing her rear because it made the tail flip about and even through the thighboots she could feel it brush against the backs of her legs.

The doors were already open and the smell of another lush warm day in the Empire managed to sneak in amidst the smell of leather to reach her nose. Candy could see the various paddocks and pens in which the other ponies had been introduced and now she was prepared to join them.

She was led towards a circular enclosure to one side and once the metal gate was opened, she was escorted in. Several other grooms were leaning upon the fence, chatting idly and pointing out interesting sights and other steeds.

Hohodemi appeared and walked past her and into the middle, paying out the rein as he went. Candy then saw that he had acquired a lengthy lunge whip when he walked past her.

There was a sibilant whistle and a raging shock of pain bored into the side of her rear. Candy jerked upright and her arms wrenched against the rings that held them at bay. She howled against the bit and as the full fury ebbed a little, the strength seemed to leave her legs. She dropped to her knees, denting the soft soil.

She wanted to embrace the throbbing weal but all she could do was cavort her torso left and right. She couldn't even bend over and fold into a ball as a defence from this attack.

The reins were given a flick and the motion flowed down the woven length before it snapped at her bit. Candy could guess what this meant and fought to rise.

With wobbling motions, she managed to get back onto her feet and immediately let out another wail when a second vicious swipe caught the exact same region to greatly improve the level of misery already lurking there.

Another hack crossed the backs of her thighs, and she ambled forward while kicking into the ground with staunch fury. She danced from foot to foot and tried to ease the pain, but there was nothing that could be done.

When another attack failed to materialise, she realised that he was encouraging her to move and so rather than endure another blow, she started to march forward while pulling outward to keep the rein taut in the hope that she might be able to stay out of easy range. She kept her eyes down and studied the terrain, afraid that any lumps or pits in the dirt would cause her to stumble and fall and thereby acquire more discipline. Although she could see the imprint of hoof and boot endlessly intertwined and impressed over each other, the pen seemed relatively flat. Dribbles of saliva escaped her parted lips and started to run down her neck and onto her chest. The heat of her breath in the snout made puffs of steam leap from the nostrils, but the same warmth vanished from her spittle much more quickly so that when it reached her skin, it was quite chill.

The whip tapped her knees and then flashed up to make itself visible to her blinkered vision before it lowered and nudged into her chin and hoisted it. Candy lifted her snout upward and although she could hold back her drool, she could no longer see where she was putting her feet. It was frightening not to have the ability to see where she was stepping, and it made her feel even more abandoned to this caste because she was now totally reliant on her trainer and had to offer them her complete trust.

A cruel upward flick caught the underside of a breast and made her squall in misery and jerk forward until the defiant walls of her corset stopped her. The whip instantly informed her as to why it had been deployed and tapped her knees as she stood and shuddered in pain.

Another swipe into her rear told her not to tarry and Candy tumbled forward into an awkward lurching march while struggling to fling her knees up and meet the demands set out by her trainer. She felt the impact when her knee hit the loitering whip and because each step met the weapon, she was sure that it hadn't been towed back to punish her. So long as she maintained the required gait, the whip would stay there as a measuring stick rather than a sceptre of chastisement.

Candy realised that not one verbal command was being offered. She was now being regarded as a beast of performance and burden, one unable to comprehend normal speech. Her education was going to be conducted through input and instinct, and no words would give her insight into what was required. If she performed correctly, she wouldn't be punished, it was that simple. However, she could not help but wonder what exemplary conduct might acquire. Did House Hohodemi reward its ponies, or were they expected to do their best and so long as they did this, they weren't punished.

Round and round she marched, and her thighs started to burn from the effort of keeping to the exaggerated strut. Several times, she lacked the energy to throw her knees high enough, and this of course led to the inevitable consequence of a sound swipe across her bottom, or if the failing were more acute, then the searing stripe her breasts acquired definitely encouraged her to throw more effort into her performance.

The whip pressed across both breasts and slowed her to a halt. Candy stood panting for breath. If it were not for the restricted vents at the end of her snout, she was sure that she would be hyperventilating. Fortunately, she could only gather what seemed to be three quarters of a breath with each gasp and this helped stop her losing control altogether.

Hohodemi marched her round and round the paddock, demanding ever greater levels of effort. Sometimes her tolerance was reached, but he was a masterful trainer, and the moment the subtle clues of her imminent dissent appeared, he applied the whip and drove her rebellion from her with the cruelest of slashes. Defeated before she even had the chance to defy him, she then returned to obeying him with a mixture of fear and respect replacing her resentment.

Her initiation took until the late afternoon, whereupon she was reeled in and then with her hooves feeling like one-ton weights, she was led back towards the stables. First though, she was shown to a small enclave to the right where she could see ponies being cleansed of the sweat of exertion and the process revived her with sudden anticipation.

The grooms removed the reins from their pony and attached a pair of chains. The clips grabbed hold of each end of their bits or their collar and left them standing in a row before a sodden wall. Hoses were then turned on the women and each jolted and whinnied with delight as they were showered. Once cleansed, their dripping bodies were taken away and back into the stable.

Candy was fastened into place, and she turned to watch the regal form of Hohodemi accept a hose and then turn the potent spray onto her. She shrieked with shock and bliss as the chill stream stole the heat of her exercise. The sparkling cascade rushed over her body, stripping away her sweat and leaving her skin tingling in its wake. She ground her teeth on her bit and skipped from hoof to hoof as she was hosed down and then casually removed from the area.

Shivering slightly, she was shown back to her stall where she was secured so that she could not leave. A few pellets were popped into the end of her snout and then Hohodemi patted her head.

"Not bad for your first day," he commented, and then left her to hoist her snout and negotiate the small morsels over her bit so she could swallow the concentrated food pellets. They were bland and dry, but as she continued to learn the process of eating, she noticed the small flexible tube jutting from the wall. She looked around and saw that other ponies were sucking on them so through trial and error she managed to insert it into a nostril hole and then get the pliant end to her lips. It was extremely difficult but eventually she managed to establish a seal and suck on the hose, whereupon she gained a small sip of water. It took her a long time just to gain a few mouthfuls, but each tiny serving was an absolute delight.

As the sun left the sky, the iron sconces in the hall were lit. They provided a token light—a warm cosy radiance that soothed the exhausted women held here. Enthralled with her new lot, Candy curled up and fell into a most pleasant sleep.

Her calendar repeated in virtually identical ways after that first day. Like almost every other pony she was taken out in the morning, exercised vigorously all day, and then after being groomed and her needs tended, she was taken back to her stall. Nothing really changed.

While it could have been misconstrued that this was a banal existence because the days melded seamlessly into one another, it was most definitely not. The simple life of a ponygirl was an absolute treasure. She pranced and stomped, she cared not for opinion or held any desires other than to comply with the command of whip or rein. The days flowed slowly by like honey, and they were just as sweet.

CHAPTER EIGHTEEN

The stable had a lethargic atmosphere at night. The ponies were all tethered in place and snoozing after a long day of relentless exertion. Everyone was exhausted, and the chance to relax meant that no matter the level of spiteful bondage applied to restrict their movement, few ponies could stay awake for long. The soft rustle when they turned over and shifted position was a sporadic accompaniment to the echoing tune of slow steady breaths and deep contented sights.

Candy opened one lazy eye and panned across the main hall and the feminine mounds that occupied each location. Her eyelid started to drift shut and she felt herself sinking back towards sleep again.

A sudden hint of movement in the shadows caught her attention and roused her a little. She was sure she had seen something but now she wasn't sure. Assuming a trick of the light, she lowered her head back to the ground and stretched before drawing her limbs back to her body to embrace a small pocket of warmth.

Another shadow moved as she lay there and intrigued, she stared to pull herself back upright. A pair of lithe forms sprang up onto a set of the dividing walls and looked across the occupant. They moved with no sound and when they did not find what they had been looking for, they leapt high into the air and landed into a perfectly balanced crouch on the next wall. Because of the grace and stealth of their motions, they seemed almost mystical, and the opaque black garb that swathed each of them only leant further credence to the assumption that there were indeed ninja.

Perhaps this was the medium through which the Moon God operated. If there were indeed a covert agency that operated within the Empire, then surely these shadow beings would be ideal. The agents that went across to Earth were infiltrators, but to police the strange realm of the Kami Empire, with its tight knit communities, immortals being, fanatic priests, and ever vigilant Wani, infiltration would take too long and be an implausible medium to gather information. Thieves in the night could monitor, copy, steal, and pilfer with ease while concubine, priest, and Kami slept soundly or were distracted with perverse indulgences.

The light that was descending on her changed in strength and Candy looked up to see a trio of the dark clad forms peering down at her from above. Crouched on her walls, they looked to each other, nodded, and before she could even gasp, they were upon her.

In a split second, everything was over, and Candy was in a different place. For a moment it seemed as though she had slipped through the cracks in reality and had again somehow shifted to another world.

One moment, she was laying in her stall, and the next, there was a flurry of black and a token feeling of falling before she landed on hard, warm stone and was somewhere else. The ninja were either gone or had transformed as drastically as the surroundings had.

She was in some sort of crude underground passage with roughly hewn walls. The corridors branched off from one another and stretched out to form an intricate labyrinth. Located on the walls were random copper flues from which flowed a slender column of flame. The dancing amber torches crated warm pools of light and located between them were bleak wells of shadow.

A pair of heels stepped out before her and Candy slowly

looked up and when she did, she gave a brief cry and promptly buried her head back down. The woman that was standing over her was a terrible image to behold and was made all the more intimidating by the bleak lighting that seemed to avail her with even more horrible menace.

She was swathed in a mixture of black latex and sections of vinyl and from the attire sprouted large conical spines of midnight rubber. These fearsome decorations changed in length and size and made her appear like some sort of porcupine woman. Gauntlet gloves spiralled up her arms and her long black nails were sharpened to wicked points.

She wore a mask that hid her entire face and much of her head, but allowed a great plume of ragged black hair to halo her head and cascade down to the middle of her back. The mask exaggerated the attributes of her face and upon the peaks for chin, cheek, brow, and temple, there sprouted another spine. The largest rushed from over her mouth like an acute snout, and the depth of the artificial brow hid her eye slits amidst copious shadow. Only the twinkle of her eyes could be discerned in them, and offered a delusion that she had luminous sight.

When she spoke, it was with a strange hissing rumble that while still strangely feminine, was a cruel and wicked sound to hear.

"Welcome to Yomi."

Candy jerked her head up and regarded the demon woman. A moment later as the words seared her brain, she yelled against her bit and tried to get up and mount an immediate escape attempt. The terror brought by the revelation of her destination was an anticipated one, and from nowhere, a trio of forms jumped forth and snared her within their limbs as a fourth brought out the means to effect a more lasting subjugation.

Each woman wore a dense leather bra, slim corset, tall

collar, and a thong that was decorated with rivets and red sections that formed into curling flame-like designs. The same decorations had been applied to the sections of leather that encompassed their forearms and shins, where smooth ankle boots or fingerless gloves loitered beneath to encompass their extremities. A fishnet catsuit left their thighs, torso, and upper arms contained within mesh, and each of these devilish females had been embellished with heavy macabre makeup to compliment the ferocity suggested by their shaven head.

A pole was set to her back and the tight belts that were riveted in foot long intervals along it were quickly thrown around her body and tightened with brutal yanks so that they hauled her to the metal. Candy struggled to get free before she was condemned but the women were as strong as they were quick and before she accomplish anything, she was being crushed to the pole and left inert. A foot of steel stretched up past her head and past her feet, and each end had moulded handgrip slotted onto to reveal that she was to be conveyed in this format.

The servile women retreated and cowered as the spike covered female drew closer. The intimidating aura of the tyrant had a similar and distinct effect on Candy. She shut her eyes and trembled as she began to weep.

The knowledge that she had been sent to Yomi was terrible. It meant that she was now lost to all and could never again see the surface. Candy had changed hands and changed facets and castes countless times, but this latest was an irrevocable transfer, one that could not be undone.

"You are wise to weep, slave. We have many more tears to coax forth though, and it is good that you get into practice."

The woman lifted a leg and placed her towering heel onto Candy's breast. She allowed weight to fall behind it and the spire started to push down into her flesh and create a mordant dimple. Candy chewed on her bit and whimpered. She shuddered and strained against the straps and the woman mocked her efforts with a sibilant laugh. With callous merriment she started to turn her extremity first one way and then the other to drag at the soft skin and make it thunder with anguish.

"Hachiman has become more devoted in his efforts to find you. Toyotama-hiko has told him that he knows not what happened to you, that you must have been abducted by another Kami. I think there is some feud between them, and he wants to make Hachiman suffer by depriving him of you. Hence he came to us of Yomi and requested that you be made to disappear into our midst. Here you will learn to suffer, slave, and never again will you know the touch of sunlight, or Kami."

Candy's distraught response only served to satisfy the woman's cruel designs. She gave a contented hiss before she cocked her head to one side, drank in Candy's sounds of despair, and then swiftly marched off into the corridor.

"Bring her. I am of a mind to commence her education in the dark abuses of the underworld this instant. But first, ensure she is stripped of her former status before she comes to me."

The ends of the pole were grabbed, and she was tugged up into the air. On quick trot she was ferried off into a side tunnel and then along a winding route that culminated in a small rocky cavern. Two men in leather trousers with the same flame design stood in the middle of the room with arms folded across their bare chests. They grinned when they saw her, and Candy was intimidated to see that they wore full contact lenses that made their whole eyes appear black.

The women set her down and started to undo the straps before they yanked her back onto her feet and then shoved her towards the men.

She fell into their arms, and they sprang into action. Slim

stubby blades appeared in their fingers, and they started to dance the silver edges upon her attire. They slashed with such skill that even though they worked with drastic and exaggerated movements, never once did they even graze her skin. Even so, the ferocity of being stabbed at made her skin go numb and her to shake and flinch as she saw the weapons continue to rage around her, shredding materials and turning her pony outfit into a collection of ribbons. The fright passed, and the last vestiges of her former caste dropped to her feet.

The eldritch tailors spun her around and shoved her back into the arms of the women. As soon as she left their care, they sheathed their blades behind them and folded their arms so they could watch in silence as she was taken away.

The females grabbed her with brute care and their disdain was shown constantly in their impatient towing of her away from the scene. The sharp corrections to her passage made her limbs flash with pain, but it was a discomfort they ignored. Such rough handling made her quail, it made her feel as though she had done something wrong. Her time as kami-tsu-ko had left the distinct impression that while she could well be tormented until she howled for clemency, this manner of barbarous handling only came about from genuine error or serious failure. This mistaken mindset made her bear their abuses without resistance.

A portal presented itself. The barred gates were flanked by similar guards to those who carried her, save that these were armed with serrated halberds. Their bodies were rigid and to attention, their eyes fixed forward and devoted to their duty.

The darkness beyond flowed onto a set of steeply descending stairs. The walls were rough and damp, and the faint smell of corruption hung in the air, tickling her nostrils with hints of some foulness as yet unseen. Fat insulated cables swung from fixed point to fixed point, swinging along the ceiling and randomly spitting out wire caged bulbs. The lights were weak and stained the areas with their dirty amber to make everything seem even fouler.

The warmth of the surface started to give way to a numbing chill but not because their descent into the depths was depriving the tunnels of the suns heated stare. The cold came because Candy was growing increasingly terrified with every step down she was made to take, because it meant that it was another step away from the surface and away from any hope of escape.

When she stumbled, they increased the severity of their grip and shook her back to an upright stance. The treatment still failed to incite rage and resentment and so they continued to escort her down.

The group emerged from the stairs onto a winding zone of convoluted tunnels. The thin passages were lit by sporadic bulbs, with sunken alcoves whose brief descending flight of steps accessed a weighty portal. The solid wooden affairs were held shut by dense beams. It was apparent that barring in this manner was another consideration to the lack of metal because the use of locks or bolts required use of the precious substance and a massive beam set horizontally across them was a far more effective and impenetrable means of securing these dungeon portals. Candy rarely saw such frugality with regard to metal on the surface, perhaps it was because the Kami were rich in the material and could squander it as they wished. Perhaps it was because of the sheer multitudes who were condemned in this hellish domain. Was there such a population down here that there simply wasn't enough metal to employ in such mundane facets? Had it all been used up on restraint and implement?

Almost at random she was presented to one of them. One of the guards pinned her arms behind her back. Her vigilance in keeping her under control bordered on the paranoid while her partner slid the beam into an accommodating slot in the wall and opened the door.

A truculent barge sent her careering recklessly down the steps. The speed caused her to stumble and then collapse to strike the floor with a harsh slap and skip to a halt. Her side bore an abrasive graze that was only eased by the strange dampness that made the stone slick.

Sat within the darkness, she curled herself into the corner and closed her eyes, riven with worry as to her eventual fate. This entire situation was a nightmare without equal. What could she have possibly done to warrant such treatment? She was no great exponent of fate or luck, but she did not deserve this.

Minutes dawdled by and the bleak isolation only helped refine her chagrin. The door gave a deep resonant thump as its weighty bar was set back and with a mewling rusty groan it swung out, letting the soft light of the corridor seep reluctantly in. The pane of light widened and revealed Candy's pale skin, exposing her fully and making her sense of vulnerability peak.

Two burly guards joined her in the cell. Their elaborate leather armour opened only to reveal the intricate flame tattoos that flowed along their arms. The stiff sections of dull black hide were fluted in places, making it appear almost like misshapen scales or protective plates taken from some sinister monster. Each wore a sturdy leather mask that gave them a subdued but nonetheless disturbingly demonic visage.

Candy wilted before their approach and then lifted her arms protectively as she began to mumble her fractured pleas for mercy. The proffered limbs were grabbed and without any display or hint of care for her plight they tugged her roughly to her feet and marched her forward. Her legs flailed as she stumbled, her panic making her movements uncoordinated, her terror making her stomach flutter and her breathing to emerge in rapid uneven pants with only the occasional despairing sob to contrast it.

The dank corridor ended with a set of double doors whose outer surface had been carved with depictions of interlocked monstrous beasts. The ornate carvings burrowed deep into the surfaces, almost lending them a grim semblance of reality as braziers on each side added animation with their flicking fires. The dancing lights cast their cavorting shadows and brought such a disconcerting half-life to the door that Candy found herself struggling even harder as she was dragged towards it.

The guards pushed open the doors and revealed a spacious hall whose low ceiling was almost within reach just from standing on tip toe. The air was a cloying mixture of smoke and incense as more braziers and smouldering sticks saturated the atmosphere.

At a casual glance and from the scents and ambience it could have passed for a temple, but this was no place of ordinary supplication, it was far darker place of grim worship. The brooding statues were engines of restraint and suffering—racks, crucifixes, crosses, with wooden limbs embellished with carvings and decoration, disguising their truth from a fleeting glance, and intimidating those who bore prolonged examination.

She was brought through the chamber and as she was led through the various horrible instruments and implements, she began to discern a looming ziggurat in the distance. When she dawdled to look upon a particularly vivid or confusing item, the guards gave her a rough shove. The disdainful treatment began to erode her fear and the fire that was her will to rebellion began to swell. Just because she had been sent to Yomi, did not mean she would stay here. She had endured so much, experienced and seen so many marvellous things. She wouldn't end her days here. If escape from Yomi were indeed impossible, then she would be the first to prove them wrong, and if not, her ability to withstand all that the underworld could throw her at her would be legendary.

As soon as that specific thought struck her, she stiffened slightly and adopted a wry grin. Candy trembled faintly as she started to saunter forward. She was no longer hunched over from the burden of her fate; she had goal now. Perhaps escape from Yomi was indeed impossible, but if she could endure, if she failed to break, if she failed to be destroyed by whatever vile machinations these demons intended, then word would spread. Her best bet to be found and redeemed by her beloved master would be to take the avalanche of depravity that was about to befall her, and stand erect and unbending in the face of the most extreme adversity. Soon, others would hear of this Hafuri-tsu-yomi who defied all attempts to break her, who did not kneel, who could not be tamed. When these words finally reached Hachiman, or Lady Uzume, then he would know for sure where she was and if his victories on Earth were as big as predicted, then allowing her to be pardoned would be a trivial favour amongst the debt that the Empire, the Sun Goddess and the Moon God owed him.

When another push had her stumble forward, she threw a fierce look over her shoulder. The savage glower caught the guard by complete surprise, and he actually froze as though she had just slapped him across the cheek. Before he could recover his pride by assailing her, she scorned him with a brief huff of derision and then started to continue towards the ziggurat. She could almost feel the two escorts regarding each other with a quizzical look before they rapidly fell in behind her. She was no longer a cowed slave being shown to her doom, she was a recalcitrant creature defiant of their power, one who would resist them at every turn.

Candy strolled casually now and let her hand trail over the odd smooth strut or beam as though she were enticed by these engines of restraint. She no longer feared these machines, in fact, she was looking forward to what the stern rulers of this place would do to her once she was on them. She was about to be taken further than she ever had before. She was in the underworld, condemned, lost, and so no pity or clemency would be shown. If she could make it through the coming trials, what a sterling slave she would be. Even the most sadistic dominant would have the luxury of not holding back. They could act with impunity in the precise manner their hearts and fantasies desired, and she would be all the more delighted at having brought their darkest dreams to fruition.

Through the smoky folds of the room's cloying air, the pyramid grew ever clearer and the ceiling started to retreat upwards until it was lost behind the loitering overhead fogbank. The pyramid loomed out suddenly and revealed itself clearly to her and Candy stopped so she could pan her gaze up the roughly cut steps. Along each corner was a slim trough down which flowed flammable liquid that blazed with a tepid crimson radiance. The four streams of fire gathered in small pools at the base where they either drained away or were steadily consumed.

Atop the eerie ziggurat was a strangely simple throne. Formed like a pair of tori-wi with a velvet cushioned seat situated across the bowed upper surface, it held the seated form of the spike encrusted mistress of this realm. Her hands were clasped to the hand rests and her legs were demurely crossed as she peered down across this field of restraint and torment.

Candy smiled and crossed her arms across her naked chest.

"Well, what now?" she said breathily. "I guess I'm supposed to beg for mercy or something?"

Her guards kicked into the backs of her knees, causing her to drop to the floor with a sharp bark of pain. She again flung a glower over at them before she returned her gaze back up to the throne.

"I guess I'll kneel then."

A hand clasped the back of her neck and flung her down onto all fours.

"Show respect to the Demonatrix!" he hissed with utter outrage.

"And what will you do if I don't!" she muttered.

Again there was a sharp intake of breath and a sudden flurry of motion suggested that they were about to pummel her where she lay.

"Halt!" came the voice of the woman. The guards stopped in their tracks, freezing in mid strike as they prepared to pound her for her vile levels of disrespect.

The creak of vinyl and rubber had Candy again hoist her head and watch as the woman sauntered regally down the steps with precise and equal steps.

"So there is some fire in this new arrival after all. How very interesting. Those that come into my personal care have such fleeting capacities to endure my affections."

"Well, maybe you just haven't met the right girl?" retorted Candy and gave the woman a coy wink.

The Demonatrix chuckled to herself. Candy wondered if the woman had seen through what she was trying to accomplish. If she was as ancient as all Kami, then it was likely that she had seen everything, done everything, perhaps even had another Earth woman kneeling before her in this very spot, showing the same pouting level of brattiness. Perhaps the laughter was a reminiscent thing for a time she had spent with someone else like Candy. A magnate from the forties? A Victorian royal from Europe? Perhaps even a feudal warrior maiden from the middle ages?

If the memory of this person were a good one, perhaps it might temper the abuses, or would it only worsen them as she sought to outdo herself in terrible acts, eclipsing the last time she had inflicted them on a slave.

Candy straightened up onto her knees as the woman reached the bottom step and then moved past her. A couple of the pliant spines brushed her shoulder, and the discreet tickle made her quiver slightly.

"You are right to tremble, slave."

"It's cold," rebuked Candy.

"Then by all means let us warm you."

With a mere nod she caused the guards to spring into action. A hand locked to each wrist and then under each shoulder. She was wrenched to her feet and drawn forcibly aside to a low rack that was supported at each corner by a squat cylindrical leg that maintained it about a foot in the air. The escort drew her onto the smooth wooden surface and slapped her hands down into a pair of padded leather shackles. They quickly applied the two dense buckles, and this left her arms spread wide over her head. Next they grabbed her ankles, and she offered some faint yanks and half-hearted defiance to make them tighten their hold and wrench her legs down so they might apply a matching pair of cuffs to her ankles.

Candy looked up and saw that a pair of chains reached from her cuffs and slipped into a dense wooden roller with a wheel on each end that would steal the slack away and stretch her.

"I always thought I was too short," she chuckled.

The Demonatrix just smiled and ran a gloved hand along Candy's chest. The touch was delicate and made goosebumps erupt across her body. Cleary the woman was appraising that which she was eager to see suffer.

The guards manned the two rollers and anxiously grabbed the extended handles before they looked to their ruler in anticipation of the command to begin.

A nod caused them to turn the wheels and a cranking grind sounded as the chain started to curl around the drums and she was immediately stretched taut.

The Demonatrix lifted her right leg and dropped her foot next to Candy's armpit before she leaned her torso down onto her knee and panned her obscured gaze from toe to finger and back again. Candy's heartbeat quickened as she wondered what was going to happen to her. This was an enigmatic and implacable sadist whose capabilities at torture were unknown to her.

Again she gestured into the darkness and one of the guards quickly vanished to appear again with a small glass jar. He unscrewed the top and held it up sideways so that the woman could push the pointed toe of her boot into the pale opaque gel within.

The Demonatrix stepped up onto the rack and stood between Candy's thighs. With her hands on her hips, she maintained perfect balance and shifted the tainted foot toward her. The toe nuzzled into her vulnerable pussy, and she moaned as the cool viscous sludge was worked against her flesh.

Suddenly her head jerked up and she released a howl of shock as a ferocious chemical heat started to gnaw virulently at her most tender regions. The liniment cream felt more like molten lava as it seared her membranes. Her muscles bucked and rippled as she hauled at her bonds and cried out. She fought to get free so she could scrape the excess off, but the blazing infernal taint remained constant. Candy threw her head from side to side and then buried her cheek into her stretched arm. She wept as she trembled and strove to withstand the horrible ethereal fires. She desperately wanted to close her thighs, but the woman was intent on taking her further with this initiation.

"No! No don't," she cried as she felt the toe return. Residual gel was caught by the fabric and rubbed into her again to revive the entire appalling event. The motions grew more distinct as the woman sought to not only apply the cream but also to punish the harried location. However, Candy had a distinct love for this mode of treatment and as the pointed toe churned against her, even as her clitoris was now being scorched by the terrible burning heat of the cream, she was brought to a heightened state of arousal. Suddenly not all of her cries were those of pain.

Gasping for breath when she could, she jerked and cavorted as the horrible anguish flowed against the sumptuous subtle pleasure.

The drums were turned another notch and Candy gave a near ecstatic scream as her limbs were racked even more brutally. Every ligament coursed with fresh mayhem. Her joints seemed to swell and began to vanish within small storms of punishing sensation.

Candy flicked open her eyes and looked up at the sublime form towering over her. The woman was silhouetted against the faintly incandescent mist as the flames of the brazier illuminated the smoke and her dark attire absorbed the light save for the odd refraction upon wrinkle, seam and contour.

The woman pushed deeper, and Candy dropped her head back, screwed her eyes shut and just cried out at the top of her lungs. It felt wonderfully liberating to just howl as she wished, knowing that no one cared, and no one was listening. The louder and more impassionate her cries, the more pleasure it probably brought these people, and it would in no way lessen what they were doing or intending.

The sight of the luscious fetish clad monster atop her was now stamped on her mind's eye and was granted an awesome clarity by the extreme distress she was in. The still image was wonderfully alluring and as she jerked and bucked from the ongoing assault, that single picture remained firmly before her to entice, arouse, and help her scrape away a definite slice of the horror and rework it into a dark delicious pleasure.

Another click resounded in her ears just as a similar nova pulse of pain thundered in her joints and coursed through her body. Candy's jaws flashed apart, her neck craned her head up, and she threw a most virulent holler into the air. When she ran out of air, her head dropped back and she quaked as the new level of distress continued to rage within her, making her thoughts swim. Again, a single look up at the woman responsible for her plight caused her opinion of the punishment to metamorphose and she groaned wantonly while she embraced the ferociously twisted pleasure.

The Demonatrix stepped onto her stomach again and just watched the captive surge and shiver beneath her. Slowly the mordant heat in her pussy began to fade as the liniment lost its ability to hurt her, but the guards administered a fresh variety when they turned the rack onwards another notch. Her body was now petrified by the tightness with which it had been drawn outwards. Only her lips, fingers, and toes moved, and even then they just quaked. Even her eyes were locked forward as they admired the sight of the architect of this agony.

Another click started to steal her cries as she was drawn so tight it became hard to even breathe. Another dropped her into a savage tornado of pain and ecstasy and her thoughts started to become indistinct as she neared a faint.

"Enough of this. I want to move on," decreed the woman.

The rack let go and the slack coils suddenly snapped taut as her limbs jerked in and she shrieked even more potently than when being stretched. The sudden freedom forced a searing sorrow through her tormented frame, and she tossed and flipped about on the rack as she tried to endure her reprieve. Being set free of the rack was even worse than being on it.

The buckles were opened as she lay in recuperative misery, and she was hauled from the rack and dragged across the floor. Her legs were limp beneath her, and her feet just slid against the flagstones. Her head hung forward and she just stared blankly at the dark ground. In her periphery vision she watched the boots of her escort stomping along and after a few moments, the sound of the steady click of her heels reached through the lingering echo of her own cries. Motivated by this sharp sound, she managed to heft her head up and regard the slinking form of the Demonatrix. Candy could not resist the allure of the sadistic villainess. The dark attire beckoned to her, the glint of light upon the wrinkles and smooth panes being almost as hypnotic as the sashay of her hips and the flow of her ragged mane of hair.

A gibbet appeared before her, and the woman swirled on her heels before she lounged against the wooden upright. She started to caress the polished black wood with her long acute nails.

Candy turned from the dark glare of the woman and regarded the apparatus from which she would soon be hanging. The gallows had a winch at the base, and it poured a single length of steel cable up through several ringlets before it fed it along the extended arm and drooled down from the end before it was fastened to the middle of a broad metal stave. Each end of the spreader bar was equipped with very sturdy restraint. These conical leather items were well padded, and Candy realised that this was to ensure that a captive could dwell in them for some considerable time without sustaining any serious harm.

The guards simply walked her around so that her back faced the gallows and then casually dropped her to the floor. Candy managed to throw her arms forward and clap her palms to the ground to ease her descent but the drop onto her breasts and belly was still uncomfortable. After she landed, she started to roll onto her side, but a heeled boot dropped into her back and pushed down. The sole turned a little to aggravate her skin and then the heel shoved into her flesh to add more fervid encouragement. Candy did not resist and floundered as the woman continued to pivot her foot to make her skin throb.

The two guards each grabbed an ankle, yanked it into the air until her joints protested, and quickly started to feed the extremity into the awaiting cuff. They yanked the buckles tight and threaded them into place to ensure she was secure, and then stepped back. One of them manned the winch, and the other stepped to the side to await any further orders form their superior.

A slight nod from the woman caused her servant to start to whirl the handle and steal away the cable. Candy's body was swiftly hauled up and when she entered the air, she swung towards the gallows. She feared that she would collide with it and threw her hands out to defend herself. In that instant, the other guard jumped forward and snagged both wrists before he yanked them back and around. Her captive arms jerked her to a halt a few inches from the gallows and as she regarded the dark wood, she felt her shoulders reverberate with stress as a pair of cuffs were snapped into place and then yanked upward towards the bar. Each leather padded steel manacle reached up with a brief section of chain and snapped onto the spreader bar. Candy gritted her teeth and huffed for breath. Her spine was smarting terribly from the acute contortion of the pose. Twisted backwards, her fingers pawed at the thick metal shackles, but she could tell that there was no way for her to get free. The pose was a horrid one that left her exceptionally vulnerable but all she could do was hang there and await her next session of dreadful education.

Candy lifted her head and watched the Demonatrix stroll out in front of her. A soft patting sound made her squint and verify what was in the woman's hands. The dark object was almost lost against the dark shades of her costume and the gloom of the chamber.

The sight of the pliant rubber truncheon had her clench her

jaw with worry, but she managed to keep her words in check as the woman merely stood still with a hip crooked towards her prisoner and continued to tap the weapon into her palm. The steady metronome pound continued to inspire malaise, but Candy just stared at the almost hidden eyes of the female and refused to show cowardice.

The sound of the truncheon and the rising pain of her bondage started to have their usual effect. The discomfort of the pose was frustratingly annoying, and Candy wanted something more vibrant than this bothersome background ache. As she regarded the salacious curves of the tyrant, she could not help but commit to improving her anguish.

"Are you going to do something with that toy? I'm bored already."

"You want attention, slave?" murmured the woman.

"Well, I w-"

Candy's words were cut off when the woman casually flicked the weapon out and had it collide with her shivering rear. The battering attack brought a wash of numbness to the region that settled in the wake of the initial shocking pain.

"Nothing to say?" asked the woman and slammed the truncheon back across her rear.

The bruising attack left a potent throb, and the sadist commenced a slow but savage beating that targeted her legs and rear and offered occasional upward thuds into her hanging breasts. The impacts drove the wind from her lungs and pummelled her flesh until she swore all feeling had been driven from it save for the relic of a deep pulsating pound.

Candy bit her tongue and took the abuse in silence with only snorts and grunts to answer the attack. A few stern swipes into her calves caused her to release brief pips of strain as she was taken further towards her breaking point.

A final volley ended with a return swing that landed in her belly and crippled her with nausea. As she hung and snorted for breath, she heard a brief crackle of moisture and gasped when viscous material was casually smeared through the valley between her parted thighs. A moment later she released a holler as the truncheon descended vertically and hauled open her sphincter as it began to enter her. Having been untroubled by trespass for some time, her rear had little capacity for this violation and as soon as she finished one cry, the woman started to pivot and churn the weapon to acquire new ones.

The Demonatrix stepped forward, ducked down a little to press her rubber smothered loins to Candy's face, and then straightened while shifting forward. Candy's howl was stifled by the abdomen of her oppressor, and she was bent back a little more sternly. With her body now pressing her face into the woman, she jerked and struggled, fighting to shift and gain air but all she could acquire were half snorts and vague gasps as she bounced and wriggled against the villainess. The Demonatrix was leaning forward so that she could not be driven back, and Candy was left pressed to her.

The truncheon was hauled out and Candy managed to snatch a decent breath before it escaped in puffs against the latex when the rounded tip dove back and pressed to her deepest regions. The woman pulled the handle down and started to draw it out, making the length stretch and pain her channel before it popped free.

"There are so many places for you to visit here, slave. And one by one we will introduce you to the catalogue of horrors we have in store for you," quipped the woman.

The tyrant stepped back and took the weapon with her. Candy dropped away and swung to and fro as she let her head hang lose while she recovered from the brief ordeal. Her skin was throbbing from the beating and her anus was pounding from the violation, but still she refused to ask for mercy.

A candle appeared in the grasp of the wicked termagant. The towering black strut was about two feet in length, and she watched as one of the guards applied flame. The female turned the candle in her grasp to watch the well of wax gather and as she examined it, the flame illuminated the eerie spectacle of her mask with its ranks of spines and acute alien contours.

Candy closed her eyes as the candle voyaged between her splayed legs and started to tilt. Insubstantial splashes landed on her inner thighs and gave way to a fierce detonation of pain. She flexed and yanked with her extremities, causing herself to bounce and sway but the woman just continued to follow her movements and steadily drip the wax. First it was only to her thighs, but her sex and the cleft of her rear were being painted with molten fluids. Candy cried out when these splashes graced her most sensitive regions and this just made the Demonatrix chuckle and repeat the application. As soon as this was done three times in a row, Candy applied all her will to refusing her sounds of dissent because it only made the woman more spiteful.

The twitch of her thigh muscles caused the wax to crack after it had hardened, and small particles drifted down before her eyes as she bounced and cried out from the maltreatment.

The villainess turned her attention elsewhere for a moment and began to drip the wax between Candy's shoulders, catching her on the shoulder blades. This tactic made her sway and jerk even more distinctly because as far as she could recall, she had never once been assailed in this particular region before in her life or during all the long days and nights she had spent at the mercy of the Kami.

When the wax landed along her spine and flowed along towards her shoulders she arched even more acutely and gasped with astonishment at how sensitive this previously untouched region was proving.

Her awareness of this attack was momentarily stolen when a flogger was grabbed midway down its bushel of leather ribbons and small swipes applied to her loins. Candy gave a shriek as the hot punishing slaps were dropped into her lewdly offered sex and each sweep cleared away more of the waxen coat that encrusted her pudenda and thighs. The guard continued to swipe the weapon into her inner thighs, the curtailed use of the mighty weapon being more than sufficient to pain her because of the delicate nature of the regions it targeted.

As she had feared, as soon as she had been cleaned, the candle returned and started to steadily drip back onto the skin, which was now raw from the application of the heat and tender from the mild thrashing it had received in order to prepare it for more cruelty.

"Feel free to scream, slave. It won't make any difference, but it might help you to endure that which I am going to continue giving you as long as you are with me."

Candy sucked in her lower lip and chewed on it as hard as she could as the drips came in two second intervals. The timing was the most vexing aspect because she knew when each was due, and it made it harder to stay quiet as they continued to hound her.

"But if silence is what you want, then feel free to indulge as you wish," murmured the woman and Candy closed her eyes as the drips continued to cover her inner thighs and several trickles made their way towards her presented pussy.

"Still nothing to say? Well, how about now?"

Candy's eyes flashed back open, and she stared wide eyed at the floor when she felt her vulva being parted by the gloved fingers of the woman a moment before she started to drip the wax into her exposed internal regions. The highly sensitive membranes reviled the wax like no other region of her body, and she immediately broke into long piercing squalls.

The steady dripping was even more a bane than ever, and she kicked at the spreader bar to try and get out from under the relentless attention. The woman kept her hand firmly in place so that Candy was left open to her intentions and could do nothing save cry out as searing impacts fell into her.

"Feel free to say anything you want, slave. There's a lot more candle left, and so much time to coat you with it."

Another series of droplets were delivered into her, but all Candy could do was snort and wail.

"Any words at all?"

Candy went berserk as the full measure of the candle was poured into her in one go. The excess rushed down her body and dripped from it as her sight swam and tears trundled from her eyes. As the agony started to fade, she collapsed and hung limp in her bonds, whimpering softly and shedding more tears.

"You must be thirsty after all your crying and screaming, but I have a desire to see you truly parched."

Candy watched in horror as a pair of braziers were collected and brought over by the guards. The large copper bowls were filled with charcoal bricks and were set down on either side of her. The candle was lowered to each and imparted its flame. The braziers quickly began to bear a towering flame that soon vanished as it ate into the coals and made the white surfaces glow from within.

The heat welled around her and began to soak into her form. At first, sweat started to form on her skin and flow down it much like the wax had, but then the heat grew to new levels that caused her perspiration to evaporate even as it was emerging.

"I think that will do for now."

The woman sauntered away, and the guards stole one last look at her and then followed.

CHAPTER NINETEEN

Candy had no idea how much time was passing as she hung in the terrible pose and was buffeted by endless waves of desiccating heat. Her skin had been abused by the heat of the wax, and now it was being lashed by waves of fulgent wrath that made her tremble and her thoughts to sway as she dizzily hung in perpetual confinement.

She strained against her bonds and tried to find some way to loosen them enough so she might wriggle free, but it soon became apparent, as it always did, that it was a futile notion.

The hours continued to trail by, and the fury of the braziers began to slowly fade. The dark coals first became a snowy white with a furious internal glow of heat and then they started to crumble and collapse into ash.

She was parched. Her throat felt like broken glass and her skin felt chafed as though rubbed with sand. She desperately desired water more than anything, and her fantasies now revolved around glasses of sparkling, clear, cool liquid. Every time she pictured the image she shook and struggled afresh in the desperate desire to try and access this impossible goal. She dreamed again of being a water concubine, of swimming in the deep, of being surrounded and immersed in that which she so desperately craved. She had reviled that lot on some occasions, but now she could not even imagine why, especially when she had been luxuriating in such splendid depths and had experienced the wondrous sensations of cool water rushing over her body in abundance.

The sound of footsteps roused her slightly and she found

joy in the prospect of being released and in her thirst being quenched. As the images of her long incarceration now formed around her, she fantasised about being thrown into a swimming pool or similar huge body of water.

The clatter of fresh coals as they were poured onto the braziers reached her ears and made her moan in apathy. Her hopes were dashed, and her resistance was shattered.

"Please! No more! I'm dying!" she implored, but the two men just laughed, poked the coals around to ensure they caught light, and then marched away.

"I need water! Please, I'm begging you! Just one drop! Just one!" she yelled, her voice now cracked from being so parched.

When their forms vanished into the shadows and became lost to her, she craned her head forward and tried to blow out the gathering flames. It was a ridiculous notion because the coals were already alight, but in her desperate state any hope was worth clinging to. When the pointlessness of this endeavour dawned, she just hung languid in her bonds, sobbing quietly in the grim quietude of the massive hall of suffering.

The two guards came to her again during the perpetual night and despite her begging solicitations they restocked the braziers. The waves of torrefying heat continued to rage against her quaking skin and her throat and mouth became arid as the hours continued to dawdle away. After a time she could not even dwell on her decisions regarding Yomi and her slavery here, every thought revolved around reviling the heat and dreaming of a drink of water.

The creak of latex reached through the crackle of the coals, and she stirred slightly. The Demonatrix sashayed from the darkness and revealed herself in a body smothering catsuit that stretched over her hands and perched her atop skyscraper heels. She still wore her ferocious mask and in one hand she drew the end of a hose.

"Is my new toy thoroughly cooked?" she purred.

A hand trailed over Candy's body and found no trace of sweat. The woman clasped at her spread thighs and then cupped her shivering rear.

"Very nicely done."

The tyrant stepped back, and her guards moved in to start to extract her. The bonds let go of Candy's body and she was lowered back to the floor where she settled in a stolid heap. A pair of steel shackles snapped to her ankles and the chain that linked them was padlocked to a nearby ring in the floor.

The sound of a few droplets of water striking the stones inspired her head to jerk up and look for the source of the glorious sound. She found that the woman had drawn forth just a few drops that she had allowed to fall onto her pointed toe.

Candy's limps operated of their own accord and had her scuttle over on her belly so she could push her lips to the cool spots of fluid and suck them free. The chain snapped taut and stopped her. The guards exploited her moment of confusion and drew her arms behind her whereupon two pairs of chain-linked shackles connected her upper arms and her wrists. Candy tugged at the ankle bonds and her balance failed her. She dropped onto her side and slithered forward to elongate her body as much as possible and reach the water she so desperately craved.

More water fell from above and the meagre rain coated both shimmering toes. Candy gave a long mew of dismay as she watched the water gather and run down the black fabric and settle on the floor where it slowly spread under her sole. She stretched her neck forward as much as possible and thrust out her tongue, but she was still an impossible couple of centimetres away.

"P . . .p . . ..pleeeease," she croaked as she stared wide eyed and delirious at the small puddle.

"A few questions first."

Candy gave another hoarse moan of despair as more water fell and tantalised her eyes. She then began to sob as she watched it slowly evaporate in the heat.

"Anything. Just . . ..I . . .I . . ." she stammered, unable to find the words to articulate the level of need she bore.

"I know, I know," soothingly whispered the evil vixen, and turned the footwear as she continued to speak seductively. "But before I let you drink this cool . . .sparkling . . .delicious water, I have to know what you know."

"Oh please, not again," blurted Candy as she flexed against her bonds and fought to slip free. She couldn't believe that she was being interrogated again. She had thought that condemnation to Yomi had ended this facet of her slavery, but it seemed that it was to unfold one more time.

"You have been amongst the great powers of the Houses of Water and Fire. The Warlord, the daughters, and Lady Uzume. We of the underworld know that you know something of importance. You are a pawn in a large game, and while *you* may be inconsequential, this nugget of knowledge you have acquired is most definitely not."

"Wh . . .why? What do you care? This is Yomi. You're not vital. You're not involved in the attack on Earth," she managed to burble.

Despite the terrible thirst that was possessing her, she had been a plaything to the Gods and had seen their intrigue. She knew that she needed every scrap of information for her defence, every trinket of secret lore, anything that could possibly help her. The Demonatrix was quizzing her, but she could also slot her own form of enquiry into the process, and the woman was so intent on getting her own answers that she unwittingly told Candy more than she should have.

"Oh Yomi may be the land of the forsaken, but not for

much longer. Now tell me what you discovered that has caused such comprehensive plots to see you lost to all."

Candy hit her smile. Even in this tormented state her mind was still razor sharp and the subtle inflections in the woman's voice told her volumes. When a century's old being was so enraged that it let this emotion slip into conversation, well, that exposed just how overwhelmingly potent it was. Yomi was resentful, and Yomi was plotting. The primary military powers of the Empire would be crossing over to Earth and that left the Empire vulnerable on this side. Was the underworld planning a revolt, to ascend when there would be nothing to stop them? If so, then it would behove them to discover all they could about the secrets of the military. Candy knew some of Hachiman's secrets, of his plans against the Eastern Provinces, and of what Lady Uzume was *really* doing. The Demonatrix would have been elated to hear these secrets, and it would give these traitors such a weapon to use. If she could hold out, she could even demand elevation, perhaps reach the ranks of the priesthood down here for handing over such vaulted and invaluable intelligence.

Nevertheless there was no way this woman would acquire the secrets of her master. It was Toyo-tama-hiko who had tossed her through the various Earth Houses until she was abducted and taken to Yomi to keep her from her owner. It was Toyo-tama-hiko who had cast her to the underworld to conceal his secret army from his brother and so there was certain sense of justice in Candy not only easing her own situation but also defending her master by betraying the very secret that the Warlord of Water sought to keep hidden. Candy had to be careful though, she had to expose this information correctly and make sure that the Demonatrix had no clue that she had more information. If the woman continued this interrogation, she would crack. She had to ensure that she convinced them that the existence of the Midzhu Wani was her only secret.

"I don't know anything. Toyo-tama-hiko is just being spiteful," she professed.

"Oh I know there's more to it than that. We of Yomi have eyes and ears everywhere. We lurk below and listen. You were tortured with Irukandji. Why would such a horror be inflicted upon you?"

Candy drew forth the thought of betraying her master. She pictured failing him, of letting him down and placing his most covert dealings out into the open for the benefit of these turncoats. The fright thundered through her like a tidal wave and even rode over her thirst to give her moments of strength.

"It just amused him," she said with a distinct tremor corrupting her voice. The deliberate ploy to slot terror in her voice worked perfectly.

"Now I *know* that you have information. You are afraid, slave. Afraid of what he will do should you expose his secret. But you are in Yomi now and no one can save you, but also, no one can reach you here. You are safe from reprisal, but you are at my mercy. Shall I show mercy? What coin will you use to pay for it?"

"Please don't make me do this," she implored, keeping the thought of Hachiman's secret in the forefront of her mind.

"Tell me and you may drink, slave. Whatever it is, I need to know, and then you will be rewarded with all the water you want."

More water flowed over the boot and Candy sobbed with panic. She remembered the meeting room where she had been bound and servicing Lady Uzume as the scheme was hatched above her.

"I . . .I saw something I shouldn't have."

"Yes, that's it, slave. Tell me what you saw. What did you see?"

Candy cast all thought of Hachiman to the back of her

mind and locked it up. She replaced this with the other secret she held, and there was enough lingering dread in her voice to shake her revelation and make it seem even more honest.

"In the abyss. There is an army. Wani that live beneath the waves. A secret army that the Water Warlords are keeping in the depths."

The Demonatrix paused and Candy started to worry that the lie had not been swallowed.

"Excellent. Well done, slave."

The tyrant stepped forward and Candy locked her lips to the boots and sobbed as she sucked all moisture free. As her sight started to clear, she began to see small perforations along the base of the footwear. For a moment she assumed them to be some sort of consideration for ventilation, to make the suit less stifling, but then she was shown their true purpose.

Without a word, the Demonatrix pushed the end of the hose into the neck of her catsuit and turned it on. She gave a soft sigh and arched her chest up against the rubber as it rippled with the introduction of cool water. Candy peered up and watched with ravenous eyes as the water swelled against her cleavage and began to clearly trickle down between latex and skin towards her feet. The woman massaged her loins when the water reached them, and her thighs twitched as she swayed her hips and stirred Candy's approaching drink.

Sparkling gems began to appear on the boots and the villainess just chuckled as Candy thrust her face to them and began to gobble up every drip she could find. The water was salty from being influenced by sweat and had the tang of latex distinct upon it. She feverishly licked and sucked on the toes and clamped her lips to the heel to devour every trickle that ran along them. As her lips and mouth were again wetted, she started to notice the other, more subtle tang of the woman's arousal from this degrading act. Squirming on the floor, she continued to drink from the woman's catsuit and body with frenzied enthusiasm until finally the tyrant turned off the hose and handed it back to one her guards.

"That will do for now, slave."

Candy pushed herself up onto her knees and although she was slightly hunched over from tiredness, she managed to try and sit as demurely as she could. She placed her hands on her thighs and stared forward at the rubber-clad hindquarters of her oppressor. One of her boots brushed Candy's left hand away and then stepped onto the thigh so she could nudge her heel into the skin.

"Touch it."

With some reluctance, Candy reached up and took hold of her calves. The latex was warm to the touch.

"Worship it."

She leaned in and nudged her cheek to the knee of the Demonatrix. The scent of the second skin touched her nostrils and her submission flared. It had been awoken by the interrogation and her recent startling abuses and now seized the chance to indulge in more fetishist derogation. Her fingers pawed at the tight smooth fabric and her lips wandered upon the impermeable skin as her tongue slowly poured out and began to trail upon it amidst adoring kisses.

"There, you now see who owns you. You are my possession. My toy."

A gloved hand stretched into her hair and began to stroke her as she continued to lavish kisses to the leg of her abuser. There was a wonderful sense of covert victory within Candy. She had kept her master's secrets safe despite the virulence of her questioning. She had wounded the man who had thrown her to this hellish domain, and now she could indulge herself with this humble devotion.

"Your information is most gratifying to hear, slave. And as a reward, I will give you all the water you want."

The Demonatrix stepped from Candy and turned to walk back towards the exit. The guards produced keys and opened her cuffs before again hoisting her up and then dragging her in the wake of their superior. Candy tried to walk but once more her legs were too weak to do anything save slip and slither under her.

The ragged tunnels of the domain passed by and finally a new location was presented to her. The domed room had walls that were carved with dreadful nightmarish imagery. Contorted screaming forms were twisted and interlocked and they flowed around a trio of smooth solid metal doors that bore no feature.

With a wave of her hand, the Demonatrix caused a scraping howl to emerge from the cavern. The foot-thick vault door started to shuffle aside into the wall and expose another corridor. As soon as the door had vanished, ranks of burners on the walls sparked of their own accord and their gas jets filled the corridor with radiance.

The passage stretched off beyond her ability to see and all along it were more featureless portals, all set within a small alcove. For long minutes she was drawn down the bland route until an open door appeared and she was shown into the dark chamber it protected.

A spotlight came on and shone down upon a smooth featureless slab of stone that sprouted from the floor and offered a smooth leather surface. She was dropped face first onto the padded table and after a brief voyage to the shadow cloaked walls, the guards returned with new additions for her body. Their life spent underground had left them with keen sight and coupled with their familiarity with processing slaves in these rooms, they could see things that Candy could not.

Unable to spy what else was awaiting her, she relaxed her physique and prepared to accept another transformation.

As though dressing her to imitate their deity they began to

slot her into a dense catsuit with socks and mittens already attached. The rear of the garment was zipped up and a hood was drawn down onto her head before it too was secured to the high collar of the suit. The hood had openings for her nostrils and her mouth, and slender slits existed for her eyes.

A single sleeve was gathered and threaded onto her arms to pin them behind her back. Several belts upon it were tightened so that she was forced to arch her chest into the table. From the upper reaches of the sleeve came two thick straps that were irrevocably fastened to a monstrous posture collar that encompassed her throat and forced her to stick her chin acutely upward.

The next portion of her attire was another sleeve that gathered up the whole length of her legs and was sealed about her waist with a densely boned but thankfully brief corset. When she moved her feet, she felt the large flipper that was sprouting from the outward sides of her extremities and realised then that she was indeed going to receive all the water she wanted, and as usual, the act of rewarding her was going to be a punishment to amuse those who owned her.

The final aspect of her uniform manifested in the form of a dense mask that resembled a frightening juxtaposition between a gas mask and that of a scuba diver. It had a transparent visor, and a plexus of straps formed a harness that would hold it to her head. The interior beckoned and she gave a brief struggle as the tubes that would enter and sustain her were gathered up and aimed at her features. The posture collar denied her any hope of resisting and so she accepted her lot willingly as the food tube thundered down her throat, making her eyes bulge and her body react violently after her initial submission. The nostril tubes were applied, and the mask was set firmly in place.

"Good. Let's show her to her new home," said the woman and with those words the other end of the chamber lit up.

Candy broke into rabid convulsions as she saw what was coming. She had thought perhaps that this was going to be some sort of punishment, or another sadistic vice of the Demonatrix, but now she realised that these were not rooms designed for fleeting supervised torment, they were rooms whose impenetrable featureless vault doors were places to dispose of a slave, to imprison them for the rest of their days.

The far end of the chamber was dominated by a great glass sphere that was filled with water. It rested upon a metal pipe that was two yards thick and allowed a pair of thick tubes to slither up through the interior and reach the lid. As her eyes accustomed to the light, she now saw that a set of stairs had been cut into the wall. They flowed along the far end of the cave before forming into a platform over the great bowl.

One of the guards grabbed her and flung her over his shoulder as they all proceeded up. Candy continued to writhe but was held tight until she was lowered and pinned down so that the last of her doom might be applied. One of the hoses clamped to the front of her mask and instantly she found herself drawing upon cool reprocessed air. Another fixture was clamped to something near the base of her spine and without even another word or care for her existence, the lid was opened, and she was tossed in.

Candy struck the surface and vanished beneath the waves. She flashed around and looked up to see the guards smile as they crouched before the Demonatrix who stood with hands on hips, glowering down at her. The lid dropped down and was sealed and Candy continued to sink down. Through the glass she watched them stroll from the chamber and the door seal and lock to leave her condemned to isolation.

She swam round in circles with her pipes flowing behind her and thought on what was going to happen next. The trouble was that nothing did. Small measures of water and nutrients were introduced to her body and were only detected because of the almost imperceptible quiver in her throat tube. She also detected that the tube to her back was gradually pumping a thin gel into her suit. Every motion made it swirl against her skin, pushing it round and round as it was also sucked out. It was no doubt a consideration to keep her skin healthy, and thus she realised just how easy it would for them to leave her in her fishbowl for the rest of her life.

The time she had spent as an animal had been laborious but had at least resulted in levels of input and occasional attention. After all her time as a slave, this was the worst fate she had endured. Even the Irukandji had been more pleasant, for at least she had the fight for orgasm to look forward to and indulge. In this bowl there was nothing.

Candy yearned for attention like never before. She ached to be touched, to be punished, pleasured, anything to break the monotony, but there was no hope. Eventually she tried to pull of her mask, to try and create an emergency so that she would be removed, but no matter what she tried, the straps refused to break, and she couldn't get free of the tube that sustained her in this hideous containment.

Unlike before, her thoughts did not diminish, she did not start to lose herself in the role of beast and think in a more base fashion. Her mind remained livid with need, with hatred of this numbing imprisonment. After everything she had done, everything that had been done to her, was this really going to be the final chapter in her life? Others had envied her for the times she had spent with the Kami, so perhaps it was a fitting end to her life as a concubine to have nothing but these memories and stark unfeeling existence as her finale. Others may not have enjoyed what she had, but they would at least enjoy sensation for life. She had binged on the most extreme forms and the most awesome couplings but had paid for it in that no other experience save swimming in circles and crying were left her.

CHAPTER TWENTY

It could have been days, it could have been years before something other than silent captivity entered Candy's shadow of life. A deep punishing rumble ran through the underground realm and shook the glass sphere. Her eyes widened with delight as she hoped that the orb would topple and smash because at least then she would be free of this thing. To her sadness it remained stable.

The tremor faded, but then so too did her breath. Candy panicked and sucked at the tubes with all her might, but the respirators were failing quickly. Another resonant clang sounded and the bottom of the tank suddenly broke open. The hatch parted under the weight of the water and as once before in the realm of the Water Warlord, she was flowing down a subterranean chute.

The tubes that were attached to her body popped free from their fixtures and Candy gave a cry when suddenly a harsh light was raging against her eyes. She kicked with her tail and found that she was in open water and even though she had been near blinded by the glare, she saw bubbles rising up around her. She held her breath and followed the direction. Her face was heating from asphyxiation, and she swam as hard as she could ever upward.

Candy erupted jubilantly from the surface and dropped onto her back. With the last of her breath she pushed the water from her tubes and snorted in a deep gorgeous breath of air. Spots of water flowed into her lungs, and she instantly broke into racking coughs and snorts. Panicked, she operated on instinct and stalled her breath until she could try and repair it in safety. She thrashed her tail, rolled, and in seconds had successfully beached herself. Her rubber-clad body had rocketed along the surface and then rushed up onto a riverbank.

So as not to be distracted by her surroundings, she closed her eyes and focused on her breathing. Hunched over into a ball, she managed to slowly recapture some semblance of normal operation. The coughing fits ebbed as she purged the tubes and her insides of water.

Calming down, she lifted her head and looked around. Her body felt unusually heavy, and it seemed that she might have been in her bowl for some considerable time if she had grown so accustomed to floating.

Candy saw that against all reason she was in an unpopulated region far from any palaces. Verdant green hills rolled off into the distance and sporadic gatherings of trees reached up towards the cloud flecked sky. The large river into which she had been ejected snaked through the hills and was fenced in by swaying reeds save for a few small beaches of grit such as the one she had managed to shoot herself onto.

She rolled over onto her back and just stared up at the sky as the droplets on her visor quickly evaporated in the warm sun. Birds flew unhurriedly overhead, and the river lapped at her tail with gentle beats. She felt her arms going numb from supporting her but didn't care. For the moment, she decided to enjoy her freedom for what it was worth.

Only once the rays of the sun had saturated her rubber skin and began to warm the gel that was still spread upon her smothered skin did she decide to return to her natural habitat. It was considerably more difficult to enter than it was to exit, and it was a particularly awkward process to wriggle and squirm her way around and then edge back into the river.

Once she was in and the gathering heat upon her was

countered, she started to ponder her next course of action. The tremor had either been seismic or military in nature, and had set off some sort of emergency sequence to preserve the prisoners. However, if this were the case, why were there no other fish women in the river? Candy wondered if the many vaults contained a variety of penitentiaries, a menagerie of bondage apparatus, costumes, and other hellish domains to embrace and seal away the hafuri-tsu-mono. This fitted with the cunning and ever enthusiastic imaginations of the Kami and could well explain her loneliness.

Deviating to a much more pressing problem, Candy had to consider her survival. Bound as she was, she had no means to feed herself. Her only option was to swim downstream and hope she came across habitation that might show mercy. It meant that she would probably be handed back to brutes of Yomi, but survival was her priority, even if it meant a return to that horrible fishbowl.

Taking the time to savour her current level of liberation, Candy kicked rhythmically with her legs and continued to swim onwards. She arched upward every few beats, shook her head and exhaled a little so she might snatch a new breath and then duck back down to continue swimming. This style of swimming was exceedingly tiring and although it allowed her to stare at the riverbed with its shoals of colourful fish and rippling weed beds, she soon decided to take a more leisurely route.

Floating on her back, she watched the skies and shifted her tail much more lethargically so that she bobbed along and went with the current. Occasionally she brushed the reeds and had to correct her direction back into the middle before she hit the bank, but there were few real hazards for her to care about.

She swam onwards until the sun started to slowly vanish from the skies and marked its departure by painting a stunning canvas of reds and pinks across the heavens before it gave way to an emerging vault of stars. Candy rolled over again and located a small opening in the reeds so she could again swim out of the water and just spend the night under the stars, snoozing contentedly. The sounds of the wilderness were a definite treat after the long silence inside her bowl, and the lullaby allowed her to gain sleep deeper and more refreshing than any she had known in a long time.

The warmth of the morning soon started to heat her bound form more than she could happily accept, and with hunger starting to levy itself all the more potently, she crawled back into the water and continued her journey downriver.

A few lazy hours passed, but then without warning she ran into an obstruction. She spun about to go around it, but found that it was not so easily evaded. The net had snagged her mask and as she whirled it came with her to catch her form and then become ensnared on her tail. With a sudden desperate lurch she tried to break free before she became even more entangled, but it was hopeless.

The waters closed over her head as the weighted lower reaches of the net dragged her down and Candy continued to fight for her freedom. As she started to fear the worst, a series of steady pulls began to drag her through the waters and to dry land. She emerged from the river and was hauled up onto the grassy bank where she found herself staring up at a rather bemused young man.

The fisherman had a sleek physique with ranks of well-developed but subtle muscles, obviously gained from arduous manual labour. His skin was tanned, and he wore a short head of dark hair. Clad in loose trousers and rough woven boots, he scratched his head in befuddlement and then began to peel her from the net.

"What is a Midzhu no me doing so far from the ocean I wonder? Or do you belong to the Warlord of the Rivers? Are you even a water concubine? They tend to have a bit more colour and flamboyance to their attire." he asked softly.

Candy dropped from the final portions of the net and just rested before him. The stranger crouched down and looked over her attire, examining the buckles and other areas that held her prisoner.

"I must admit, I am intrigued," he muttered.

The stranger grabbed her about the upper body and heaved her over his shoulder before he began to stroll off towards a slim dirt path that crept amongst some nearby hills. Candy did not resist, without food and water she had no hope of lasting much longer, so she needed to surrender to whoever she found in order to try and find a route out of this costume or least someone to provide her with sustenance.

The fisherman walked down the path for several minutes, whistling a merry tune as he bore her away from her habitat.

"What have you got there, Sato?" asked a chirpy female voice.

"Not all the fish I caught today were edible," he replied and dropped her down onto a small pile of hay.

Candy peered around and saw a small discreet cabin with modest fields of crops spreading behind it. A young and slender woman was setting aside the basket that she was currently weaving and was currently looking across her contained form with a wicked leer. She had long dark hair that was fixed into a meticulous plait and cheery green eyes.

"I don't know about that. I find her quite delicious," she purred.

"In that case, let's have a real look at her," replied Sato.

"Isn't she a water concubine?"

"Who knows? And there's only one way to find out."

"Her owner might be upset."

"Well, Muso, then her owner should have kept a better eye on her. See these," he said, and prodded her mask's fixtures.

"Feeds for air and nutrients. She was being sustained by them, and they either came lose or she broke free of them, either way, she needs help."

"Mmmm, so she's a prisoner in there then," said Muso and sank down onto her knees at Candy's side. The woman's hands began to explore the tight cell that held to Candy, and her hips swayed as she found such captivity titillating.

"What a callous thing to do to such a pretty toy."

"I'll open her inside. Care to join me?"

"As opposed to finishing this basket for Oshinataka's sister? Hmmmm, let me consider this for a moment."

Sato gave an amused chuckle and lifted Candy in his arms, this time cradling her before him and carrying her into his home as though he were bringing home a bride. Muso followed close behind and was visibly quivering with excitement at what would be found in the dark rubber cocoon.

Candy was laid down on the kitchen table and flipped onto her front so that they could begin work on her freeing her.

"Actually this shouldn't be too difficult. It's quite a simple outfit."

"Maybe she doesn't belong to a Kami after all?"

Sato said nothing and began to unfasten the straps and peel away the latex. Candy liberated from her tail and catsuit, and her arms coursed with residual pain as they were finally set free of the sleeve.

Her face mask was opened, and when Sato saw the tubes that entered her features, he drew it away and let them pull out of her body. Candy shook as they left her and then sagged onto the table as her skin tasted fresh air for the first time in an unknown duration.

The hands of Muso were upon her in an instant and started to slither upon the gel and appraise her curves. The delicate touch was most welcome, and Candy remained where she was and just luxuriated in this long-desired attention.

"So who are you?" asked Sato, focusing on fact as his partner busied herself with fantasy.

Candy had been considering what she should do. At present she was anonymous, with an unknown owner who had shown her an almost criminal level of neglect. Sato and Muso seemed to be mere peasants, but they had a kindly demeanour that she found almost intoxicating.

Candy perked her eyebrows and shook her head before she looked around at the simple kitchen. It was a rustic scene, quite unlike the opulent and exquisite palaces she had dwelt in or the eerie domains to which she so often found herself delivered.

"She's mute?" asked Muso.

"So it would appear."

After a moment to think on how to overcome this language barrier, he sprinkled some flour onto a cutting board and etched his question into the powder. Candy stared at it with an exaggerated look of confusion and then stared at Sato with an imploring look to express how frustrating this was for her.

"It's okay," he said and physically expressed this sentiment with a gentle pat of her head and then a stroke of her cheek. She rested her features into the soothing palm and continued to enjoy his partner's slow groping interest. "Looks like she's illiterate to."

"So we have no way to find out who she belongs to?" asked Muso.

"So it would appear."

"Then we should look after her until such time as her owner comes looking or we find out where she may have come from."

"I concur," he answered with a titter in his voice from his partner's intense excitement. Clearly Muso was going to seize any opportunity she could so that she could get to keep the new arrival.

"We should get this goo off her first."

"I'll boil some water," offered Sato and moved to the stove.

Muso took Candy's hands and started to help her off the table and back onto her feet. When her body weight came onto her soles her legs buckled slightly, but the woman's support prevented her from falling over.

"There we go," she said as Candy started to gather a little more balance. "Let's sit you down before you fall down."

Muso hooked a small stool with her foot and dragged it over to them before steering Candy around and down onto it. She dropped onto the smooth wood and sagged while breathing heavily. It felt so strange to finally be a bipedal creature again, and there was a sense of nakedness that was far more powerful than from just being without clothing, it was because that for so long she had been encased in the most binding costumes, been devolved by them, been controlled by them, tended by machines and automated systems. To be actually exist without any impediment or any invasion into her body was most unusual and oddly enough, quite disconcerting.

While she continued to try and process her freedom and what she might do now, the couple held each other and watched her recover. Her every movement seemed to entice them, and their hands began to wander upon each other as fantasies of what she could do crept through their minds.

When the water began to reach a suitable temperature, they brought the large bucket to the floor and gathered sponges that they then started to dip in and rub across her body. Candy shuddered as the glorious warm water started to take away the nutrient slime that had stopped her skin from being damaged. Sato attended the task with a view to finishing it while his partner handled it with a far more self-indulgent hand. Candy allowed her thighs to be parted and with Muso kneeling before her she closed her eyes and enjoyed the feeling of the woman repeatedly cleansing her skin there.

"She looks tired," said Muso.

"Okay, then. Let's get her to bed," answered Sato with a resigned huff. There was no way to dissuade Muso from experiencing their new playmate.

They each took a wrist and guided her out of the kitchen and to a small bedroom whose windows allowed the sun to stream in and pour across a simple double bed. Candy felt as though she were in a dream. They were not restraining her, not towing her at the end of a lead. Her compliance was being asked, not demanded, and this was such an unusual event that Candy had little idea how to react to it.

She flopped onto the mattress and remained where she was as the couple shed their clothes. Muso prowled onto the bed with a ravenous look in her eyes. She leaned down and kissed Candy's shins while peering up along the length of her body and to her eyes, never once breaking visual contact with her.

Fingers rushed up and down her calves and the woman began to kiss a route upwards. The slow rise towards her thighs seemed deliberate so as not to unduly spook a skittish creature.

Candy felt Sato sit down beside her head whereupon he drew her chin around and sought a kiss. For a split second she was reluctant, but the feel of a feminine tongue clearing her knee and voyaging onto her thighs dispersed all feelings of antipathy. Lips met hers and lingered until by her own choice, she opened her mouth and responded. Resting his head on one hand, Sato's other reached in and cupped a breast before his thumb began to toy with her ring and to stroke her nipple.

Candy's eyes jolted open, and she swung her stare down as much as she could without breaking her passionate kiss with Sato because she felt the delicate hands of Muso lay down onto her thighs and press thumbs in to ask her to spread her legs wide and allow access.

No sooner had her limbs drifted apart than the woman stretched herself forward and offered a few precursor kisses to the soft skin before her tongue tip began to draw circles around Candy's sex. Running around thigh and stomach, she allowed Candy to become used to the feeling before she kissed her navel and then had her tongue sway from side to side and commit to a zigzagging downward path. The warm, wet organ crossed onto her pussy and slid through to tantalise her clitoris with some highly stimulating swirls.

Candy gave a long sultry mew and kissed Sato with more abandon. Her stomach muscles rolled, and her thigh muscles flicked and clenched. Her own hands reached around and encompassed Sato. She held tighter as the enthusiastic tongue of Muso gathered new degrees of effort.

Inspired by Candy's response, the agile tip raged against her clit and Candy jumped to attention as she came. After her long duration of imprisonment, it felt wonderful to climax again. She screamed aloud with victory and rhapsody, and this caused the couple to move with energised haste.

Muso grabbed Candy's left ankle and cast it over to roll her onto her front. Sato shuffled down the length of the bed and slid his hands beneath her hips to hoist her rear into the air just as his partner collapsed before Candy and cast her own legs wide.

Elated to be free and eager to please, she reached up and began to tease Muso's breasts as she nestled between her thighs and started to diligently adore the woman's pussy. Candy resonated the intimate flesh with a long moan when Sato's engorged shaft brushed against her and then committed to a steady driving thrust. His hands clenched to her sides as he withdrew and again sheathed himself within her, and each gradual plunge caused his length to twitch within her.

Muso's hands clawed into the sheets and her head rolled upon the pillows as she cried out from Candy's eager attention. The woman began to thrash around so much that she had to let go of her breasts and clamp her hands to her thighs to keep her in place so she could work effectively. Candy could almost believe that this woman had never before been attended in such a way, such was the extremity of her response.

Sato flopped back and propped himself up on his arms so he could launch his hips up into her. Each potent slap made her squeak as she was relentlessly pummelled. When she felt him swell within her and flick with the onset of orgasm, she squeezed her channel to him and sucked ferociously on Muso's clit to inspire her to scream and join the two of them in mind-bending release.

"By Izanagi and Izanami she is an astounding concubine. What sort of fool would let her slip through his fingers?" gasped Sato.

He slid back and collapsed onto the bed at Candy's side so he could embrace both women. They all lay panting with their strength sapped by the energetic experience.

"Oh we'll make sure that her days of neglect are over," murmured Muso. The woman pulled a blanket over all three of them as the sweat of their exertions started to flee and give way to a slight chill.

CHAPTER TWENTY-ONE

For the next few weeks, Candy enjoyed a carefree and wonderful life on the farm of Sato and Muso. The couple were sweet and tender in their affections, and even when they tied her up so they might flog her, spank her, or torment her with pegs, it was a spry and frivolous form of abuse. They may not have been ageless masters in the arts of bondage and domination, but for now, Candy was glutted from having endured the dark depravities of Warlord and Yomi. The innocent dalliances with this couple were a welcome relief from the highly ritualised and intensely experienced machinations of the Great Houses.

When she was called upon to service them, she performed cunnilingus and fellatio with such gusto that she could have been attending Hachiman or Uzume. Her gratitude to the couple was immense, for they had liberated her from the one place in the Empire from which no mortal ever returned. Sometimes in the aftermath of sex, it was a serious fight to keep her words in check. She yearned to reply to them, to thank them, and strained not to reveal that she was anything other than a mute who did not understand the Imperial tongue.

Candy just wanted to stay on the farm. She knew too much. By accidentally discovering the mass secrets in the Houses, she had placed herself in a level of sexual jeopardy she hadn't thought possible. Rulers sought to pry her secrets from her or hide her away behind a bit, in a fishbowl, in a sarcophagus. She didn't want to be a pawn anymore. She would willingly endure the loss of her hope of ever seeing Hachiman again just so long as all the other darker personages of the Empire never again crossed her path.

Sato would sometimes fish the river and she and Muso would make love on the riverbank, their antics being a means to entertain him as he sat and waited for something else to blunder into his net.

Sometimes they bound her in the barn, other times to their bed, but always she was drenched in attention and lavished with kisses and affection. Several times, she was tied to a yoke and used to plough some fresh fields, and her time as a pony had her recalling the infinite satisfaction she had enjoyed in losing herself within that simple and rewarding role.

One morning, Masu had tied her to a low stool and then settled into an armchair to do some sewing. By pulling in the stool, she enveloped Candy in her thighs and had her perform at a slothful, delicious rate. When Candy became too excitable from attending her, she would prick her with a pin to make her squeak and slow down. Sometimes Candy misbehaved just to acquire this minor chastisement.

Sato stormed in unexpectedly and remained in the doorway. He was out of breath.

"What is it? I thought you were heading to the village for some more seed?"

"This, you will not believe, my love."

He extended a piece of paper and Muso accepted it with a frown. She scrutinised the contents and then pulled Candy's face up by the back of her hair.

"You've got to be joking?"

"It explains everything. Why she doesn't understand us. Why she's so skilled. Why she's so beautiful. By the Sun Goddess, I have passed this reward poster almost every day and never given it a second glance.

"She . . .she belongs to the Supreme Warlord of Fire?" said

Muso, a hint of sadness quickly creeping into her words. As though to banish them, she pulled Candy back between her legs, whereupon she instantly began to lap with a more vigorous rate.

"She is the lost property of Kami! And not just some Lord of an Earth House, but the Supreme Warlord himself."

"I don't want to give her up," muttered Muso.

"We have to, my sweet. It is our duty."

"But I love her. She's ours. We rescued her," implored Muso.

"This is not a case of *finders keepers*, she is important to a ruler of the Empire. Who knows what role she serves? We cannot jeopardise the realm by transgressing against the will of the Gods."

"I know. I know. It . . .it's just not easy to let her go."

"Then let's enjoy her one last time before I head to the palace of Hachiman."

Candy felt tears well in her eyes as she was taken to the bedroom. They were a strange concoction, inspired by radically different mindsets. On the one hand she was grief-stricken to lose the couple, but on the other hand she was elated because after all this time, finally, she was going to be returned to her one true owner. She had not felt such mental joy in a long time, and the love she made with those who had brought her to this state was as sterling as it was honest.

CHAPTER TWENTY-TWO

With her arms bound behind her with rope, Candy bore witness to another eerie sight. She was already familiar with one aspect of this manner of orchard, although from a far different life than the one she had lived since falling through the vortex. The Sakaki, or sacred evergreens, were visited by women who much desired harmony with their husband. Each meticulously tended tree was marked with a small red tori-wi in front of them to reveal their stature. Before several trees she could see bowed females in deep mediation and prayer.

Also situated amongst the grove were other forms of trees where women learned to appreciate their husbands in a far sterner way and also perhaps to inspire less felonious visitors to greater heights of commitment.

The contorted polished sculptures were formed from invaluable steel and rose up from the grass to embrace and contain a single trapped form. They were crushed into immobility by a number of severe metal bands that were decorated to resemble twigs and thereby make it appear as though the metal trees had grown around and encompassed them naturally. The hints of tubing revealed that the channels within the trees fed them and disposed of waste so that they were left to suffer and endure their demeaned isolation in silent contemplation.

Sato led her deeper into the large orchard and past countless suffering women as well those who bowed before the organic versions in the hope of avoiding the fate of those hanging about them.

A small clearing beckoned and standing in streams of golden light was Warlord Hachiman. Dressed in his battle armour, with daisho at his side, he stood next to a waist high tori-wi. Candy closed her eyes and cleared her mind of contrary thoughts. She feared that her hunger to see her master again was resulting in hallucinations, but when she opened her eyes, the image remained.

Sato stepped into the grove and sank down until his forehead was pressing to the lush green carpet. Candy followed suit and prostrated herself before her beloved master.

The sound of his methodical tread closed in and stopped before them. Both remained where they were, and Candy trembled with anticipation, excitement, and absolute lust. She had almost given up hope of ever seeing him again and now he was here, right before her. The aura of his dominance washed over her and made her want to grovel and beg, to sink into the soil in cowed awe.

"Rise, Sato," he said gently, and when the words graced Candy's ears, she had to fight to suppress her licentious moan of rapture.

The farmer drifted up onto his knees and Candy remained where she was.

"You have done me a service for returning to me that which was misplaced. I will see that you are rewarded for your service to the Kami."

"You are too kind, Warlord Hachiman. I merely wish to serve the desires of the Gods and need no reward."

"Nevertheless, to know the value of this kami-tsu-ko and bring her to me with no petition for compensation proves your loyalty to the Empire and so it shall be blessed. My Mikado will ensure your comfort and he will meet you at the main gates."

"My absolute gratitude for this generosity, Warlord

Hachiman," announced Sato, and started to retreat from the grove, leaving Candy and Hachiman alone in the quite.

"Rise, Candy."

She drew her knees under her and fought her way back up onto her feet. She kept her head lowered and swayed as she saw him standing before her. A hand reached up and lifted her chin. When her eyes met his, she immediately started to cry with jubilation. Hachiman just smiled and let his gaze stroll across her physique.

"Still as luscious as I remember. Your hardships have done nothing to mar your beauty, slave."

Candy's tears increased immediately as she heard the term she so revered slip over his lips and announce that she was truly his again.

"Thank you, master. It . . . I'm just so . . . I . . ." she spluttered, unable to find an appropriate sentence to express her joy. Words could not encompass just how much she adored him and how happy she was to once again be in his presence and know that she was owned and his.

Hachiman let go of her chin and wandered behind her. Hands took her shoulders and pushed her towards the tori-wi. Her stomach met the curved horizontal upper strut and her torso folded over it. It was then that she noticed the leather fetters in the grass. Attached to the base of the two supporting beams, they were semi-hidden in the greenery and were quickly buckled about her ankles to leave her legs spread wide and her chest hanging over the other side.

Hachiman strolled around the symbol to which she was bound and stepped out before her.

"Tongue."

Candy flung the organ out with such reckless abandon that it hurt the root. Hachiman produced a pair of slim wooden struts and used them like pincers to capture the length. One rubber band was closed about one end, and then another made the jaws close tightly into the flesh and enclose the other. Candy gave a soft mewl of discomfort and pleasure as the wooden jaws dug into the corners of her mouth and her strangled tongue was left hanging forth on display. It throbbed with a keen ache that started to gather new potency with every passing second.

Hachiman stepped back and from the grass drew two leather thongs. Already fastened to some hidden anchor, they reached out and after pulling Candy towards them with a pinch to the tip of her tongue, she quickly tied them to each end of the struts. Any attempt to wilt or retreat now hauled painfully at her captive organ and enhanced its suffering. Her spine started to smart from having to hold her torso up and her thighs flexed with the effort of retaining the stressful position.

"Many wives have had to prove their devotion to their husband upon this symbol, slave," he announced.

Hachiman removed one of his armoured gloves and tossed it over her. She saw it land in the grass and then gave a jerk when the naked palm slapped to her rear. She gave a shocked squeak and then whimpered as warm bliss seeped through the spanked skin.

"The form of their testing depends on how much disrespect they have shown."

Another heavy-handed smack landed on the other cheek and Candy cried out with elation as he continued to spank her bottom as she writhed and revelled in the salacious chastisement.

"The cane, the crop, the paddle, perhaps even the bullwhip for the truly erroneous. However, you have been through more than even the most outrageously wayward wife, so I will be gentle . . .before I take you."

Candy gave an elated howl at the thought of being spanked and then ravished by the being she worshipped. She pulled back to stretch her tongue and make it pound with new har-rowing. She embraced the misery and surged within her bonds as another swift trio of slaps greeted her juddering rump.

"You have been through many facets of the Empire's kami-tsu-ko. You have tasted the twisted desires of the Wani daughters, swam in our oceans, served in our fields, and even been owned by a mere citizen."

Another rapid deluge alternated from cheek to cheek and then a hand cupped the crease of her rear and squeezed her inner thighs. Candy arched up with a shriek of satisfaction as she felt the grip tighten so it could feel her flesh twitch and struggle. Her tongue paid the price for this movement, but the pain only exaggerated her libido.

"You have seen the Empire as no other slave has, and your journey is now complete, and you are returned to me."

Six more stern slaps were brought to her rear and then another six were bestowed to the backs of her thighs.

"It is time for you to know the truth, slave," he stated and then paused for a moment before offering a mild chuckle of amusement. "Well, perhaps not all of it, but the part that is relevant to the moment."

Candy sagged as the heat swelled within her skin and made her float upon an intoxicated haze of lust. A hand cupped her pussy and started to stroke her. She almost climaxed from the first touch.

"Everything that has befallen you has been according to my will. Toyo-tama-hiko had my permission to give you to the Houses of Earth, to make you a beast, so you would experience all, while also serving our other plans that are still in motion."

The hand came away and was replaced with an engorged cock. His sterling manhood ploughed into her channel, and Candy almost tore her tongue out as she jerked up and screamed from such heavenly fulfilment. The rapture of his entry into her body was almost more than she could withstand.

Hachiman paused and savoured the feel of her channel squeezing and flicking, adoring his cock with a muscular dance.

"When we invade, I want someone who knows Earth, and I need them to know that the Empire is far superior," he said, and slowly withdrew before he again rushed back into her. The slow methodical drives made her body quake against the bondage as the savagery of the delight raged within her, making her squawk incoherently as she tried to come to terms with the rapture that possessed her. So many times she had dreamed of this moment, and to have such a potent and long held fantasy realised, especially after such lengthy and arduous separation from him was uncannily satisfying.

"From what you have been through, I know that there will be no lies, no distortions. I know that you belong heart, body, and soul to the Empire and to me. What better advisor could I ever hope for when we cross over and subjugate your people?"

Hachiman continued with steady rhythm and relished her impotent thrashing. Candy screamed when she felt him starting to stiffen within her and her whole body vibrated feverishly as she felt a new orgasm suddenly loom.

The ends of the wooden pincers opened and dropped away. Her tongue exploded with a surge of terrible anguish, and as Hachiman came, she detonated with a delirious mixture of pain and absolute pleasure. Her body bent upward and fell into his arms. His brawny limbs instantly enveloped her and held tight as he continued to thrust into her. Pinioned to his armoured chest, with the back of her head resting on his shoulder, she stared up and squealed at the top of her lungs.

An armoured hand cupped her jawline and held her in

place as his naked extremity caressed and squeezed her breasts. Every thrust seemed to take her to new pinnacles of elation, but Hachiman never slowed in his steady rate. His lust dragged her through an orgasm the likes of which she had never before encountered.

He jumped back and his flight brought another nova burst of bliss that seemed to suck the energy from her body. Candy collapsed forward and hung on the tori-wi, twitching occasionally as bursts of sensation tightened her startled physique.

Hachiman unfastened her ankles and Candy slithered back until she dropped back onto the cool grass.

"While you have been passed from House to House, Uzume has instigated war with the Eastern Provinces, and this will lead to their defeat. Engineered dishonour for Uzume has allowed her to accept Toyotama-hiko's offer of co-rulership of a new House of Wani without suspicion. The House of Wani is readying to join the Mitama in the destruction of the Provinces and this will sharpen their war skills in readiness for the invasion of Earth, and once there, because of their position in the frontline they will sustain heavy losses and endure a measure of disgrace. I will remain unaffected by this since they were removed from my command. Then, when House Hachiman defeats Earth, and cements our hold on Pangaea, I will have earned a great and absolutely flawless favour from the Sun Goddess. My request is simple, slave. Lingzhi. For Lady Uzume and me, for all time. And such a wish will readily be granted."

Candy was suddenly assailed by a fear that after all her trials, she was to be used and then discarded when her usefulness came to an end. She was to be at his side through the war with Earth, but then what?

"But what of me, Warlord?" she asked meekly.

"When I retire from the realm of Earth, I will need to

appoint a Mikado to rule in my name. Ame-waka-hiko will be needed to run my House on Pangaea, and deal with the responsibilities and securities of this homeland. However, I have already groomed someone for the position. He has spent time on Earth, he knows the intricacies, the culture, the people, and will be most adept at ruling that land. I believe you are well acquainted with him . . ."

She looked up and then followed Hachiman's stare as he looked to the edge of the grove. From amongst the trees emerged a visage she had not seen save in dreams of a long-forgotten life.

"Lei!?!" she exclaimed, her mind recoiling at the intrusion of something from her life as Candice into her depraved existence as Candy.

Joseph Lei's face had changed little, but the corporate raider she had first known and been attracted to now appeared ferocious and deadly in the bold armour of the Kami with swords at his side and holstered firearms holstered upon his person. His dark hair was tied back into a high ponytail and his elegant features were riddled with satisfaction.

"I told you that I was hunting for acquisitions for my sempai, Candy. But it wasn't your portfolio that was my target, it was you," he announced. His voice was potent, full of confidence and authority. The innate charm he had displayed on Earth was still there, but now he could reveal his true power as an agent of an immortal Kami.

When he had mentioned his sempai — the older individual who guides, defends, and mentors the younger and less-experienced individual, she assumed a Japanese executive or other high ranking and important official in his company, not that his sempai was a divine warrior-general from a parallel world planning conquest of Earth and her enslavement to facilitate his ruling of the entire planet. The absurdity of the thought almost made her break into cracked laughter.

"Wh . . . why?" she began, trying to find the words to encompass the sudden turmoil in her head. Sex with her owner had left her aglow and sated, if she were not, she swore she would have swooned from sheer puzzlement.

Lei marched over and bowed deeply to his sempai, who offered him a nod before turning his attention back to Candy.

"I prepared my kohai to rule Earth in my staid when I retire from Imperial life to live out the endless years with my agent. It was I who asked Amatsu mika hoshi to accept Lei into his House, to train him in the ways required to operate as a covert agent, and then send him across to fulfil those obligations while familiarising himself with the ways of your kind. I have a great responsibility to my kohai and even though he learned much, I encouraged him to seek an advisor, an agent, much like Lady Uzume, but one clearly not as elevated and from the land we intend to invade."

Candy looked to Lei and saw the glee in his eyes before she turned back to her master.

"Lei saw the potential in you. You were accomplished, and smart enough to remain behind the scenes. A wily political creature with skill and accomplishment, but ultimately hollow inside. Clearly you had to be filled, and by being trained and used by the various powers and beings of the Empire, you would be enlightened as to the superiority of our ways and thereby show them, and Lei, the proper reverence."

"Bringing you across under the guise of acquiring your yacht and new genetic stock was simple enough, unfortunately, we were not expecting you to go Stray on us. Ultimately not a terrible occurrence for it allowed us to expose you to Uzume's passions as she was sent to collect you without knowing the role you were to play in our schemes."

"However, if I were to openly acquire you for my kohai, I would offer others hints as to my eventual plan. After all, why am I arming my subordinate with experts on Earth if I am committed to ruling it myself? If others even suspected me of wishing to retire, it would show weakness, and plots to enfeeble my House or even destroy me would immediately ensue."

"I decided to keep you under the pretence that you were to be mine, but then I encountered unexpected bidding from agents whom I suspected of working with the ruling elite of Yomi. This aroused some suspicions that my brother and I have long since held secret, that Yomi harbours desires of revolt and usurpation."

"My brother and I planned to work together on our goal to cement our power, and I handed you to him so he might "accidentally" expose you to some of his secrets. A few of his trained concubine elite hounded you until you reached the abyss, pumping you up until you saw what we wanted you to see."

"With hidden matters relating to the Houses of Water and Fire, the powers that had tried to outbid me to acquire you would expose themselves, but nothing happened. To make you even more tempting, we decided to send you through the care of the Houses of Earth, but still nothing occurred. We feared that we had overplayed our hand or were wrong, and decided that under the pretence of keeping the secrets of the Houses of Water from me, Toyo-tama-hiko would condemn you to Yomi."

"I continued my supposed search for you, adding weight to the supposition that I was either besotted with you and would be a valuable coin that I would pay anything for, or that you held secrets I could not risk being divulged to others—making you equally valuable. And so I trust you have heard from their own lips what is planned, and who is involved?"

"I have, master."

"As I knew you would, and to keep you safe and to continue your education, I arranged an explosion and your "loss" into the rivers. I knew that your beauty would ensure that you were well taken care of by whoever found you, and I knew that my former quest to reclaim you would eventuality filter down through the priests and slaves and reach the citizens. Yomi searched for you amongst the Houses, fearing that you would betray what you had heard, and did not think to seek amongst the citizens where I had hidden you. Now that I have reclaimed you, we enter the final moments of our long game."

"As an agent for the Moon God, Lei has been working diligently on the other side and this is a prelude to him taking the reins of power once I have finished suppressing all resistance. Toyotami-hiko and his Wani will bear the brunt of the failures, Lady Uzume will be embraced by me to protect her from the dishonour as I forgive her for her engineered earlier failures, and with a flawless battle record, I will be in the position to ask my favour of the Sun-Goddess."

"I will lead the subjugation of Earth, and you will be at my feet as I do it. Afterwards, I will retire, and Lei will become Supreme Warlord of Earth. You will remain with him, and be his. With you as a source of knowledge, he will be most effective, and I am sure he will continue to educate you in our passions, especially after having had to abstain for so long."

"Oh my kohai is going to make good use of you, slave. I taught him well, and he will be most eager to avail himself of your body in ways you've never experienced, you-"

Hachiman froze as something caught his eye. All joviality vanished from his face, and he started to slowly straighten as he stared into the tree.

"Sempai, what is it?" asked Lei, scanning for what had perturbed Hachiman so acutely.

"Yatagarusa," he said flatly. Lei gasped and as his eyes widened and darted around at the perimeter of the grove.

Candy remained still and peered into the trees where she saw a crow perched atop an evergreen. It was staring at them as though it was well aware of what it was doing and was actually enjoying the anxiety its arrival had caused.

Hachiman took several faltering steps towards the crow and then flashed around to Candy with a look of concern corrupting his features. The sight of this expression brought an icy terror to Candy's heart.

"The Sun-Goddess is about to bless us with a visitation. If you love me, show absolute respect," he stated forcefully and dropped to his knees so he might press his brow to the soil. Lei instantly copied him, and Candy sank down to once again prostrate herself.

It was strange to see Hachiman revere this woman with such piety, because surely he knew that she was just another artificially created deity like himself. Yet somehow, he regarded her as actually divine, in the same way the citizens and slaves and priests regarded the Kami.

Candy watched carefully using her periphery vision. It was a talent she had acquired as a slave, to study in the corner of her eyes so as not to annoy her superiors. It was what made the slave caste such valuable sources of information and the inspiration for so much plotting.

From amongst the trees emerged figures. They were all tall and powerful of build, with clothes that were manufactured from sturdy hide. The white skin was adorned with only token portions of lacquered armour — shoulder guards, breastplate, greaves, and vambraces, and these silver plates were marked with a red ideogram for Yatakagami, the Sun-Goddess herself. Where armour or leather did not cover them, their skin was coated with a comprehensive sheet of tattoos. The complex and elaborate patterns and pictures of mythology were sprawled meticulously across their frames.

Each wore a featureless helm, the smooth dome lacking even eye slots so that an opaque polished steel face was all that could be seen. They all wore paired katana at their sides and moved with a slow methodical precision that gave them a seemingly ghostly quality.

The warriors formed into a circle about them and then sank to one knee as a gently measured tread sounded against the grass. The crow cawed and took flight, swooping over the humbled forms and settling onto its owner's shoulder.

"Warlord Hachiman, it pleases us that you have reclaimed your property," came a sultry and aloof female voice.

"Your servant is overjoyed to have brought you pleasure, divine one," replied her owner and used such reverence that Candy was sorely tempted to look and see what manner of beauty could humble a man like Hachiman so flawlessly.

"Then you will be equally pleased to know that by our decree and the mutual consent of Tsuki-yomi, she is pardoned from Yomi. You may give her to Lei when you deem appropriate."

"My most reverent thanks, divine one."

"And on matters of Yomi, I understand you have suspicions about the realm below, suspicions that your brother and you have been probing into."

"We have suspected whispers of revolt, divine one. But wanted to be sure before we brought the matter to higher attention."

"Your dedication is most appreciated, but the situation with Yomi is known to us, and in truth was orchestrated."

"I . . . I do not understand, divine one," said Hachiman.

"Amatsu mika hoshi acted under the orders of the Moon-God and began a campaign of misinformation when we first learned of the rising plot beneath the Empire's feet. The Dread Star of Heaven was performing flawlessly, and then your investigations and own schemes became aware to him."

"If I have caused offence, divine one, I will end my life immediately," he decreed with absolute truthfulness.

"There is no need for apology. Your convoluted schemes

have aided us immeasurably. Your plans with your brother, your use of this slave, your intrigue concerning the Wani, Lady Uzume, and the Eastern Provinces, all have assisted the greater goal by causing confusion and distraction. By focusing on what you and your brother were doing, they have failed to notice the destructive machinations of the Dread Star."

"May your humble devotee be permitted to know the truth of what has transpired, divine one."

There was a pause as the woman seemed to consider whether to let her subject know what he had helped bring about. She then spoke with a lighter tone that suggested just how pleased she was that Hachiman had acted as he had.

"The disaffected of Yomi have been given false hope. When the Great Houses of Water and Fire advance on Earth, they believe that they can rise and take the surface. To ensure that the Great Houses are in no condition to retreat and engage them, they have been leaking vital data to those of Earth — to those who can best make use of it. They believe that they have offered enough information to ensure catastrophic losses when you and your brother commence the campaign. They believe their scheme secure, but in truth, it is all part of our attack plan."

"The governments of Earth have many entrenched covert divisions that have been operating with impunity for many decades. They could have been a threat to us, and so, these forces have been slipped portions of supposedly vital data from traitors in our midst, and have been dedicating all their resources to this conspiracy."

"Supreme Warlord Toyo-tama-hiko's secret development of the Water Wani and the skill with which he hid them has greatly impressed us and no doubt intimidated the traitors of Yomi. So, we engineered samples that were stolen and then leaked to the appropriate agencies. The biological agents those of Earth have been perfecting will be useless against his forces."

"And Supreme Warlord Hachiman. Psychological and tactical data on your Wani and cavalry has similarly been falsified, reproduced, and leaked. The traitors in Yomi have passed it to their Earth agents, and they will find their arrogance turn to despair when their machines and machinations fail them."

"The corrupted Kami of Yomi will be removed, and replacements established. There will be no cause for fear from Earth or from Pangaea. The time is upon us — war begins now."

The crow took to the wing and the sound of the ruler striding away reached their ears before it was eclipsed by the soft rustle of departing guards.

Hachiman and Lei clambered back to their feet, not one of them having seen who it was who held such authority over all.

"We had best make haste for the palace," said Lei.

Hachiman laughed and strode over to Candy. He grabbed her by the shoulders and pressed her back to the wooden symbol.

"Kohai, one must take the time to enjoy the simple pleasures. Earth will still be there in an hour, so let us bind your new toy as tightly as we can, and then take our pleasures from her."

Candy grinned as she felt them once again capture her ankles. Lei's hands flowed against her hips as Hachiman stepped before her and hoisted her chin. She was going home, and soon everyone on Earth would know the rapture of being owned by the Kami Empire.

Epilogue

Candy once again stood before the sprawling desolate plain that was Izanagi except that now she was looking out at the ferocious perimeter wall from one of the warships.

She was happily naked on a leash and huddled at Lei's feet as he sat bold and defiant on the bridge. The large throne was established atop a flight of three steps in the centre of the command room and the vantage point allowed him to see everything.

Each of the battle hulks was built like a gargantuan super tanker with hulls adorned with an interlaced shell of ceramic plating. At least fifty stories tall, if it were not for their obvious ocean-going design they could have been misinterpreted as buildings and the plane itself as some sort of eerie city.

Through countless gun ports jutted artillery barrels. Locked drawbridges could be seen along the front and sides to permit the poised forces to spill forth as soon as they arrived.

Battlements and other hard points were stretched around their deck, which hoisted several fort-like towers where missile launchers peeked through openings next to catapults. This was not the only contradiction in eras of technology, for machine guns and howitzers could be seen dispersed amongst ballista and cannon.

Rising amongst the cluster of rotund buildings was a single rough tower. It was in this elevated location that the primary bridge was located. There was a secondary version located deep within the heart of the vessel where it could not be easily attacked, and it had been the first location they had visited. An exclusive lift had brought them to their current location, proving that in a split second, they could evacuate and sacrifice their exemplary view for superlative security.

The ring of large windows that surrounded the uppermost level granted a panoramic view and from it she could see the dozens of monstrous craft now land locked and awaiting their voyage through the vortex. Between the windows were large consoles that were tended by technicians in light armour with side arms. Again there was the strange splicing of machinery in that circuits and computer screens were lodged amongst great industrial gauges whose needles wavered and fluctuated as a steady hum began to fill the air. Keyboards were placed within clusters of levers, and rows of switches and buttons lurked amidst large and awkward seeming valves and dials.

Her side was getting a little cold from leaning against the chill metal of the deck plates, so she huddled closed to Lei's armoured leg. Her new owner was flicking his gaze from the consoles to the view with concerned intensity but still he absently started to stroke her head as she nuzzled in.

An intercom blared into life and the words issued in the room and roared across the whole plain.

"Attention assault fleet. Confluence detected. Vortex is imminent."

Lei reached to the side of his throne and pulled out a corrugated pipe with a mouthpiece at the end. The primitive communication system allowed him to address the bowels of the ship.

"Activate the generators and hoist the goads," he said firmly and then settled back to hold tight to his throne with the hand that held her lead while he continued to pet Candy with the other.

Deep metallic peels flowed across the land as each of the behemoths started to respond. The forts atop them began to open their roofs. Powerful hydraulic rams broke the domes into triangular sections that opened out like flowers. Arcs of lightning jumped from within the exposed core and lapped at the metal as the hum in the air intensified and was joined by a dull squeal.

Each vessel shook slightly as a huge copper orb almost a

hundred feet in diameter appeared. Rising upon a telescopic pillar, the polished surfaces started to crackle with arcs of electromagnetic energy.

"Shut down all non-goad related electrical systems. Activate EMP countermeasures," announced Lei.

The fear that the electrical surge would destroy the delicate computer systems and microchips suddenly made it clear why they still employed the devices and machines that would have seemed more relevant to a steam engine or similar Victorian style creation. Even if the swell of power scorched and destroyed their modern systems, their backups would always serve them just as effectively.

The computer screens went blank and the lights and signs of activity in the other modern systems dwindled and went out.

"Alignment is commencing. All vessels begin countdown to full goad surge," decreed the intercom.

"Here we go, Candy," he said with an excited smile.

She looked up and saw that he was staring down at her. He extended his hand, and she stretched her cheek into it.

"Bring the generators to maximum in three-second increments. Watch for power spikes and shunt them to the energy sinks."

Candy held to Lei with utter adoration. She couldn't wait to begin — not the attack on Earth, but her ownership under Lei. Her affection for him had been massively enhanced by his exposure as the agent that had been responsible for bringing her to the Empire. Everything she had undergone here, every delight, every torment, the core of all had been his doing.

Her master had given her to him. Lei had been trained by Hachiman, just as she had been. So here they were, both students of a giant in the fields of sensual depravity and bondage. Their appointment to Earth meant that they had at least in some way, graduated. They both still revered their master, but now the two of them would engage in a war of their own. As Earth and the Empire fought each other, so to would they. She would struggle and defy, make Lei train her, have him defeat her, prove his power, and coerce her complete abandonment to his rule. Just as she had been seduced by the captain, by Uzume, by Hachiman, she would demand that Lei confirm his credentials if he were to relish her true submission.

A dreadful shriek filled the air and the orbs above each ship exploded into life. Each one became a screaming electrical nova that lashed at the ships, the ground, and the sky. Candy closed her eyes, but the light still managed to pour through her eyelids.

"The Vortex is forming!" roared a technician, fighting to be heard over the brutal din. Lei jumped up and threw his stare from one console to another as warning signs caught his attention.

"Fire a level five pulse into goad's three and five!" he bellowed. "Stabilise the port cells!"

A pair of technicians each opened hatches and started to spin the large metal wheel that lay within. The ear-piercing scream that rent the air made Candy clap her hands over her ears.

"Dimensional stability is definitely in flux. We're going through!" said the technician with a wonderful mixture of ebullience and dread.

The scent of ozone once again ruled her nostrils as her hairs stood up. Candy chuckled at the return of a sensation that had almost been forgotten, and just like that first time on the Pacific that had brought Candice to Pangaea, there was a final flash, and her stomach seemed to rise from a moment of free fall. With a stern jerk and the sound of monstrous splashdown, she was delivered to Earth.

The fleet had arrived, and she eagerly looked forward to a whole new series of adventures.

GLOSSARY FOR THE KAMI EMPIRE

Izanagi and *Izanami*: The creator deities, the names of the two forces whose interplay create and move the vortex between Earth and Pangaea.

The Kami: the various deities of earth and heaven. The lords and manifestations of thought, deed, and substance.

Mitama: The essence or emanation of god or spirit. The name given to the Imperial Army that enforces the will of the Kami and marches under the banner of *A-Katsu* (I conquer).

Shintai: The God body, the earth form, or symbol of a deity.

The Primary Powers of the Kami Empire

Yatakagami: The Sun Goddess. Supreme Ruler of the land who is always accompanied by her sacred crow — *Yatagarusa*.

Musubi: Lord of growth. He is the tactician, the planner, and chief advisor to the Sun Goddess.

Tsuki-yomi: The Moon God. The lord of darkness. He is the keeper of time, and his House plots the path of the vortex on Earth. His House alone is not subject to the rule of the Sun Goddess.

Amatsu mika hoshi (Dread star of heaven): He knows all, but cannot leave his shrine. He controls a vast and highly secretive spy network that watches the Empire, the lands about them, and trains the operatives that go across to Earth to send ships and planes into the vortex. He is the chief advisor to the Moon God.

The Kami of Water

Toyo-tama-hiko (Rich jewel prince): Supreme Warlord of the Water.

Naka-tsu-wata-dzu-mi (Middle sea body): His House conducts submerged patrols in the ocean waters. His troops ride aquatic Dinosaurs such as the seventeen-metre long Kronosaurus.

Uha-tsu-wata-dzu-mi (Upper sea body): His House provides surface vessels and reptilian steeds to protect and patrol the ocean traffic.

Soko-tsu-wata-dzu-mi (Bottom sea body): Warlord of the deep. His House oversees seabed construction and harvesting, along with ocean bed mining for valuable minerals.

Midzu-chi (Water-father): Warlord of the Rivers. His House conducts river patrols to maintain security and order either by boat, or on trained fifteen-metre long Phobosuchus (Horror crocodile).

Midzuha no me (Water-female): The concubines of the Great Houses of Water.

Idzu no Midzuha no me (Sacred-Water-female): Concubines that have been elevated through exemplary conduct, like Kamube.

The Kami of Air

Ame no minaka-nushi: Supreme Warlord of the air

Shinatsu-hiko: Lord of the Wind. His House is responsible for the sending of all radio communication.

Shinatobe: Lady of the Wind. Her House is responsible for the receiving of all radio communication.

Hayachi (Swift father): The Messenger. His House handles all overland messages and items of import, and sees to their safe delivery.

The Kami of Fire

Take-mika-dzuchi (Brave-dread-father): The master of thunder, Warlord of the artillery regiments.

Hachiman: the Warlord who commands the Mitama.

Ame-waka-hiko (heaven-young-prince): His Mikado and highest-ranking general.

Uzume (Dread female): His most feared and ruthless agent.

Ashua: Guardian Warlord of the courtyard, protector of the inner lands. His House is the police force of the Empire.

Toyotama-hiko: the Dragon Warlord. He is part Wani and second in command to Warlord Hachiman.

Wani (Dragon): Eggs of the Dinosaur tribes were taken centuries ago, and the offspring raised as Wani. From the best of these warriors were bred more until an army was created. They are now fanatically loyal warriors. They are fierce, fearless, and serve as the backbone of the Mitama.

The Kami of Earth

Kagu-tsuchi (Radiant father): The fire god. Lord of power and energy, his House runs the nuclear plants.

Kamado no Kami: The furnace deity. Lord of the furnaces of wood, oil, coal, and hydroelectricity.

Inari: The Lord of the rice fields. His House sees to the feeding of the general population.

Susa no wo: The Lord of rain. His House oversees all plumbing and irrigation.

Oho-toshi (Great harvest): The lord of gathering. His House sees to the harvest and the safe storing of all food.

Uka no mitama: Lord of the food spirit. His House ensures good crops and plentiful harvests. They provide knowledge, equipment, and expertise to guarantee growth. They breed and raise the best herds for slaughter. They also train humans to fulfil the role of beasts.

Ho no Susori: Lord of the fishermen. His House builds

boats, provides equipment, and sees to the smooth running of the fishing fleet.

Hohodemi: Lord of the hunt. His House hunts Dinosaurs to replenish the stock. They also see to the breeding and training of new steeds and herd animals for domestic use. They also train human ponies.

Sukuna-bikona: (Little prince): A House of dwarves that see to the brewing of wines and other drink. They also produce many medicinal remedies and maintain a large medicinal thermal springs. It is in his underground palace that the sacred spring of longevity is located.

Temmangu: The Lord of learning and calligraphy. They are the teachers of the young and old, and indoctrinate and educate new slaves.

Ishikoridome: The stonecutter Lord. His House is one of architecture and building.

Toyo-tama: (Rich jewel): His House are jewellers, and makers of finery.

Ohonamochi: Lord of physicians. His House tends the injured, the sick, and the many slaves of the Empire to ensure their health and survival.

Yama tsu mi (Mountain-body): Lord of the trees. His House is responsible for tree-cutting, lumber, timber, and the maintaining of forests.

The ranks of the Kami Priesthood

Mikado: Chief Priests of a Kami. They see to the running of the House and its affairs and responsibilities.

Nakatomi: Mediators between the priests and the Kami. They regulate and assign the slaves of a House as the Kami or Mikado decree.

Imbe: The preparers. They ensure that the lower ranks see to the preparation, cleanliness, and order of slaves, equipment, and chambers.

Hafuri: Inferior grade priests that see to the basic tasks of the House and its responsibilities.

Negi: The lowest priestly rank that is responsible for the most mundane functions of the House.

Kamube: A slave who has earned freedom through exemplary conduct and service and now tends the House as the priest's dictate while still holding authority over other *Kami-tsu-ko*.

Kami-tsu-ko: A slave dedicated to a House.

The Underworld of the Kami Empire

Yomi: The land of darkness where slaves and criminals are banished. Once sent to Yomi, one may never return unless via personal pardon from both Sun Goddess and Moon God.

Bimbo-gami: The Lord of poverty. The Kami of sexual frustration, teasing, and enforced chastity.

Naki-sahame: The Lady of weeping. The feared sadistic dominatrix of Yomi.

Ashiki kami: The rulers of Yomi.

Oni: The inhabitants of Yomi. Many are former *Hafuri-tsu-mono* and have been elevated from that caste to assist in the running of the realm.

Hafuri-tsu-mono (flung away things): Those sent to Yomi.

About the Author

Born and raised in San Francisco, Talia Skye spent part of her early career living and working in Japan where she discovered her passion for writing, scifi, and BDSM. She currently lives in London, and continues to explore those worlds.

www.ingramcontent.com/pod-product-compliance
Lightning Source LLC
Chambersburg PA
CBHW061611170626
46811CB00001B/391